A DIFFERENT TRUTH

CHRISTINE MILLER

A DIFFERENT TRUTH

ISBN 978-1906221-713

A Cataloguing-in-Publication (CIP) catalogue record for this book is available from the British
Library.

Mixed Sources
Product group from well-managed
forests and other controlled sources
www.fsc.org   Cert no. TT-COC-2082
© 1996 Forest Stewardship Council
FSC

Typeset in 11.5pt Book Antiqua by Troubador Publishing Ltd, Leicester, UK
Printed in the UK by The Cromwell Press Ltd, Trowbridge, Wilts, UK

Matador is an imprint of Troubador Publishing Ltd

ACKNOWLEDGEMENTS

There are few people among my family and friends who know that I have written this book, but I owe a debt of gratitude to those whom I did take into my confidence.

I had thought about writing the story of some Staffordshire Quakers, especially Alice Bowman and Peter Littleton, for many years. Without the help, guidance and encouragement of Philip Emery B.A. (hons), M.A. tutor and the members of Keele University's Writers' Workshop, Lichfield, Staffs, which I joined on a whim, it would never have got off the ground.

My thanks are due to Ruth Robinson of Rugeley, Staffs, who helped with her notes on the seventeenth century agricultural year and Rob and Chris Brittlebank, of Walton-on-the-Hill, Stafford, experts in the subject, who, after reading my made-up description of a non-existent Moorlands Wassailing Ceremony, pronounced it convincing.

In addition I should like to thank Rita and Tony Newman of Mold, Flintshire for their encouragement after reading what I had written up to June 2005, and Dorothy Seedhouse of Hednesford, Staffs for reading the whole book in its almost final state and for her continuing support and encouragement.

Following the closure of the Keele Course some of its members re-formed and became the 'Well Cottage Group', also based in Lichfield. Special thanks to Andy McNaughton of Stafford and Paul Lewis of Rugeley for transporting me to and from Lichfield. I couldn't have done it without them.

I would also like to express thanks to Thea Randall, County Archivist, Stafford Record Office, Eastgate Street, Stafford and Martin Sanders, at that time Area Archivist, Lichfield Record Office, The Friary, Lichfield, Staffs for permission to quote from the documents listed below and the help they and the staff at both record offices have given me over the last few years.

References:
Quarterly Meeting Minutes Book (D/3159/1/1); Stafford Record Office.
Stafford Book of Sufferings (D/3159/2/18); S.R.O.
Leek Book of Sufferings (D/3159/3/3); S.R.O.
Wills and Inventories: Alice Bowman (1690); Peter Littleton (1690); Lichfield Record Office.

FOREWORD

Alice Bowman and her family and Peter Littleton and his wife were real people.

Alice did harangue the priest in his Church on Easter Day 1664, spending time in gaol before imprisonment in the House of Correction, where her suckling baby died. The names of her children are all taken from her Will, in which it appears that only one daughter was married. Alice was a comparatively rich woman when she died. The rest of her story, including her mental instability, is imagined.

Peter seems to have been a prominent member of the Society of Friends and is well documented, but I have used my imagination too. He visited other parts of the country, including London, often as part of an advisory group. His terms in prison, including his early releases on the payment of his fines by his cousin and later by Charles II's Declaration of Indulgence and his serious illness are all in the record. An Inventory taken after his death showed that there were a lot of beds in the house, this, together with a note that 'two ancient persons' were staying with him, suggested to me that he helped poor and infirm Friends by offering accommodation.

Other Quakers named, even if briefly, all lived at the time and their story is yet to be told.

Staffordshire, especially the area around Leek, was home to many Quakers. Those that I've written about lived many miles apart in various towns and villages throughout the whole of the county. I therefore invented the village of Branslow and the nearby town with a courthouse, so that the characters I wished to concentrate upon were all in the same place.

The Reverend Thomas Fletcher is another real person. The records show that he was fiercely anti-Quaker and may almost have had a personal vendetta against Peter Littleton.

PREFACE

Saturday May 7th. 1664

Alice is howling. She is in the House of Correction. Her two-week old baby is dead. She gave up holding it to her when she realised that it was cold; wasn't making its usual mewing cry for the food she couldn't supply. It now lies on her lap. She can feel its flaccid body lying across her knees. She doesn't know how long it's been dead. Doesn't know how long she had been in this hellish place of unrelenting, enforced and useless drudgery. Her body aches with wishing to be released from the torment of this place. Her breasts and belly ache with the loss of her child.

She knows that some of her family, most of her neighbours and all of the people in the House of Correction regard her as a madwoman. Henry, her husband, is regarded as mad too. So is his brother Anthony, who is in prison with him. But she's madder than either of them. She tries to remember how she came to find herself in this terrible situation, this awful place. And she is anxious about her other children, Henry the younger, called Harry, Ellen and Cornelius. She wonders too, about how other Friends have been affected by her violent behaviour. She even wonders about the lad, Daniel Brass, who is not a Quaker but is a good boy nevertheless, helping about the farm for his board and lodging.

℘ ℭ

CHAPTER ONE

Wednesday, January 9th 1660/61

The nervous young man stood in front of the small table which served as a desk. He stooped a little and shuffled his feet, as he clutched his hat in cold-blued hands. At first the Reverend Thomas Fletched had regarded William Jenkins without warmth. Will was not among the most enthusiastic members of the congregation at St. James's Church. He attended only the minimum number of services to keep him on the right side of the law. But he was offering information. Informers were despicable but useful. What they had to say was usually of little value; they only did it for the money, but it was as well to listen, just in case. This time it was worth the wait.

"Sittin' ducks, they was, Reverend Fletcher," Will said, excitedly. "I've seen 'em before, assembled there, at what they call their religious meetin's. Quiet as mice, men, women and children, but no parson, no altar, no singin', no prayer book, no candles - that's not religion. Not sayin' or doin' anythin'."

As he gained confidence in himself he continued, "They don't even go to a proper church. It could be in somebody's kitchen, like it was this time, at Master Fernyhough's, or they could be standin' outside in a field. All's quiet, and then one of 'em ups and starts preaching. It could be anybody, man or woman, a child even. It doesn't matter; they're listened to as if they was proper clergyman. It's not right".

"You are quite correct in your supposition, Jenkins", Fletcher had replied. "What they are doing is unlawful, unlicensed preaching. What's more it is blasphemous, and cannot be allowed to continue. Dissenting religious conventicles such as these meetings must not be allowed to continue. Now, my boy, where is the next unlawful, abominable meeting to be held?"

Will faltered. He'd overheard a whispered conversation between two of those Quakers outside his father's ironmonger's shop. They were good customers. If they got into trouble it could be bad for trade. But the Reverend Fletcher wouldn't tell, he was sure of it.

The Rector, waiting for the vital name, was becoming annoyed. "Come, Jenkins. These people are criminals. They are an affront to Almighty God, His Blessed Son Jesus Christ and the King," he continued. "They insult the decent law-abiding people of this land, and if such - " he spluttered as his anger increased. " - such demons are not destroyed, they will infect this whole country of ours." Beside himself with rage, he'd almost forgotten the presence of Will, who, before he lost his nerve, suddenly almost shouted the name.

"Master Richard Buxton."

With an effort the Reverend Fletcher pulled himself together. Sometimes he found it difficult to remain a calm and serene member of the ordained clergy, especially when, in his parish, the activities of these sacrilegious criminals were brought to his attention.

"Of course you've done right to inform me of this disgraceful behaviour". His voice became calmer, but his plump body was still shaking with residual agitation. "I shall inform the Constable without delay and he will arrange with the proper authorities to seek out the perpetrators of this incident. If necessary, the militia will be called out".

At last once more in total control of himself, he'd risen from his chair, and turned to open the door for Jenkins, who had been standing awkwardly, still twisting his cap in his hands and not meeting the parson's eye.

"Er." Will had said, "Er. What about -? "

"Oh," the Reverend Fletcher suddenly remembered what the young man had visited him for. "Be assured that you will not be forgotten. As soon as the miscreants are convicted you will be paid for the great service you have done for the village, the county, your King and Country. And God. It is your entitlement, and it is the court's duty, to see that you receive your - er - reward. Now do not hesitate to let me know of any other incident which may occur." He was ushering Will out now. "Goodbye young man. You are a credit to your mother and father."

"Thank you, Reverend Fletcher," Will muttered, nodding his head respectfully and replacing his battered felt hat as he left. Conversations with the gentry, for that was how he regarded the clergy, were a rarity for him and he was always glad when they were over. If they went by in their carriages he could manage to nod his bared head deferentially, but when they talked to him he wasn't sure whether they were speaking English or some other language.

Reverend Fletcher had talked about a 'dissenting religious convent -' something or other. Was that the same as the religious meeting he'd reported? He wasn't sure. Convents were for Roman Catholics, weren't they?

80 CR

CHAPTER TWO

Sunday, January 20th 1660/61

Ah, Alice. Remember the violence suffered by the peaceable people.

First Day Meeting had been assembled in Richard's kitchen for about half an hour and would probably continue for much longer. Meetings took as long as they may. Through the single window, the weak winter sunlight moved slowly across the silent room.

Suddenly the silence was broken as a Constable thrust the door open with a violent shove. He struck the stone floor sharply with his staff. Almost no one gave any sign of awareness that they had been interrupted. Most of the Friends, including Alice, her husband Henry and seventeen-year old son Harry, controlled their startled reactions quickly before resuming their quietness. Everyone knew that the situation was likely to become dangerous and Alice put her arms around Ellen aged eight and Cornelius, seven years old.

The Constable surveyed the people before him. He reckoned there were about forty or forty five packed into the room and overflowing into the adjoining dairy. There were men and women, even children, there. The most elderly sat on any form or stool available, while the rest sat on the floor or the table, or simply stood. All heads were bowed. Most eyes were closed. All, after the first momentary shock, were motionless. For a fleeting second he wondered why he was there. They were no threat. He knew some of these people. He knew Richard. He pulled himself together.

Once more striking the floor with his staff he pulled a Bible out of his pocket. Then he realised that before he could open it he would have to put the staff down. He looked for somewhere to rest it, dithering a little. One of the younger men opened his eyes, saw the Constable's difficulty and, with a gentle gesture offered to relieve him of his encumbrance, then, holding the staff for him, resumed his silent waiting on the Lord.

The Constable opened the Bible at random and prepared to face the Meeting, which was continuing in its accustomed way. The Friends weren't ignoring him. They had simply returned their silent worship to the stage it had been at before his entrance. Alice didn't always find the silence easy but now, strangely, she felt that it was more important than ever to bring her whole mind and body to the patient waiting for God's inspiration.

Remember that day, Alice?

Oh, Alice. Now, even in this miserable place, wait on the Lord. Remove from your mind all thoughts of what is happening to you now. Remember the peace of Richard's house. Wait, wait, oh, wait on the Lord, Alice. Peace. Remember.

The Constable gave up trying to engage the Meeting's attention and decided instead to continue with the duty with which he had been charged. He cleared his throat and held out the opened Bible.

"I am ordered by Law to request that each and every one of you swears the Oath of Allegiance to our gracious Lord, Charles the Second, King of England, Scotland, France and Ireland."

The heads remained lowered, hands stayed folded in laps, eyes continued closed. No one moved. The fire crackled while a hambone and some vegetables boiled in the pot suspended above it. Here and there an empty stomach rumbled. Outside, heard through the open door, a horse whinnied and hooves rattled on the cobbled yard. The sound encouraged the Constable and he tried again. Once more he cleared his throat and shifted his weight from one foot to the other. Once more he showed the Bible to their closed faces.

"I am ordered by Law to request that each and every one of you swears the Oath of Allegiance to our gracious Lord, Charles the Second, King of England, Scotland, France and Ireland," he repeated.

Unnerved and feeling a little silly, his face reddened. He decided to abandon the repetition of the speech he had prepared so carefully and which had produced such a negative effect. He decided to try to make these people understand the situation they were in. He lowered the hand holding the Bible, but still holding it in one hand, he stooped slightly towards those nearest to him. His posture was conciliatory.

In the silence muttered voices could be heard outside and the jingle of harness.

The Constable tried again, "See here", he said. "The Law says everyone in the country must be prepared to swear allegiance to the king. At any time. It's just to show your loyalty to him. It's - it's just something everyone has to do, now." He raised his voice a little. "Everyone, not just you people".

Richard Buxton realised now that somebody would have to say something. He rose to his feet and attempted to explain why no Friend would swear an oath. Outside the voices were still, although the sweet jingle of harness remained. There was the sound of hooves and an occasional soft exhalation of a horse's breath.

Richard's voice and manner was quiet and reasonable. Almost, but not quite, in the same way as he would have explained something to a child, he said, "Luke Carter, we do not swear oaths. We are loyal to the King and to our country. As Children of the Truth our word is sufficient, without needing to swear on the Bible. We follow the words of our Saviour Jesus Christ who said, 'Swear not at all, but let your yea be yea and your nay, nay'."

He appealed to the Constable, "Luke, you know I was as relieved as you were when the King was restored to his throne."

In spite of himself the Constable nodded.

Richard turned his attention from the Constable to the Meeting, "Are we loyal to our King and country?"

There were immediate murmurs of assent, "Aye". "Most certainly". "God bless him!"

"There, Luke," said Richard. "You have our word."

"But it's not enough," the Constable shouted, drowning their voices. He was anxious and confused. Suddenly he lost control. "The Law says you've got to swear the oath," he shouted. "Now. This very minute. Or God help you, because if you don't you will destroy yourselves!" In a moment of complete frustration he almost screamed, "You stupid half-wits!"

Suddenly, Harry Bowman who was standing near the window, started to shout a warning over the Warden's bellowing, but his words were, in turn, drowned in the storm of shouting and heavy footsteps as soldiers burst through the door.

There were about twenty of them. The local militia and not totally untrained. They were foot soldiers customarily drawn by local muster for military duty in wartime and now being used for such extra law keeping as may be required in peacetime. They all carried weapons of some sort, mostly cudgels, or muskets left over from the Civil War. Some even carried swords and other weapons from earlier battles in which their fathers and grandfathers had fought.

Antagonism towards religious dissidents, Protestant or Roman Catholic, was high among many people, as the Church of England became established. The restoration of Charles II to the throne after the Civil War had also restored maypoles to the village greens and Christmas celebrations to a populace starved of enjoyment during the strict Protestantism of the Commonwealth. It was with ferocity, born of the fear that those repressive times could return, that the soldiers started laying about themselves, beating the unresisting worshippers with their weapons.

The militia shouted at them to take the oath and swear allegiance to the King. They forgot that many of these submissive people had been their friends, had helped them at harvest-time. Even that some of the Quaker men had fought at their sides in the War. Shouting obscenities and blaspheming, they crashed around the kitchen, smashing or overturning furniture, pulling their seats from under the elderly people and laughing as they fell to the floor.

Harry, in the first seconds of the uproar, saw his father being beaten and ran to help him. A soldier was holding Henry with one hand and punching his body with the other. Henry gave his son an agonised look. "Get them out!" he managed to say before a blow to his mouth silenced him.

Harry knew what he meant. With a rapid glance around the ravaged room he located his mother, cowering with her arms around her two younger children. He raced towards them, landing an inexpert but effective punch on the nose of one surprised soldier who got in his way. Reaching his mother and brother and sister, he dragged them, somehow, out of the wreckage.

He avoided the main outside door of the house. It opened onto the frosty yard, where the soldiers created too high a threat. Henry knew this Friend's house well. It was an advantage many of those who had travelled from other parts of the county, didn't have. There was a door opening into the garden on the other side of the house. To get his charges through it and out of the building would quickly put them out of sight of the militia.

As soon as Alice realised what her son was doing she relaxed a little. She also knew the house well and hurried along the passages, Ellen held tightly in one hand and Cornelius in the other. There was one anxious moment when they were confronted by a frightened maidservant, who, recognising them, quickly got out of their way and disappeared through a nearby door.

Once outside they all ran as fast as they could, across the icy garden and over the dry stone wall, slipping a little; then through the adjoining field, scattering the sheep recently brought down from the hills, until they had put a good space between them and the militia. Slowing down to a walk and getting their breath back, they talked for a while, but soon lapsed into silence. Only one thought in all their minds. How was Henry senior faring?

Oh, Alice, Alice. While you are in this place, how is Henry faring now? And Harry? And Ellen? And Cornelius? Susan would have been a sister for them. Oh, Oh, Alice.

Despite there being little or no resistance offered, Friends who had remained in the Buxtons' kitchen were being treated roughly, with blows to face and body.

Some, their religious consciences understandably overcome by their instincts for self-preservation, tried to avoid the violence by running out through the main door to the yard, where they were trapped by the group of mounted soldiers waiting there. On sight of them the order was given and the horses were driven forward. Frightened men in their path and the women and children they were trying to protect, were knocked over and many were injured under the horses' hooves.

Oh the screaming and the crying and the begging for mercy, Alice! How can men, made in God's image, do such things? Why could they not leave all of you in peace? Why didn't they try to understand?"

At the end of the attack, for that is what it was, thirty-five Friends had been taken prisoner. As each was taken hold of they had offered no resistance and now stood, grouped together, heads bowed, eyes closed. The Meeting had been resumed. Out of doors. Cold. Silent. Submissive. Waiting on the Lord.

They were loaded into carts and taken away, to be committed to prison for refusing to take the Oath of Allegiance. Later in court they pleaded their obedience to the teaching of Christ, "Swear not at all", to an unsympathetic Justice of the Peace and were whipped before being returned to the gaol.

They were among about one hundred and eighty men from various other local towns and villages, violently removed from their separate Meetings for Worship and arrested that day.

***

After everyone had left the maidservant came into the kitchen, where the contents of the overturned cooking pot had sizzled briefly before putting the fire out.

'It'll snow tomorrow', she thought.

෨෬

CHAPTER THREE

Monday, January 21st 1660/61

Harry Bowman sat opposite Tom Wells at the cluttered kitchen table. Harry's right arm was outstretched, tapping a devil's tattoo with his stubby fingers on the clean wooden surface. Tom Wells, who worked on the Bowman's steading, showed signs of having been in a fight. He had a rough bandage around his head, his face was lacerated and his left eye was swollen closed. He'd also taken a severe blow on his back and to ease it a little he leaned forward with his arms across his knees, uncomfortable on the rickety stool. Both of them were lost in their thoughts, trying to make sense of the dreadful happenings of the previous day.

Despite his aching body, Harry suddenly leapt to his feet and paced two or three rapid steps backwards and forwards before returning to the table and thumping it with his fist.

"I can't rest, knowing what 'appened yesterday," he shouted, "It was savage, cruel! So many of our friends taken from Meeting - I was lucky not to be taken meself! And all because some little pipsqueak of a parish Warden informed on us. Tom Bott! 'E's only been doing the job five minutes, and suddenly 'e thinks 'e's the law. I'd've 'ad a go at 'im myself if I 'adn't looked out of window and copped sight of soldiers first and got out as soon as I could".

"Thee always was a slippery mover", Tom observed dryly, "Best lad round here for getting out of way of trouble, leaving others to take blame". He straightened on his seat, and looked up at his younger friend. "I stayed long enough to get a walloping, but managed to get away before they started rounding people up. I should 'ave been at home anyway, looking after Grace, but where was thee? Why didn't thee stay with thy father, instead of running off with thy mother and the children? Thee thinks such a lot of 'im, to 'ear thee talk, but 'ave thee -" he stood up and jabbed a finger at Harry's face - "'ave thee bin dragged out of the Meeting to get the butt end of a soldier's gun across thy 'ead like thy father did before they threw 'im in gaol?"

He warmed to his subject.

"No, " he shouted, "Thee ran away and now thee's 'ere shouting odds to me in a nice warm kitchen. The Grindy brothers and their dad stuck together and've gone to gaol together - " He stopped himself suddenly, turned his back on Harry, took a deep breath, then turned to face him again. Not being one to talk much, he'd run out of steam and now felt slightly ashamed of himself.

Surprised by the injustice of this outburst, Harry was flustered and indignant. He could feel his colour rising and his collar suddenly felt tight. Leaning forward he held his hands out towards Tom, wishing the older man could understand how torn he had felt about leaving his father to the mercies of the militia.

"I saw a soldier taking hold of Father and beating him and I wanted to go to help him. He shouted at me to get hold of Mother and Ellen and Cornelius and take 'em with me. So that's what I did. I could see he was in trouble and I wanted to help him, but there was so much noise and shouting. I didn't know what to do. I thought I would go back after I'd got Mam and the little 'uns away - but I was frightened". He suddenly started to cry with the crackled sound of a young man whose voice has not quite changed

" I'm sorry, Tom, I'm sorry", he whispered, wiping his nose on his sleeve, "Mam's had a right old go at me. She nearly threw me out when I got them home yesterday, and told her I'd punched somebody on the nose when I was trying to get to her. Then she said that when all's said and done, the truth is that there is that of God in all men, including me." He sniffed once or twice, then grinned, his natural buoyancy returning. "She gave me extra beer at supper."

Tom found himself smiling back. "I'm sorry, lad. I

shouldn't be so hard on thee. She's right. We're supposed to be peaceable people, to love one another," he sighed and held out his right hand to shake Harry's. "If we fight amongst ourselves, we're done for. When we went to that first Meeting, we knew what Friend George Fox said was the Truth and some folk wouldn't like it. But we live in the Light, now, whatever may happen to us."

"Well said, Friend Tom", said a voice from behind them.

Harry and Tom turned to see Alice in the doorway, leaning against the post, exhausted. She closed the door on the bitter moorlands wind and the flurry of snow which had blown into the room with her. As she took off her shawl and tucked strands of damp hair back into the confines of her cap, Harry caught sight of a bruise on her left cheekbone. Shocked, he realised that his mother had received one or two bruising blows during the raid and it was only now that he noticed.

Alice moved to the table, gesturing nervously to the men to sit down again, the movement exposed more bruising on her right arm. When she spoke it was agitatedly.

"How is Grace, Tom, and is the babe better now?"

Ah! Tom and Grace's newborn, a hope for the future. One of your little hopes for the future, your babe, your Susan, is dead, Alice. Her father doesn't know. He never saw her. He didn't even know when she was being born.

"Thee must keep them both warm, this winter weather."

Your babe is cold, cold as ice, Alice. She will never be warm. Alice, she never was warm, in her whole life.

"How is thy mother, Tom? Have thee enough candles?"

It is so dark where you are now, Alice. Dead and dark.

"Where are Ellen and Cornelius, Harry? She couldn't help but be anxious about the children who had been so fearful the previous day.

She was clearly trying to control her distress by enquiring after others. Harry, not completely understanding the signs, tried to put his mother's mind at rest by reassuring her that Ellen and Cornelius playing in the barn. Tom, the more perceptive of the two, realised that there was another reason for Alice's unease. He rose from his seat and came round the table to where she stood. He leaned forward and took her nervous hands in his.

"Is there any news of thy Henry?" he asked quietly.

Oh, Alice, your heart must scream out for your Henry!

Alice's shoulders drooped and releasing his hold, she started to fiddle with a spoon lying on the table in front of her. "They've got to pay for the carts that took them away. Some didn't have the money for that. They'll probably be fined for that on top of what they owe for the cart. They won't have money for food while they're in there either. I think Henry would have the money for the fine, but he would refuse to pay."

She drew a deep breath. "He'll say that having done nothing wrong, he shouldn't be going to gaol, and shouldn't have to pay to be transported there." She gave a half-smile. "They'll all say the same thing and they'll all receive the same punishment"

Once more they fell silent. Alice started to play with the spoon again.

Then, tentatively, Harry asked, "Who else was taken, Mam?" asked Harry.

Alice was tired and her patience was waning She had been out all day gathering information from friends and neighbours living in the area. Most of them knew at least one or two people who had been arrested. She put the spoon down and, stretching her arms out, with her palms flat on the table in front of her, said, "Thee knows what happened yesterday. There were scores of Friends there, met to worship God quietly and peaceably. Waiting on His Word."

Restless, she stood up and starting pacing backwards and forwards across the stone-flagged floor. The two men watched her a little helplessly. Even Harry knew this would not be the right time to interrupt. They had both been at the Meeting with her for all or part of the day and knew or could easily imagine what had happened to end it all. They bided their time.

Alice needed to talk.

"Informers. They're all around us, aren't they?" she said, "Watching, waiting for any chance to tell the Priest or his Wardens if we don't go to church, tell the Constable if we preach in the streets. For the slightest reason they call in the Constables or the Militia as soon as they can. For money." She turned to face Harry and Tom, remembering, recalling the horror. "And some of them are our neighbours and so-called friends"

She hadn't then heard of the extent of the arrests, or of the whippings which followed.

***

Alice had been pacing back and forth across the length of the kitchen place, but now she resumed her seat, and sat for a moment, thinking about the previous day's events. Her face was distorted with the effort of holding back the tears. Usually she never shed tears, no matter what distress she suffered.

Harry, a little embarrassed by his normally placid mother's unaccustomed passion and distress, was becoming restless. Nervous energy prompted by fear had helped him to get his mother and younger brother and sister away from Richard Buxton's house without being badly injured. Shaken by the raid, the first that he had experienced, now he wanted to know more about what had happened after they had left.

"Who was taken?" he asked again, trying to control his impatience for more detail.

Alice quietened, then with a sigh, she recited the names of those who had not been lucky or quick-thinking enough to avoid the inevitable consequences of such raids.

She counted them off on her fingers. Thirty-four names, ending with "And my Henry". She whispered his name sadly, shaking her head.

Remember that, Alice? They were in gaol for eight weeks, weren't they? They went before the Justices and then they were whipped through the town. People jeered and threw filth at them. Then they were thrown into gaol. Oh. Alice! Your Henry! His beautiful back scored and bleeding. You'll see the scars on his back when he comes home and there'll be scars on his mind, too.

Turn your mind away from that thought, from the place where you are now, Alice, back to that day in the warm kitchen at home.

The room was almost dark on that winter afternoon. While she thought about those left behind as well as the men taken away, Alice rose from her chair to light a candle. The simple domestic duty was familiar and soothing. Sitting down again, she said, "Thee knows about the Grindys, does thee not? " They nodded. She had quietened down a little by now, but suddenly she was fiery again.

"And little Susan Ward! So quiet and frail, but strong in the Light until now. Those soldiers they beat little Susan!"

She was interrupted by a noise outside and turned to look through the window. What she saw terrified her and for a horrifying second she thought she was still experiencing the previous day's disturbance; then came realisation. "The bailiffs are come here!" She shouted as she recovered her senses and ran to the door. She intended to throw her weight against it, but as she did so it was roughly pushed open and she was thrown to one side.

"What dost thee want?" shouted Harry. "There's precious little left here after last time!"

"We're takin' everything", was the short reply. "Your daft dad says 'e's got no money and even if 'e had 'e wouldn't pay the fine. Says 'e's done nothing wrong. But the law says 'e 'as been a naughty boy, and if 'e won't pay no fines, goods 'ave to be taken to the value. Right, lads, clear the place - and take no notice of these loonies".

Tom saw an opportunity and ran to the door, "I'm sorry, Alice," he shouted. "I've got to get back to Grace and little 'un," and leaving Harry to protect and support his mother, he slipped through the door to return to his sickly wife and newborn as quickly as he could, before his own home was invaded.

Although Henry and Alice had attempted to replace much of what the bailiffs taken away previously, many things were irreplaceable. Their religious principles did not encourage love of material things, but they could not help but regret the loss of the little desk, which had been in Alice's family for many years and which her mother had given them when they married. Gone too was the great brass pan which Henry's parents had passed on to them at the same time. Henry's and Alice's pewter plates, cups and bowls, symbols of their then modest prosperity, had also been taken away leaving them with nothing but wooden vessels to eat and drink from, and now those, too, were being carried out, thrown on the cart, with all its bedding. All the straw mattresses in the house were taken out.

This latest merciless confiscation of goods didn't take long. As Alice and Harry stood in shocked and motionless silence, the men roared through the small house like a whirlwind, sweeping up with them anything they could carry. The cart outside in the yard began to fill with bedding. Linen, bolsters, pillows were taken from the beds in the curtained-off space in the house room where Alice, Henry and Ellen slept. A cupboard containing the family's few items of clothing was emptied. The cradle, previously used by Cornelius had been taken in the last raid and now the truckle bed, which he shared with Harry was carried down from the loft.

Alice protested at the sight of her sons' bedding being put on the cart. She shouted, "Thee would rob children?" and made to attack the man carrying the blankets and covers. Harry stepped forward quickly and put an arm around her shoulders to restrain her.

"My mother is upset," he said, quietly. Then, gently, "Have thee taken enough yet?" His protest was greeted with jeers about his strange speech, and he and Alice resumed their bewildered, silent watching.

The table in the kitchen was too heavy, but the benches and

a chair were taken, with the stool which was kept by the fire. Fire irons, tongs, the iron cooking-pot, spoons, knives and a sieve were thrown into the box, which held the kindling, and taken out to the cart.

From outhouses the bailiffs took any small tools they could carry, a grindstone, iron hooks, six cheeses and a tub of salted pork.

After Alice's one shocked reaction, little or no resistance were offered to the intruders other than occasionally registering their protests. Their quiet pleas for mercy ignored, the men left leaving them standing helplessly in the emptied cottage.

"What are we going to do" Alice whispered. They both looked around the room, now lit only by the moonlight. Their only possessions, were the few worthless items left behind by the bailiffs and clothes they wore. The livestock, a few sheep and cow, had not been touched, for this they thanked God in their evening prayers, but their home was ravished.

Even the candles had been taken, the fire put out, and the charred wood thrown on the cart.

೮೨ ೦೪

CHAPTER FOUR

Tuesday, January 22nd 1660/61

A few miles away, the next evening, three men sat comfortably at the local Green Man, enjoying their beer, with the satisfied air of those who have worked hard, and done a job well.

"Well", said David Davis. "I reckon it'll all be over by now. For that lot, anyway. And the sooner they're all out of the way the better. They'd be fools to carry on the way they are doing. Why can't they be the same as everybody else? What do they get out of being different to everybody?" he looked at the other two with an expression of half-amused bafflement. "What makes 'em carry on like they do? They must know that they'll get into trouble if they keep on breaking the law".

"But that's the point, Dai", Edward Morris said, leaning back on the settle, arms folded across his chest, and with the air of a man in full knowledge of all the facts.

"They don't think they are breaking the law. They think they're right, and other folk are wrong. They say they stick to what the Bible says, and they say the law doesn't always go by the Bible. This thing about not taking the oath of allegiance. We're all glad that we've got King Charles back in his rightful place?"

It was a question by implication. The other two nodded, staring glumly at the table.

"We don't all agree with 'im all the time, but 'e's better than Cromwell and 'is cronies. The Bible's right, we know that, but you can take things too far. Any way", Eddie was warming to his subject now, feeling even surer of his ground. "I know they've got it wrong about swearing on the bible, and taking the oath. When Our Lord said 'Swear not at all', he meant not to use bad language. That's what he meant. And that's the truth. And anyone who won't swear allegiance to our new king is a traitor, and deserves all 'e gets".

There was a general murmur of agreement followed by an equally universal direction of three pairs of eyes towards three empty tankards.

"Oo's turn is it?" said the previously silent third man, hopefully.

"Yours, George", the other two replied in chorus.

***

Earlier, on that same day, in the darkening late afternoon, Peter Littleton and Elizabeth, his wife of two years and their dog, Bob, stood side by side looking at the devastation that had been their home. Their cottage was now almost empty. Most of their possessions had been taken away the previous day, by the same bailiffs who had raided the Bowman's house, three or four miles away across the moor. The raid had been in reprisal for Peter's refusal to pay fines incurred for non-payment of tithes. Fines had been imposed on him before, for refusal to attend church, or refusal to promise not to attend a dissenting religious meeting. The outcome had been the same then as now, distrainment of goods to the value of the fines.

Peter, a tall, well-built, fair-haired, fair-skinned man with the reddened, almost sore-looking complexion of the man who works outside, was trying hard to control his anger and distress. It would be of no use to express such feelings to Elizabeth, as it would only increase her anguish. He had his arm across her shoulders as she leaned against him.

The youngest son of a modestly successful yeoman, he had married Elizabeth two years earlier, and to support themselves they grew some cereal crops on one good piece of land and had kept a milch cow, a mare, a few sheep and a couple of pigs on another. Both pieces of land were rented from Peter's father who also owned the cottage in which they lived. On another piece of land, which Peter's father had given to him when he married, was a barn where harvested

22

crops could be stored. This was now empty. Everything removed by the bailiffs. Today their cow, their last item of livestock worth, he reckoned, about three pounds ten shillings, had been distrained in lieu of fines of five shillings, for refusal to pay tithes.

"What are we going to do, Peter?" Elizabeth whispered. She was tired by the struggle going on in her mind. Her body ached with anxiety for the future and she felt weak.

"We can thank God that Bob wasn't anywhere to be seen", he replied, trying to lift her spirits a little. The dog had been intended as a protection for the holding but had proved inept. He was too friendly and therefore useless. They only kept him because his puppy-like behaviour often made them both laugh. "They would have taken him too and likely treated him badly for his daftness."

He tried desperately to think of a past incident involving Bob which would amuse Elizabeth, in the hope that he could cheer her, but he failed. As if he realised that he was being talked about, Bob flopped onto his back wriggling with ecstasy and waving his paws in the air. Peter glanced at his anxious wife. She was looking at the dog but not seeing him. The hoped-for signs that her gloom was subsiding were not there.

Peter was silent for a moment, then he said quietly, "We will wait upon the Lord." Together they fell silent, standing hand in hand in the empty room, eyes closed, waiting for whatever God-sent solution or thought should come to either of them, if such was to be.

After a while Peter opened his eyes. He'd found it difficult to clear his thoughts in order to receive any more inspiration. A practical solution had occurred to him before he'd even suggested that they ask God for His help. The thought would not leave him and it was now a most difficult one to express.

He waited a second or two longer then said, "We can't ask our parents again, they have done all they can for us, and they put themselves at risk helping us. There's only one thing we can do. We'll ask Friends for help".

"Oh Peter", Elizabeth opened shocked eyes. "We can't. It would be begging. We can't."

"What else can we do?" he replied. "We have nothing until harvest. We have nothing we can sell. What else can we do? We need money for rent, seed, food. In between working our own bit of land, I'll offer to work for any Friends who can pay me a few pennies, or can spare us a crumb of food. God will help us, if we have faith."

"I suppose I could help, too." Having the few minutes of quietness had helped Elizabeth's mind to clear. Peter was such a calm, strong man and always knew what to do. She felt more confident now.

"Perhaps I could offer to sew or clean for Mistress Chinnock. I worked for her sometimes when I was a girl, and she was Widow Lawton. She might need a little more help now that she has a new husband and a bigger house"

"Good," Peter smiled for the first time in a long time. "Tomorrow we will start all over again. With God's help". He kissed his wife gently on her cheek. "God is good", he said.

Wednesday January 23rd 1660/61

The following day, Peter, accompanied by Bob, went to visit a cousin who was also one of his closest friends. Thomas Hickock had started in life with the same prospects as Peter, but had not had the disadvantages that Peter and Elizabeth had incurred by the promptings of their religious consciences. Tom's and his wife's cottage was as comfortable as they could make it. Some produce of the fields they worked helped to feed themselves. Other crops together with eggs and the occasional half-dozen sheep or couple of calves, were sold on the open market.

Peter was greeted warmly when he arrived. Though fond of his cousin and his wife, Peter's response was quieter. Friends were not given to conventional greetings, believing that getting down to the business of the day was more practical.

"We're so happy to see you, Peter," said Joan Hickock, who was used to what could be regarded as Peter's lack of polite manners. She took his hand and led him to the warmth of the fire. "We heard about the trouble the day before yesterday, and we wondered how you had fared".

24

"Badly" was the short reply. There was no sense in prevarication and drawing a deep breath, he came right to the point. "We've lost everything. Even pots and pans in the house. Everything. Elizabeth is at her wits end. She didn't sleep last night. Neither of us did".

He brought himself to a halt. He had not intended to complain so much. He believed that trouble should be borne silently with patience and fortitude. He now forced himself to continue, haltingly, "I've come to ask if thee could give me any work. We need money for food and seed and - " He stopped himself again. Of an independent nature, this was one of the hardest things he had ever had to do. Tom sat looking at him, quietly thoughtful. Neither of them was aware of Joan bustling about on the other side of the room, until she spoke.

"Well", she said over her shoulder, as she reached into a cupboard. "Food you shall have right away. I made bread yesterday, and Tom can you reach a side of bacon off the hook and cut Peter a piece off it? I'll get some cheese from the cockloft."

She bustled away while her husband saw to cutting the bacon. Minutes later she came back with the cheese, took a clean cloth from the press, and laying it on the table, put the food in the centre of it and tied it up in a bundle. "I'll come over tomorrow with some other things. Have you got wood for the fire?" Peter shook his head. He could have gone out to get some, but it would have been useless; the axe and saw had been taken.

"Tom will bring some over tomorrow on the handcart." Joan said decisively, "I'll go and see if there are any eggs."

After Joan had gone out to the henhouses, Tom gave a wry smile, "My wife, always ready with a solution to the problem".

Peter returned the smile. "She's a good woman, like my Eliza", then, serious again he said, "I need paid work, extra to the farm, to keep us going until we are on our feet, again. Can thee give me any, Tom? Please?"

"I can't see how I can," was the reply. The reply that Peter had dreaded. "Besides Joan in the house and yard, I've got an old boy and a lad helping me in the fields, and between us we can get all the work done without too much trouble, at this quiet time of the year. I'm sorry, Peter."

A smiling Joan came back into the house. "Only three eggs, but you can have them. There'll be more in the morning." The smile faded when she saw the demeanour of the two men. She guessed immediately what had passed between them, but left Tom to explain later.

Listening to his cousin's retelling of his story, Peter felt hopeless. Fatigued by the physical as well as emotional strains of the previous two days, the present additional effort and embarrassment of asking for help was now unbearable. Abruptly he said that it was time for him to go home, adding that he would see Tom the following day, then he made for the door. Tom followed him, expressing his regret for Peter and Elizabeth's present difficulties and with hopes for better times to come.

At the threshold, Peter turned towards his cousin. A few conciliatory words were exchanged, then, sombrely, the two men shook hands. Peter went home trying to retain the small glimmer of hope in his heart that perhaps Quaker Friends might help.

***

"No work?" Joan was plainly surprised. "There's work all over the place that Peter could do."

As Tom started to protest, she continued, "There's the window-frame in the little room over the kitchen, the gate to Stoops Field needs re-hanging, the fence round the kitchen garden needs repairing, the - ". Her husband made an impatient gesture, but she, anticipating what he was about to say, continued, "I know you haven't the time. That's why paying Peter to do this work would be worth the expense," and then, in a gentler tone, "You have been friends to one another since you were little children. You have always helped each other, but this time your cousin and his wife really need help and it might seem little to your advantage, but Peter and Eliza are worth it".

Tom, not looking at her, shook his head slightly, and the slightly severe expression on his face now caused Joan to regret her outburst. She had actually raised her voice to her husband. A thing she had never done before. She had also nearly lost her temper with him which, had she done so, would have caused both of them a great deal of pain.

Tom wasn't angry. He was, however, surprised by her expressing herself so strongly, which was making him consider again the sense of what she had been saying. A non-Quaker, but a regular churchgoer, Tom was fond of Peter and had some limited sympathy for the religious path which he was treading, although he secretly thought his cousin was somewhat touched in the head.

While Joan busied herself around the house waiting for her husband's reaction, Tom sat and considered his cousin's request. Peter's abilities extended in other directions than agricultural labour. He was good with his hands, particularly carpentry and repairs and renewals in the house and outhouses were required before another winter. Like most farmers he usually did such work himself, but Peter's help would mean the work would be done sooner, and, if he was honest with himself, better too. Initially doubtful that he could help in any way, Tom now felt more enthusiastic about the idea, suspecting that it could be of benefit to both families. If Peter did the work as his wife suggested, it would free himself to do work in the fields and with the livestock, without the anxiety of knowing these vital repairs to boundaries and property were waiting to be attended to, often when he was already exhausted.

The decision was made. "Well, Joanie", he said, "We'll help them. I'll give him the work." He smiled at her and she was relieved. "I knew I'd married a good 'un when I married you. Sensible, hard-working woman, a little money of your own. Oh, and good-looking too. 'Course, I never knew what a scold you'd turn out to be!"

CHAPTER FIVE

Sunday, June 9th 1661

After Evensong, in the vestry of St. James's church a conversation was taking place between the Reverend Thomas Fletcher and Will Jenkins, the young married son of one of his parishioners. Money was changing hands across the small polished table. The Justice of the Peace had entrusted Fletcher with this duty.

"Some for the King, some for the poor of this parish and some for you, Jenkins", said the rector, handing over a small, pleasantly chinking, drawstring bag. He placed another bag containing more cash, in the table drawer, and leaning forward on his elbows and clasping his hands together in front of him said, "I'll make sure that after I take what is to be distributed to the poor, the rest will go into the right hands".

The Rector's voice was reassuring; his smile benign; his whole attitude benevolent. Despite this, Will had his doubts, but so long as he had his share he wouldn't trouble himself about whether the King and the poor had their thirds of the proceeds or not. So far as he was concerned his payment was his rightful reward for the risks he'd taken.

So far as the authorities were concerned, the matter of the illegal religious conventicle had, for the time being, been resolved, and action against miscreants had been carried out according to the law of the land. In turn, his contribution to the process recognised by Church and State had been rewarded.

As he walked home along the muddy road under darkening night skies, he tried to evaluate exactly what the effects of giving information to the Rector had been. People had been arrested and although some had managed to get away, others had been treated roughly before being taken to the gaol. As it turned out they had been whipped through the streets for their wrongdoing - and wrong thinking.

With the money in his pocket, he felt that he should be feeling pleased with himself, happy to have been rewarded with the coins that were chinking with each step he took. He should even be feeling proud of himself. The parson had said that there would be more money for any future information given, and he and Margery needed money, of that there was no doubt.

There was a sudden chill disturbing the mild air of the June evening. The summer breeze was shifting its direction slightly. Will shivered and drew his shirt closer around his neck.

The trouble was that now it was all over, he felt bad. Those people had been his friends and neighbours, but now they knew what he'd done, they had withdrawn their friendship. One of the young men who had gone to prison, had helped him with odd carpentering jobs around his cottage, but Will had not seen him since he came home. He'd lost a good friend. That's what those peculiar people called themselves. 'Friends'.

The confusion about his feelings persisted. He remained confused and vaguely unhappy. Never mind. His Margery was at home. She would make him feel better.

***

Margery was ready to dish up their supper when he walked through the door. As she turned away from the fire to greet him and saw his expression, Margery could tell that Will was troubled about something. He had been in high spirits when he set off to see the parson. "We'll soon have a bit of spare money, love," he'd said. "We can buy those things for the 'ouse, that you've been goin' on about, and p'raps even a little trinket or two just for you. Some pretty ear-bobs, like those Mistress Chinnock was wearing at church that time, p'raps. Whatever you like".

Margery had laughed, protesting that she was sure that there wouldn't be that much money and, in a cheerful mood, he'd left for his meeting with the parson. The change in him from then to now worried her. His shoulders drooped and he sighed deeply as he turned to take off his shabby jacket and hang it on the nail at the back of the door.

Carefully removing the pot from the fire and placing it in the hearth, Margery went over to Will and put her arms around him and kissed him. Then she rested her head on his shoulder for a second or two, gently patting his back with one hand.

"What's wrong, love?" she asked, straightening up and looking into his eyes. "I know somethin's upset you. Didn't parson pay up like 'e said 'e would?"

Will pulled away from her and walked over to the fireplace, where he leaned forward to warm his hands. "Oh yes," he said. "He paid up and we've got a bit to spare, now."

Like most working men born in humble circumstances, he was condemned to a life of drudgery working in the fields. He was intelligent, but not used to dealing with the deep mental conflict he was now experiencing. He was also reluctant to talk about his feelings.

"Yes" he repeated. "He paid up, but I feel bad about it"

"Why should you?" Margery was surprised by what he said and waited for him to speak again, but there was that particularly closed look about his face, which she'd rarely, if ever, seen before and she instinctively knew that, for now, he'd said all he was going to say.

She turned back to the hearth. Supper was ready. They would eat it, she thought, and then it would be time to go to bed. He'd be happier in the morning.

Thursday, November 8th 1661

Today, five months after leaving the vestry with money in his pocket and a strangely unsettled feeling in his heart, Will Jenkins couldn't get the uncomfortable conversations with Thomas Fletcher out of his mind. The passage of time hadn't dimmed the memory or the feelings.

He was sitting down to supper with Margery when he suddenly felt that he could bear the anxiety no longer.

"I'm going out", he said suddenly, rising to his feet and rushing out of the house.

Margery, astonished, said "Where to?" to the empty room then, resigned, set their supper by the fire to keep warm.

***

As darkness deepened, Peter and Elizabeth Littleton ate their last meal of the day, bread, cheese and small ale. In answer to Peter's requests to the Meeting for help there had been small monthly payments from a Disbursements Fund, collected from all over the county for the benefit of needy Quakers. In addition there had been various donations of seed from individual Friends. All of these debts he had promised to repay either with money or seed, as soon as finances and the weather allowed. As had been his custom for the last two seasons, his fields had been turned over using Tom's borrowed plough. The difference being that this year, he'd had to borrow his oxen too

Now, ten months after his appeal to his cousin, in addition to work on his own account Peter had made his presence felt on Tom's holding. The roof had been repaired, and was good for a few more years. The gate was re-hung and fences were being mended. Other repairs that had come to light would be completed before the onset of the following winter. Working on Tom's holding as well as his own was exhausting, but the money was helping to keep the Littleton's land working. New livestock, a few cows and sheep, and a horse, at least were needed as soon as possible, and Peter and Elizabeth were confident that, with the Lord's help, they would replace what had been taken away from them.

Elizabeth had used a few pennies to buy a couple of broody hens and some geese to provide eggs for sale as well as the couple's own use. Offspring from both hens and geese were being grown on, while the older poultry were now being prepared for sale at Christmas. She had not been so successful in her search for employment. Mistress Chinnock had been sympathetic, but was unable to give her work, although she had said that there might be some in the future. This had been the stumbling block, which dampened Elizabeth's enthusiasm, but then she had an idea.

Elizabeth's visit to her previous employer's house had reminded her that she had an ability which she could pass on to others and for which they could pay a small amount. When she was a girl she had worked for Widow Lawton, who was now Mistress Chinnock. The youngish widow, looking for consolation after the untimely death of her husband, had taken it upon herself to teach some of the village children to read and write. She loved children and had unlimited patience with them, but her success was limited as many of the children were being used for seasonal work at home and on the land. Others simply had no interest, or their parents thought such activities were not suitable for their offspring.

Elizabeth, however, was proof to the widow that it was possible to teach children of the 'agricultural class' the joys of book learning. She had progressed to such a degree that she was allowed to take selected books from the shelves, to read at home when she had finished work. When Elizabeth married Peter and left Widow Lawton's service, she was no longer able to borrow books, but as a result of her reading, she had learned something about the wider world.

As a child Peter had been taught his letters and, like many others, could read well enough but had not learned the skill of writing. In any case it was numbers that he had more use for, when he was working out his accounts. Since their marriage Elizabeth had encouraged Peter to improve his reading and writing and these became skills he would use to great advantage for the rest of his life. She realised it was an advantage she could make use of too and decided that in addition to teaching children she would offer lessons to any adults, men or women, who wanted to learn.

At present she had two or three people who came to her occasionally for an hour or two of reading and writing. She had hoped for more after visiting many of the houses in the village telling friends and neighbours of her scheme. It was disappointing when some laughed outright at her audacity, saying either that she had ideas above her station or theirs. Others had shown interest and a few of them had tried one or two lessons and given up.

The two or three who remained were enthusiastic, but duties at home did not always allow for regular attendance. Sometimes it was difficult for them to find the payment and Elizabeth had been offered anything from very small coin to a basket of fruit or half a pound of ham. Her pupils knew that in other areas there were great risks involved even in only being associated with the 'peculiar people', but here in this remote region, the danger was not so great.

***

Their meal finished, Peter and his wife held hands across the table for a while as they silently thanked God for their food, then Elizabeth rose and started to clear the pewter plates and cups, knife and jug away.

A few minutes later Peter sat in relaxed silence by the light of the fire, half-asleep. Their useless dog, Bob, who should have been tied up outside, had slipped his tether and was lying across his feet. Elizabeth sat at the table in a pool of candlelight mending the sleeve of her husband's smock, torn during the day's work, so that it would be ready for the morning. The fire was beginning to die down. Before they went to bed it would be carefully damped down, so that it could be revived again in the morning.

Only the sound of Peter's almost soundless snoring, the tiny click of Elizabeth's needle against her thimble as it went through the coarse cloth and Bob's soft, dreaming yelps disturbed the quiet evening.

A sudden loud knock on the door startled all of them, waking Peter up with a start and disturbing Bob's slumber. Elizabeth's heart thumped and she looked quickly at Peter, seeing her alarm reflected in his eyes. Both were nervous that it was the prelude to further harassment from some official.

Elizabeth stood with nervous fingers pressed against her lips as Peter, as apprehensive as she was, went to open the door. Bob ran out into the night.

"I've come to say sorry!"

It was Will Jenkins standing in the doorway, looking anxious and ill at ease. "I shouldn't 'ave done it." He was almost shouting now, "I feel really bad about it. I want to make it right. I'm sorry! I'm sorry!"

Peter smiled at him "What is making thee sorry, Will?" he stepped back into the room. "Come in awhile. Calm thyself, then tell us."

Will walked in clutching his hat and looking about himself apprehensively. He was in the house of one of those strange people. He nodded to Elizabeth. "Evenin' missus," he said. Elizabeth gently gestured towards a bench "Sit down, Will." she said quietly. "Would thee like some ale?" She poured him one anyway, handed it to him and sat down beside him. Peter closed the door and came to stand by the fire, facing them.

Will assumed, correctly, that neither of the Littletons were ignorant of the reason for his visit and was taken aback by their tranquil reception. He had expected confrontation and anger. In unspoken agreement both Peter and Elizabeth were leaving him to explain himself; though they realised that a little prompting of the young man may be necessary. After a small pause, Peter spoke.

"Now, Will," he said, "What can we do for thee?"

Will didn't know how to deal with this benevolent approach by one to whom he had done harm, and from whom he expected reprisal. He felt a strange mixture of fascination and apprehension. He felt like a trapped mouse, as the cat, crouching, eyed him, poised before the pounce. These were people had been described as dangerous and wicked law-breakers they didn't seem that way to him now.

"Why are thee here, Will?" Peter spoke quietly and when Will remained tongue-tied repeated his question and pushed Will's beer a little closer to him.

It was time for Will to take his courage in both hands. He

drew a deep, quivering breath and opened his mouth to speak. To his horror all he could say was "I'm sorry" again and to make it worse it was in a voice that was nervously high-pitched and tremulous.

"Thee told the parson about the Meeting, did thee not?" put in Elizabeth, encouragingly. Will nodded.

"And that caused the law officers and the militia to be brought in, didn't it?"

Again Will could only nod unhappily.

"And some people were hurt. Some others had their things taken away. Worse still, some are now in gaol, are they not?" Elizabeth's voice was still gentle.

"And now thee are sorry, because thee thinks that it was all thy fault, does thee not?" Peter put in quietly.

Will looked agitatedly from one to the other and back again.

"But why are thee here, Will?" repeated Peter. "We were not at that Meeting"

"You're the only ones of them people I know to speak to!" Will stammered, "I thought you'd be able to tell them as've been to prison, that I'm sorry for it."

"And thee are truly sorry, Will?"

"Oh, yes, sir, missus, sir!" He found his voice again. His real voice this time. "I don't blame you or any of them for 'ating me. It was a wrong thing to do to anybody, especially people 'oo 'ave been friends to me and me dad."

"I am Peter and this is Elizabeth. There are no titles here.'" said Peter. "We are all equal in the eyes of the Lord. As for thy betrayal of us, thee are not the only one, Will," said Peter. "There have been worse things done all over the country, to people who don't want to worship God in the way the Law says they should. To people who want religious freedom. And this suffering is caused by people who think that they, and only they, practise the true religion and then persecute, torment and slander people who seek another truth, like my wife and me, who only want to live quiet and peaceable lives, practising that truth."

Peter's voice was raised now, and Elizabeth stood up to

put a restraining hand on his arm. She looked up at him and the expression in her eyes cautioned him. When he continued, Peter spoke more gently.

"Thou art only doing what many others have done. Thee thought thee were doing the right thing. In many peoples' minds, thee were. In Friends' minds you weren't doing right, but that's not important. If it will make thee happier, because you repent, I am sure the Lord forgives thee, Will Jenkins. None of us in this room now will ever speak of this matter again, and it will be as if it had never happened to us".

Will's agitation, which had subsided a little, now returned. He was bewildered by their passivity. He had come to their house tonight expecting loud voices, scoldings, blame, even violence, but there had been none. He ached for a more vigorous reaction to his confession, but they were acting almost as if it was of no consequence. Even when speaking of the repercussions following his informing on their friends to the Rector they had shown no anger.

Frustrated, now he too stood up, picked up his hat, which he had put on the table and walked towards the door as if he was leaving, but then, determined to break their wall of gentleness, turned round to face them and try again.

"But that isn't all, Master Littleton," he said, desperately pressing his point, "There's the money. Parson gave me some money for - 'informing', he called it. Some for the church, 'e said, some for the King, and some for me". He fumbled in his pocket. "'Ere it is, " he said. "You 'ave it. I don't want it no more, and you need it!"

"Neither do we want it!" Peter's face clouded over and his voice was stern again now. "We don't want money gained by evil dealings. Neither would any other Friend. Thee must relieve thyself of it by some other means."

Once more Elizabeth intervened with that look towards her husband, which he knew meant that he must calm himself. He waited a little while before continuing and then he said. "Thee are forgiven, Will. But remember that today thee has proved that thee are a free man, who can make his own decisions. Thou decided to come here today even though thee were frightened. Thee are a brave young man who today conquered his fears and recognised the promptings of his conscience."

Peter walked towards the door, signifying that Will should leave. On the threshold he shook Will's hand and, looking up at the clear sky, said, "It's a fine night, young man. As regards the money, it is true that we and many other Friends are in poor state, but thee will do all of us more good by letting us be, to live a peaceable life. If thee be pleased to help my wife and me, thee could let people know that I am available for work, if they should have any for me to do. Now, go home to thy wife. Good night".

ॐ

CHAPTER SIX

Thursday, March 3rd. 1664

George Palmer was angry. Not given to talking much about anything, he was even less likely to talk about his feelings. Now he was very angry indeed. He was also frightened. As well as being frightened he was also sad. He was angry because Frances, his only daughter, had gone against all the advice he had ever given, which wasn't much, but what he had counselled was important. He was frightened because she was putting herself into great danger. And he was sad because he loved her more than anyone else in the world. He had no other family besides Franny and, the way she was behaving, he thought he would soon be losing her, too.

Since the death of his wife Margaret, his daughter had become the one light in his life. Franny had been a beautiful child and had grown into a beautiful young woman. George didn't know how he had managed to be the father of such a miracle. In fact, because he regarded himself as not at all handsome, he even occasionally wondered whether he really was her father. But, in his heart of hearts, he knew that Margaret had been totally faithful to him.

A plain woman who smiled only rarely, Margaret had devoted her whole married life to keeping their tiny cottage clean and keeping George and later, little Franny, well fed and clothed. She would never raise her eyes in the presence of anyone who was not a member of her family. Consequently she could sometimes appear to be a rather unpleasant woman. Only George knew the real warmth of her nature and the beauty of her spirit.

Margaret had died of a fever when Franny was seven years old and George had been heart-broken. A quiet man before this, afterwards he became even more so. A wheelwright by trade he was able to earn a reasonable living doing work in the surrounding area. All his energies now went into providing a good home for Frances, now 20 years old, who, in his eyes, was perfect in every way.

Or had been until now.

Frances was standing in front of the fire looking at him, her fists clenched and shoulders hunched. There was an expression on her face which he had never seen before. She was trembling slightly and looked close to tears.

"These are good people, dad", she said. "You should be pleased that I know them"

George exploded with an amazed "What?" But she continued.

"You've always brought me up to speak the truth, be kind to everyone, respectful to my elders, try to live an upright life. That's what these people are doing". Her father made an impatient movement and started to speak, but she interrupted him.

"Listen to me, dad," Frances persisted. "They would never 'arm no-one and only want to live a quiet peaceable life."

George could remain silent no more. He stood up and faced her, grasping her upper arms.

"They are wicked, wicked people"

He was shouting now. Their faces were inches apart as he held her.

"They break the law. Their religious meetin's are illegal. Some people even think they practise witchcraft. They're disrespectful to God and man, includin' the King and they rightly go to gaol for it. They rightly get whipped for it, too. They have all their belongin's taken away and I say good luck to them as takes 'em. They get deported overseas and that's the best place for 'em. They are evil criminals. They are wicked, sinful people and I don't want you to have anythin' to do with 'em, especially this boy, John Taylor. E's one of the worst. Already been in trouble for refusin' to swear allegiance to the King. He's a traitor."

"Stop it, dad," Frances screamed. "You don't know 'im.

He's the sweetest, kindest boy round here. 'E's honest and true. E"'s an 'ard worker. A carpenter, a wood-worker, like you, learnin' what was his dad's trade. Like you did. That Robert Davis you're always tryin' to get me off with can't keep his 'ands to 'isself when you're not around. John wouldn't 'urt a fly, and 'e treats me with more respect than any of the other lads round here. Don't you talk about 'im like that. I won't 'ave it. E' does what 'e does because 'e thinks it's right, and if such a good lad thinks such things are right they must be right. Any way, I love 'im, and 'e loves me, and we're goin' to get married".

George, who had been half-expecting that the subject of marriage would be raised at some time, was nevertheless taken aback. He released her immediately. As Frances ran out of the room, her father sat down heavily on his chair. There was no sound in the room but her almost inaudible sobs, his heavy breathing and the crackling of wood on the fire. Outside, in the cloudy late March sunshine, an early lamb bleated and a blackbird sang. Tap, the dog, scratched at the door.

෨ ෬

CHAPTER SEVEN

Easter Day, April 10th. 1664

Sunlight made diamond sparkles of the raindrops held in the folds of leaves and on the bending tips of grass blades. It caught the glittering edges of crystal fragments in the rough stone of the walls and the ancient Saxon cross, mutilated only a few years earlier by Cromwell's men. A light breeze murmured in the trees and the raindrops, harboured in the branches, showered onto the steep path below, where they dried almost immediately.

After the hard winter, this promise of spring renewal echoed the Resurrection being celebrated inside the crowded church, where the Reverend Thomas Fletcher, in his richly embroidered Easter vestments, was laying his hands on broken pieces of bread upon the golden paten, consecrating them.

Alice Bowman, standing at the rear of the church, head bowed over her clasped hands and indistinguishable from the rest of the congregation, raised her eyes and through her fingers, looked towards the altar. She had mustered all her courage to come here today, but she felt compelled to make her protest. It was, perhaps, a sort of revenge for earlier harassment by both church and secular authorities and she was not sure that her conscience would allow it.

'Vengeance is mine, saith the Lord'. Isn't that so, Alice?

The priest, whom Alice knew to be a persecutor of Quakers and an idolater, was reciting the most holy words in his lexicon:
"We do not presume to come to this Thy Table, O merciful Lord, trusting in our own righteousness..."

It is malicious actions by Thomas Fletcher and all those other evil men, Alice, which have sown these seeds of righteous anger in your brain.

***

At the beginning of March she and Henry had been fined eight shillings for not having attended the steeple-house during the previous month. When they had refused to pay the Churchwardens had forcibly entered their house and taken away household goods, including Alice's largest cooking-pot, worth at least eighteen shillings.

"We are not worthy so much as to gather up the crumbs under thy Table..."

Two years ago Henry and seven or eight others had refused to swear on the bible and were sent to prison. They had all been asked to pay four shillings each for the transport to gaol, but all had refused to pay on the grounds that they had not committed any offence. In consequence Henry and the others had been distrained of household goods. The constable and another officer had forcibly entered the house, to Alice's alarm and removed two cooking pots worth over 16 shillings and other items in lieu of the charge.

***

"...Who, in the same night that he was betrayed, took bread and brake it...

Many of those gathering here are known to you and your husband, Alice, and they shun you because of your beliefs. They scorn you both because of your trouble with the law. Now these same people are honouring the Messiah, a simple-living carpenter, Alice, whose only sin was preaching love, forgiveness and mercy, like Friends do, but whose teaching was despised and at odds with the law. He would be angered to see this pagan ritual practised in his name.

42

"...This is my Body which is given for you. Do this in remembrance of me. Likewise..."

'Alice! It will soon be too late. Now, you must do it now! Alice!'

Her stomach fluttered. Her legs felt weak

'There is only one way to release yourself from this fear, Alice. It is to face this other fear. Do it now, Alice! Now!'

Alice was making small agitated movements now, looking around herself nervously. She needed to gather even more mental strength and boldness, soon, before it all evaporated and the moment escaped.

In his hands the priest was holding the bright jewelled wine cup, its golden shine amplified in the sun's rays.

Now!

"Drink ye all of this, for this is my Blood of the New Testament which is shed for you..."

Now!

Now was the time. For the gathered congregation the holiest time. For Alice the time of most hypocrisy, the most intolerable time. She pushed past surprised and outraged worshippers, uncaring of toes trodden on or bodies collided with, until she reached the central aisle of the church.

"There is no true Worship in this evil Steeple-house." She screamed at the priest, who, though alarmed, continued, tremblingly, to complete the Easter rites. "Your words don't come from the mouth of God; they are invented by the imaginations of those in the darkness of ignorance, who haven't seen the Light. They cannot see the Light for all the trappings which hide it."

She ran down the aisle, with a speed she had not known she was capable of, especially since she was so far gone in her pregnancy. She even had breath enough to shout, "You clothe your priests in rich raiment, while the poor and hungry go naked. You drink wine from a golden cup while beggars pick your unwanted scraps and drink water from the gutters."

Before she could further give her voice to the urgent callings of her conscience, rough hands were laid on her, she was brought to the ground and she was held there.

"Hypocrite, liar, thief!"

She managed to shake off her captors, sat up and spat the words at the priest who had hurriedly completed consecration of the sacrament. Now he stood over her, his face twisted with anger and disgust. He gestured to those who still held her to raise her to her feet and sent a Churchwarden for the constable before he addressed any words to her.

His dignity regained, he considered what he should say. He looked at her properly for the first time and saw a panting, wild-eyed young woman, with dishevelled dark hair surrounding a pale, defiant face. He thought, 'Forgive me, Lord, but I hate this woman and all the fanatics she represents.' She looked back at him without a trace of shame, regret or remorse, ready to harangue him again given the chance, but he spoke first.

In a voice loud enough for the entire assemblage to hear the priest said, sternly, "You shall be taken by the constable and locked up. The law of the land will deal with you. You will probably go to gaol, where you and your like belong," then, while the congregation murmured their agreement, in a lower voice that only she could hear, Thomas Fletcher whispered, "And I hope you and your brat rot there"

***

Outside, in the churchyard, birds sang, early bees busily tunnelled into spring flowers, and on Alice's arms the bruises started to form.

***

After supper on the evening of the same day, Mistress Ruth Chinnock sat comfortably in her favourite chair by the side of a bright fire. On the opposite side sat her husband, Abel, moderately successful farmer and youngest son of a local landowner. Although the weather had shown pleasant promise of the coming of warmer weather, a chill came with the lowering of the sun. Some days Ruth felt the cold very much indeed and today had been one of those days. The disgraceful incident in church this morning had frightened her a good deal. For at least an hour after dinner she had continued to experience occasional chills that she was sure had been brought on by the shock.

Dear Abel was a good man, but not always a sympathetic one. His view was that a disagreeable event, if it was a short-lived thing like the behaviour of that madwoman this morning, should be of no concern at all once it was all over.

"Come, come, my dear wife," he had scolded her, on their short arm-in-arm walk home after the service, as she clung to him, shivering and weeping a little. "It's all over now and you are perfectly safe again." He pressed her arm closer to his body. "Not that you were in any great danger, anyway. I am always there to protect you, my dear"

"Oh, I know, I know, Abel." Ruth turned her face towards Abel and he thought to himself, ' She's still pretty, you know, even though she's nearly thirty-two. That little smile that lights up her dear face ...' But Ruth brought him back to the present.

"I cannot help but think about what might have happened," she said. "What if the Constable had arrested us all? He might have thought we were in league with that wicked woman. We might all have been taken to the lock-up. She will probably be whipped, and I could not bear to think that you or I might be whipped. -" At which point her husband's tolerance started to falter.

"What a silly way to think, Mistress Chinnock. Indeed it is." He spoke sharply now. "You have too much imagination. Indeed you have. Much too much imagination. Shame on you for allowing such silly thoughts to enter your head." His tone moderated suddenly, when his wife began to cry again. "There, there, now," he said more gently. "Where's your handkerchief?" They stopped walking and she handed a tiny square of embroidered lawn to him. "There, there," he repeated, as he tenderly wiped her wet eyelids and cheeks, then, "Blow, my dear."

***

Now Ruth was warm and comfortable again, all fears cleared away by the ministrations of her husband. He had continued to be most unusually considerate to her all through dinner, after which he had retired to their bedroom for his usual Sunday nap. The rest of the afternoon he spent as usual, with his dog, walking some of his fields. On Sunday it would be wrong to work, but 'There is no better fertilizer that the farmer's boot,' he thought.

As the darkness deepened, when the curtains were drawn and the candles lit, it was very pleasant to sit in each other's company. Abel was reading a farmer's almanac and Ruth was embroidering colourful fanciful flowers on the third of a set of twelve chair seat covers for the elegant dining-room they hoped to have one day. They talked occasionally, when each rested their eyes, while the fire danced and crackled in the hearth.

Later, when they retired to bed, Ruth was restless. Troubling thoughts of the day's occurrences, which had been calmed by Abel's reassurances earlier, wriggled their way back into her brain now that the quietness of the night released them.

Ruth was not used to being wakeful. She remembered that, as a child, if she was restless her mother used to make poultices of pounded blue violet leaves and poppy seeds. To these she added a little grated nutmeg then placed the warmed cloth upon her daughter's temple. It smelled beautiful and it soothed her, but there was no one to fulfil that function for her now. A friend had once told her that counting backwards from one hundred was a good remedy if you could not sleep, as it occupied your brain with quieter thoughts. She tried it now. That didn't work either.

In the night-covered fields a ewe, one of the many brought

closer to the house in anticipation of lambing, changed it's position, bleated twice, and quieted down.

Sleeplessness was so lonely.

Ruth gave a small, testing, cough. Abel did not move. She tried again. He gave an extremely theatrical snore. Despite herself she started to laugh and so did he as he turned towards her.

೫ ೫

CHAPTER EIGHT

Tuesday April 12th, 1664

Alice is huddled in her corner of the cell. There is no light or heat, and fever is rife. There are probably fifteen or more other women and children in this confined space. Most are ill, moaning, crying, and praying, some are cursing. The comatose and dying are the luckiest, they feel and know nothing.

The clamour of the voices fades, as she fights down the waves of pain, which are invading her body. The woman they call Goody Barton is doing her best to help her, but Alice knows the baby will come in its own good time. She just wishes it could be soon. She doesn't know how long this has been going on. She prays that it will not be much longer. She can't remember how long any of her three other birthings took. In a brief moment of relief between pains, she thinks, wryly, 'Labour, travail, it's that, to be sure!'

Later, looking down at the screaming red-faced scrap in her arms, she wishes her husband was with her and bites back the tears. She is so tired.

Goody Barton is still hovering nearby, hoping. 'If I wasn't in this place, if I'd bin begging in the street, this madwoman would've given me a penny or two,' she's thinking. 'No chance now, though.' She took a covert glance at the now silent baby lying in Alice's lap. 'An' that babby aint long for this world,' she thinks. 'What a place to be born. What a mother to be born to! P'raps the little 'un's better off where it's going'.

Goody catches the eye of a more likely benefactor and hobbles nearer to her. "You wouldn't have a bit of food about you, would you?" She doesn't hear the mumbled reply, but the meaning is clear and she looks around for someone else. She is starving.

Friday May 6th 1664

The constables had taken Alice from the church to the gaol, before she appeared in court for sentencing. While there she began to develop strategies to help her deal with the consequences of her actions. Today she was as tidily dressed as she could manage, she had combed her hair with her fingers and was carrying her three-week-old baby in her arms. She hoped her assumed submissive manner would show that she recognised her lowly position in the presence of their honours the Justices of the Peace.

Ah. Quietly Alice.

Remember those manners your mother taught you to observe in the presence of the gentry. 'Yes, sir. No sir. Anything you say sir.' Don't let your feelings show in your face. Stay quiet. Polite.

It's hard not to hold yourself proudly, but hang your head.

Don't let your eyes tell them what you are thinking. Remember, these people can do what they like to your body, but your mind is your own. Inside you are a proud, intelligent, sensible woman. Be true to that woman, but don't allow these despicable people to know that woman. Hold on to that woman for yourself.

She was charged with vagrancy and disturbing a priest in his church. It was decided that with the right instruction she could mend her ways. A merciful Justice decreed that she was not a hardened criminal, but needed both guidance as to good behaviour and the discipline of hard work. For these reasons and for the sake of the baby, she would not remain in gaol, but be moved to the House of Correction. There she would be given useful and improving work to do.

She had found it difficult not to laugh out loud. What sort of punishment was this? What did the Justice think she did when she was working on the farm? Good sense told her to control herself and she managed an expression of humble gratitude, for the first and only time in her life.

Sunday, May 8th 1664

Sitting on the floor of the cell, Alice remembers returning home that January afternoon three years earlier. Her feet had hurt and she had felt dirty, but not as dirty as she felt now. She still holds her lifeless baby. Nobody had offered to help her. She doesn't want help.

She wants to go home.

After a while her dead baby went stiff like a doll. Not like her other babies had been at three weeks old. Soft and warm. A living promise of the future. A sort of immortality. But now it's gone floppy again, loose-limbed, damply cold. She doesn't like the feel or the colour of it.

***

They've just come and taken it away from her.

She raised no objection.

***

Soon after her arrest Henry and son Harry had asked permission to see her in the gaol and had visited her again on other occasions at the House of Correction. They always left her food, a little money and told her news of the steading at The Ridge, the children and her friends. Visits were less frequent now as it was a busy time of the year. Lambing was finished, so was muck spreading. The hayfield was soon to be closed off from animals and sowing in other fields needed to be done before sheep shearing started. Because of this neither Henry nor Harry had ever seen the baby. A situation that touched them only a little.

Babies were women's work. It was best left for them to attend to the business of caring for children. Most men, Henry among them, could not fully understand their wives' grief when a child died or a pregnancy did not reach completion. It happened so often that it was normal in the first few weeks, days, hours even, after birth. The Bowmans knew they were fortunate to have reared all but two of their children and daily praised God for His bounty.

Today Harry arrived at the House of Correction on his own. He had been told about the baby's death before he saw Alice and was horrified by the condition he found her in.

She was sitting on a low stool, separated from the other inmates by grief and supposed madness. Her arms were crossed over her chest and she rocked silently backwards and forwards, staring ahead, unseeing. All his life Harry had been used to seeing his mother labouring on the farm, even when she was pregnant. She would be dirty, wearing her oldest, most tattered clothes, cleaning out the cattle stalls, helping at lambing-time, even taking on the ploughing if necessary. He had seen her too exhausted to move, too tired to speak, but the next day she would recover, her natural good health and good nature restored.

At her trial. Alice had been told that she would be undertaking 'corrective' work, not knowing what such work could be. She was to discover that women were expected to work at spinning, weaving or cleaning; Alice's work was consisting almost entirely of wearisome, constant spinning. At home this was a pleasure, it was for the good of the family, but here all her waking hours were being spent in useless, mindless activity for the benefit of strangers. It was supposed to have an 'improving' effect, but, because of the pain and distress surrounding the birth and loss of her baby, the strong spirit that had always been at the core of her being was lost. The constant noise of looms and spinning wheels by day, the sleepless nights listening to the sighing and sobbing of her cell-mates and, above all, the loss of her freedom tormented her.

Harry had never seen his mother like this. He felt that he hardly knew her, almost unrecognisable, as she was now, through intense tiredness and exhaustion. Hesitant, reluctant to disturb her, he wished his father had been able to come with him.

She did not stop her rocking as her son approached her. She did not turn her head or look at him. Her eyes remained fixed on some point in front of her, miles away on the other side of the cell walls.

Harry put a timid hand on her shoulder. "Mother," he said softly. There was no reaction. "Mam," he said, a touch louder. The rocking continued. "Mammy!" There was desperation in his voice as he reverted to his baby name for her. First she turned towards his voice then she looked down over her crossed arms to her empty lap.

"Susan's gone." Her voice seemed to come from a long way away. "She's gone," she repeated and turned to look at her son again. This time she seemed to see him. Harry was unsure of what he should do. She was drifting away from him again, repeating, "Susan's gone, she's gone."

Harry was puzzled. "Who's Susan, Mam?" he said.

Her reply was a painful cry, "She's gone!"

"I'm here, Mam," he said, attempting to console her.

She turned towards him once more.   "Have thee come to take me home?" she asked.

Do you remember how glad you were to get home that January day, three years ago, Alice? After trudging across the frosty fields. Remember, Alice?

Thursday, May 19th 1664

Alice has cramp and shifts a little to ease it. For a brief moment she remembers again the viciousness of the disturbance that day when the Meeting at Richard Buxton's house was broken up; the revulsion at the knowledge that informers were about who, for money, would take took news of Friends' activities back to those who could cause them harm, the Constables, the Churchwardens. She dozed.

***

One of the gaolers shouted across the room to her, rousing her. "Your son's bin 'ere. 'E's left you some food. I told 'im about you bein' sick an' bad, an' 'E's gone to get some medicine. 'E'll be back in a bit."

Alice smiled for a moment at the thought of seeing Harry. Harry. Her surviving first-born. He had been the saviour of his mother and brother and sister that day. He'd been brave and frightened at the same time, which made his bravery the more remarkable. Yet the following day he had been unmanned by such a little thing as his mother's distress. During her imprisonment she'd become careful not to expose her misery to anyone. It was becoming easier to hide it. In a restricted environment she was learning to restrain herself further.

Oh Alice, you are putting yourself in another prison. A prison of your mind.

Saturday, July 9th 1664

Henry and Harry went to the House of Correction to collect a wife and mother and brought home a broken shell of a woman. Either husband or son had visited Alice whenever they were able, following the death of the baby in May. She had suffered greatly during those eight weeks, sufficient to break anybody's spirit. Now her advanced mental agony, caused in the first instance by her loss of freedom and increased by the loss of her baby, had left her a timorous, trembling and emaciated figure.

The gaoler thrust her roughly outside the gate, where her husband and son were waiting for her. At first she appeared unaware of what was happening and looked around her, eyes wide with incomprehension.

"What are thee doing?" she murmured as the two men came and stood on either side of her, drawing her arms through theirs. "Thou'rt coming home," said Henry. "Thou'rt coming 'ome where thee belong," and they started to walk to their horse and cart, which was waiting a few steps away

Alice was having trouble walking and Henry realised that it was going to be a long time before his strong, healthy Alice would be restored to him. He lifted her up and attempted to carry her the short distance, but Alice, suddenly agitated, started to struggle.

"What are thee doing?" she repeated, trying to shout in

protest, but her voice was too weak to rise above a whisper and her feeble struggles were like those of fly caught in a spider's web; frantic but useless. She tried to strike her husband with her fist, but the blow carried no force and the effort reduced her strength further.

"Where are thee taking me?" the voice remained an agonised whisper, and the terror showed in her face.

"We're taking you 'ome, mam, like dad says." Speaking quietly to her, Harry attempted to calm his mother but she was now extremely agitated, although too weak to offer much resistance. A moment later despite her protests, she was lifted up onto the cart. Sitting on the seat between her Henry and Harry, she seemed to quieten. The truth was that her terrified exertions had worn her already tired body out completely. By the time they reached the farm, she was asleep with Harry's arm around her waist and her head resting on his shoulder.

She awoke for an instant as the sound of the gate to the yard being opened disturbed her. Raising her head a little, she whispered, "Are Ellen and Cornelius all right?" before slipping back into a doze.

You're home Alice, back with your family, all will be well now. Won't it? Alice?

***

Night time.

Henry, for the first time since their marriage, was not sharing the bed with Alice. He wanted to fold her in the comfort of his embracing arms, but she had shut herself away from him. Instead he was on the truckle bed in which Ellen usually slept. This, he reasoned, left space for Alice to sleep undisturbed. Nine-year-old Cornelius was sleeping on a makeshift mattress, sharing the loft, still fragrant with the remains of last year's apples, with Ellen. She was home from their grandmother's, asleep in Harry's truckle-bed. Harry, deprived of his usual sleeping place, had chosen not to sleep in the house. He was enjoying the advantage of sleeping without disturbance from his younger brother, comfortably curled up in the nest he had made for himself in the summer-scented hay barn.

Alice, unaware of her surroundings, lay, neither awake nor asleep. It made no difference, asleep or awake; she was always partly in the numbed world she had created for herself. It was an empty place, an attempt to protect herself from the other world, the one into which she was forced on that Easter morning. Now she was unable to free herself from either of them. They battled with each other for her mind.

Now faces loom out of the darkness of the empty place, drifting towards her.

They're coming for you Alice. Those faces. Staring eyes and malevolent. Men. Women. Even children. Evil faces born in your poor tortured mind. And the hands, Alice, stretching out towards you, intent on harm. Pale, ugly, hands and faces.

The noise emanating from these beings pulsates around her.
Voices.
Loud voices, soft voices.
Loud and threatening.
Soft and menacing.
Rising and falling against a background of twittering demons.

The soft voices are the worst, aren't they Alice. There's one in particular. So gentle, insistent, never letting go.
Ambivalent.
Is it friend or foe, Alice?

And pain, always there is pain. Everywhere. Her head, her legs, her belly and back. Nowhere is there any respite from the faces, the hands, the noise, the pain, the voices. She will never be free of the abyss into which she had been thrown.

Mercifully she is drawn, at last, into the empty place. She sleeps

Sunday, July 10th 1664

She wakes and opens her eyes. The light hurts them. She hears noises. Men, talking. Alarmed, she wonders what they are going to do to her. She tries to get up, to rise from the bed, but the sheet has twisted around her in her dreaming and she is too weak to extricate herself from it. She tries to call out but her voice is too weak. She falls back and is asleep again before her head touches the pillow.

***

Alice hadn't imagined the voices this time. Henry and Harry, up at their usual time, the early morning chores finished, were sitting at the table trying to reconcile themselves to the knowledge that the Alice in the curtained-off sleeping place was not the Alice that had previously slept there.

"Is Mam going to be all right, Dad?

Harry was doing his best to keep his feelings under control. The last few months had been distressing for all of them. Both he and Henry had tried as well as they could to keep their anxiety for Alice away from the younger children. When, at the age of fifteen, Harry had rescued the family from the soldiers who disrupted the Meeting at Richard Buxton's house, he had been treated as an adult. He was pleased even a little proud that he had earned this place in the family, but his emotions now were still those of a boy and his mother's obviously serious illness frightened him.

Henry chose to cloak his feelings of fear and anguish with a pretended lack of concern.

"Course she will, lad," he said with exaggerated brightness. "Now she's 'ome she'll be well in no time. Truly, she will." With an awkward movement he put an arm around his son's shoulders. "Dunna fret," he carried on, attempting cheerfulness he did not feel. "She'll be on 'er feet in no time, and like as not ordering all of us around again."

Harry, young as he was, doubted the truth of this but nodded silently. Henry moved his arm. Such overt expressions of affection were unfamiliar behaviour for either of them and made them both uncomfortable. They remained standing side by side for a moment before they moved apart again.

Henry took his jacket off the hook and turning to Harry before he went out, said, "Will thee go an' 'ave a look at 'er? Ask 'er if she wants to break 'er fast?" Going through the door, he said, "I'm going to see if Elizabeth Littleton will come and see 'er once in a while. She's going to need a woman around the place for a while, and Elizabeth's a good woman, very sensible." Then he remembered Alice's mother who had died earlier in the year and for whom the new baby would have been named. "If mother-in-law were still alive, she would have 'elped too. Another good woman." He thought for a moment, trying to get the biblical text right in his mind, then, paraphrasing said, "A good woman's value is above rubies".

After his father had left, Harry looked around him. For the first time he saw the untidy and uncared-for room as his mother would see it when she came down. Henry and his sons had tried to keep the house in order but without Alice's presence it had become a shambles.

Before her imprisonment there had been a young girl named Hannah who helped Alice in the house. In Alice's absence Hannah's parents had removed her, conscious of the impropriety of their daughter being alone with the two men. There was also a growing boy only slightly younger than Hannah, not to mention the men who worked on the farm.

Henry had thought of getting an older woman in to help, a presence which would have allowed Hannah to stay with the Bowmans, but he had never put the thought into action. All their efforts had been put into getting the Ridge steading back into full working order after the bailiffs visits. They were beginning to see the improvements they had hoped for, but it had been hard work, with little or no time for anything but farming matters. The truth was that Henry and his sons were all miserable during Alice's absence and exhausted at the end of a working day. Neither man cared what sort of squalor they lived in and their occasional clumsy efforts at house-work had been ineffective in removing the aura of neglect that hung over every room.

Against her will, the Bowmans' twelve-year-old daughter Ellen had been sent to stay with Henry's mother while Alice was away. Although she was now supposed to be at home to help care for their mother, she and Cornelius, after eating with their father and brother had slipped out and taken themselves to see what mischief the new day had to offer them. Ellen had missed their mother but was taking a last chance to enjoy freedom.

Cornelius, in his artless, heartless way, once over the initial shock, had relished the freedom from Alice's discipline. Despite Henry's pleading with him to behave, he regularly ran amok with his friends from the village, despite his father's pleading with him to behave. Harry, anxious to maintain his newly achieved adult position in the family, knew that it would help his father if he could have had more control over his brother, but Cornelius was strong-willed and in the face of the boy's high-spirited naughtiness Harry felt powerless.

Stirring himself, Harry set about getting some food for his mother. The family, depending on availability, sometimes breakfasted on a slice of bacon cut from one of the sides hanging from the kitchen ceiling. This, a chunk of bread and the weak beer they brewed themselves completed the meal. Today all the bacon had been used up and it would be December before the next pigs would be killed, so he climbed up to his parent's room, carrying just bread and beer.

Pausing before he drew the curtain aside, he was surprised by nervous thoughts of what would face him when he saw Alice and was instantly ashamed of himself. This was his mother he was about to see. The mother who had played with him when he was little, who had comforted him when he fell and grazed a knee or a hand. She had made his baby clothes. Tiny clothes which had been passed down to his sister and brother, now lying in the chest, waiting for the next baby.

He opened the curtain wide, dreading what he should see, but this woman in the bed was not the screaming, confused woman he had helped onto the cart yesterday. This woman lay on her side in the bed, her dark hair, without its cap, loose and lying across her face and the pillow, sleeping peacefully, her bony shape outlined in the sheet which covered her. She lay there, looking simultaneously like a sleeping baby and a frail, sick old woman. He felt overpoweringly sorry for her and knew, in that moment, that there was nothing he wouldn't do to help her. Suddenly he realised, for the first time, that the feeling he was experiencing wasn't pity, it was love.

He walked over to the bed, the cup of small beer and piece of bread on a platter in one hand and with the other he gently touched her shoulder. She was instantly awake and sat up, startled and alert. With the surprise of her sudden movement Harry nearly dropped the food and drink but composed himself quickly. Alice was staring at him. When she spoke it was in the same feeble whisper as on the previous day. "Harry?" she breathed, "Have you come to take me home?" Then she looked around the room, which had once been so familiar to her. "Where's this?"

"Home, Mam," the boy replied. He sat on the bed beside his mother, looking at her; looking for signs of the mother he knew. He had got used to her physical deterioration while visiting her in prison and the House of Correction. Although it was distressing, in those places where everybody looked the same, it had been possible to accept the change in her to some extent. He was sure she would be her old self when she was released from that awful place. But here, in her own home, his mother's emaciated form and distracted behaviour seemed more strange and difficult to contend with. His lips quivered, and his eyes filled with tears.

"Thee's 'ome, where thee belong," he said again. She was not listening and continued to look uncomprehendingly around the room. Harry tried to draw her attention to the food, which he had put, beside her.

"There's bread and beer for thee. Eat it up, Mam, thee will feel better for 'aving something to eat."

"Yes," she whispered absently, "Yes, yes, thee's right, I will." Her voice became a little stronger. "Harry, where's thy father?"

59

"Dad's gone to see Elizabeth Littleton, to ask 'er to come and look after thee a bit," he said, smiling at her, thankful for this tiny sign of comprehension. "It won't be long before 'e's back."

He broke off a piece of bread, dipped it in the beer to soften it and held it out to her, but she was uninterested. "Eat something, Mam, please." He had a sudden remembrance of other times when she had been the coaxing one, trying to get a fractious Ellen or Cornelius to eat their dinner. This time the son was persuading the mother to eat. It felt wrong, awkward, and he wished his father would hurry up.

He was stirred out of his thoughts by his mother's sudden movement. She stopped surveying the room and turned to look at him, a sharp, angry expression on her face.

"What are thee doing here? The voice remained weak, but the tone was demanding. "There is nothing for thee here. This is my house. Get out!"

Her voice rose, "Get out, get out! Out!" She was trying to scream at him now, attempting to untangle herself from the sheet and get out of the bed. She aimed feeble blows with her fists against his head and body. He stood up and tried to restrain her. "Get out! Get out! "she screeched and, with a shock, he noticed some of her teeth were missing. "There is nothing more to be had." The food and drink fell to the floor as Alice railed against hallucinatory bailiffs.

"Alice! Alice!"

Never had Harry been so pleased to see his father and in the doorway close behind him, Elizabeth Littleton.

Henry, hiding whatever surprise and distress he was feeling, walked over to where his wife was still beating their transfixed eldest son with ineffectual blows from fragile fists. "Leave him alone, love," he said quietly. It had no effect. He raised his voice a little, "Leave Harry alone!"

He was by the bed now and taking hold of both Harry's arms above the elbows, firmly moved his son out of the sleeping-place, turning him round to face the doorway. "Out of the way, lad. Out of her sight for the moment. Thee can come back when she is calmer." He turned to Alice, who now transferred her aggression to him, while he continued in his efforts to soothe her.

***

Trying to separate himself from the disorder and confusion at the other end of the room, Harry sat staring at a spider scurrying across the table. He put a finger in its way, and the tiny creature crawled onto his hand before moving onto his sleeve. He encouraged it onto his other hand, from there onto the sill of the open window and away. He thought about his mother. She had taught him the names of the birds and the trees, flowers and insects. She had taught him how to tell what weather was coming by looking at the clouds, by listening to the wind, by observing the movements of birds or leaves on trees.

Would she ever be the same again?

Would he ever be the same again?

Meanwhile, Elizabeth Littleton picked up the bread and broken pottery from the floor and set about tidying the whole room. She thought, 'Poor soul. How much agony of mind thee must be in, and what will become of thee?'

***

For most of July Alice was subject to periods of complete indifference to her surroundings, alternating with times of mental clarity so acute that all her senses seemed more alive than they had ever been before. At such times everything she looked at seemed brighter, more clearly defined, as if lit by a stronger light than had been there before. Then she was being, as Henry described it, 'my Alice once more.' It wasn't only her vision which seemed so profoundly affected. Her hearing seemed more acute, sounds were not just a little louder but, according to their nature, sweeter than usual, or more jarring, or slightly more or less beautiful than she had ever previously heard.

෩ ෨

CHAPTER NINE

Thursday, July 28th. 1664

One day when she was grown physically stronger, she walked with Henry up on to the top of the nearby ridge which gave the steading its name. Together they had looked out over the moors laid out before them, shimmering slightly under the July sun. From far above them came the joyful song of a skylark, a tiny, hovering spot, pouring its heart out into the sky. Henry's eyes searched the turf around their feet. "We must be near its nest," he said. But Alice was not listening to him. She was entranced, bewitched, by the sound of the bird and wanted to tell him how she felt. Instead she burst into tears and could only say "It's so beautiful; so beautiful."

Hold on to the sky full of music, Alice, hold on to the skylark. In your darkest times, remember a tiny bird filling the firmament with beauty.

Afterwards, whenever she remembered the lark's song, she smiled to herself at the thought. It hadn't just been that heavenly sound; it had been everything that she saw and felt at the time. The wideness of the open green space and the blueness of the sky; the delicious sensation on her neck as the breeze released tendrils of hair from the constriction of her cap. Even just the knowledge that beloved Henry was standing beside her. All these things were part of the magic of a particular moment. In that moment she knew that the combination of the things making it; the time of day, the weather and her own responses, were unique to that moment and she recognised it for what it was. Pure happiness.

There were black moments, when she was frightened of the slightest sound or movement. When she felt that the only way she could react to the fear was with aggression, even against her children. There were times when she was so confused that she thought that she was back in gaol screaming her anguish at the physical restriction. Mercifully, such times were only remembered afterwards as if part of a dimly lit dream and she was only faintly aware of how she had behaved. All she knew was that she had been through the 'black' time and this was because of the depression she suffered afterwards.

At these times, like an automaton, she took part in the familiar world around her, following the routine she had been used to. Helped by Elizabeth Littleton she went through the familiar preparation of meals and keeping the living place clean and tidy. She even helped a little with the farm work although without enthusiasm, as she was still not yet restored to full physical health. Often, like a grey residue of the blackness, she saw everything through the misty veil of depression while her family waited until the happiness returned.

The skylark, Alice, hold on to the lark, the blue sky, the space, the air.

***

As July moved into August, Alice's mental and physical health continued to improve. She gained a little weight; her dark hair lost its lank dryness, some of the fire returned to her eyes and her general well being improved. The manic episodes diminished although they did not cease entirely. Neither did the depression.

As her recovery progressed she was better able to analyse her situation. She recognised that when she started to feel a certain lowness of spirit, the best way to combat it was to work.

So she worked.

Pewter and copper, replacements for much of the household goods taken away by the bailiffs two years ago, sparkled, rubbed with stems of horsetail plant, or cleaned with boiling vinegar. The inside of the cottage, neglected by her husband and children during her illness, became tidier. Even the inside of the stone walls were brushed down with a bunch of feathers and Henry was directed to cut a bough of holly and sweep the chimney. In a festival of laundry lasting days, all of everyone's clothes were washed and mended, along with the bedclothes.

Wednesday, August 31st 1664

At the end of the month came the blow. Henry and Alice were arrested. Alice remained calm, which pleased Henry. There was good in everything and the especially good thing today was that Alice seemed certainly to have regained her full strength. She was early in pregnancy and a little sickly in the mornings, but she had shown today that she was fully herself again. A strong woman taking everything in her stride, even this unfortunate situation.

Henry was asked to pay the fine for not attending Church. He refused and the constable turned to Alice and asked her the same question. Her answer was a firm, quiet "No" even when it was pointed out that the penalties would be the invasion of their house and removal of goods to the value of the fine, the answer remained the same.

After questioning they were allowed to go home, for which they politely thanked the Constable and blessed him in the name of the Lord. Despite this they were manhandled out into the street, amid loud jeers and a hail of stones and street filth thrown by the small crowd that had gathered.

Thursday September 1st 1664

When the bailiffs burst into the house all Alice's anxieties returned and they didn't leave her when the bailiffs left. She carried on trying to prevent the men taking her belongings even after they had removed what they wanted.

Alice, Alice You run from room to room, like a trapped bird that the wind has blown through a window.

How desperately you gather up disparate belongings. A pot here, a pair of pillows there, a jerkin, a plate of apples, anything. Because today the nightmare returned and you're trying to hold your home together, aren't you?

Don't you care that you suddenly seem to have lost all the restraint and dignity that came back with your return to health?

It's because of the bailiffs, isn't it, Alice?

Please, please, Alice. Calmly, quietly.

Alice!

"Alice!"

Henry, confused perplexed and bewildered, followed her on her progress through the house. He watched, baffled, as she scooped up a handful of spoons and bowls from the table. So far as he was concerned the matter of the fines was at an end. The punishment had been administered by the bailiffs and the two of them were free to resume normal life.

He had thought his wife recovered from the temporary madness brought on by her imprisonment and the death of her baby. But here she was, all control gone. Eyes staring, the wild black hair framing her white, open-mouthed face.

Alice couldn't understand his calmness.

Once more there had been noise and commotion; loud voices and harsh words and through it all Henry had remained so calm.

Who is in the real world, Alice? Is it your dear husband, so steady and true and faithful, strong in the light of the Lord? Accepting as if it were normal that peaceable Quakers should be fined for not going to church. Be distrained of goods worth more than the value of the fine. The bailiffs have been, taken what they wanted from the house and left, but still he is peaceful and composed.

Or is the real world where you are? Noisy and dark, confused and frightening, where God holds no sway?

A terrifying thought came into Alice's head. Could this be the Devil's work? Was she in Hell?

Henry put his arm around his wife, quelling her agitation a little and gently drawing her to him as she trembled and wept. He and his children would have to start all over again, bringing Alice back to her senses. It wouldn't, couldn't, be so bad this time, he thought. They knew how to do it this time. With God's help they could, must do it.

80 03

CHAPTER TEN

Thursday, October 27th 1664

John Taylor stood facing five of the Meeting's Elders and its Clerk. They were six men, who'd been among those converted to Quakerism at one of George Fox's outdoor Meetings in the 1650s. Deeply respected and profoundly knowledgeable in all Quaker practises and principles, their severe, unbending approach to all aspects of life, in as well as out of the Meeting, was evident in each of their unsmiling countenances.

They were subjecting John to concentrated interrogation about his association with Frances Palmer. Every one of their questions and John's replies were being carefully being written down by Peter Littleton, acting as Clerk. Once or twice he asked for a little pause in proceedings, so as to complete his note-taking accurately. For John, these brief pauses had been the only respite from his ordeal, which had been going on for nearly three hours.

He could not help but be overawed by the company he was in and his anxiety was obvious. He tried to stop trembling, to steady his breathing and conceal his nervousness, but he was sweating profusely and that he could not control. He felt as if his face was shaking, while his heart thumped in his chest. He didn't know what to do with his hands. He also needed to pass water.

The most senior Elder present, Isaac Brown, raised his head to look at the young man before him. Having a son of his own, he had a certain amount of sympathy for John's youthful discomfiture, but not for the course of action he was proposing to take. The duty of the Elders today was clear, unpleasant though it may be. It was time to make a decision.

"I ask thee again, Friend, is this young woman an honest,

righteous and respectable woman?"

"Yes, Friend, " John replied. He had lost count of the number of times the question had been put to him. Now already much-repeated questions were asked again.

"Does she love God, follow His Commandments, and pray daily for her soul's salvation?"

"Yes, she does, Friend."

"She is a good Christian, is she not?"

"Yes, she is, Friend."

"Is this Christian woman, who loves the Lord, says her prayers and, by all accounts, lives a pure and innocent life willing to become a member of our Meeting?"

John was struggling to keep what little he had of his composure.

"It would be against 'er upbringing and 'er conscience, Friend," he stammered. His mind was now entering a dream-like state, in which he was becoming increasingly unsure about whether this was reality or a dreadful nightmare. It seemed to him that he had been answering the same questions with the same responses for an eternity. The image of a dog chasing its tail came into his mind. Round and round and round it went, in an unending circle of frantic, brainless activity. He was startled out of his waking nightmare by Isaac Brown's voice.

"... Her conscience!" The Elder's indignant voice thundered into his bewildered thoughts. "What of thine own conscience, Friend, in the face of her foolish adherence to a wicked and unenlightened religion? Thou tells us that thee has put aside all the flummery of religious ritual and ceremony, recognising it as the invention of at best misguided, at worst evil, men. Thee says thee has no use for arrogant priests, whom ignorant people see as the only ones who can call upon God. Thee knows that everyone has God's spirit within them, and can, in turn, call upon him themselves, without a priest's intervention, the only true intermediary being Christ himself"

Isaac had risen to his feet while he was speaking and, although looking at him, hadn't really seen John, until now. Once again, observing the miserable young man before him, he was brought to mind of his own son, as a five-year-old, tearful and woebegone, because he had disappointed his father for some now-forgotten transgression. For a fleeting moment he wished he could put an arm around the lad's shoulders and tell him all would be well, but his was no minor childish prank. Principles, hard though they were to live by, had to be upheld no matter what the cost. John would have to put all thought of marriage to Frances Palmer out of his mind. If he could not he must suffer the consequences.

"If Frances Palmer will not become a member of this Meeting, and thee wishes to marry her against the wishes of thy parents and this Society, John Taylor, thee will be cast out of it." Isaac paused for a few moments. The silence rested heavily on the meeting.

"Think again, lad, "Isaac said in kinder tone, "and come before us at next Monthly Meeting".

℘ℛ

CHAPTER ELEVEN

Saturday, October 29th 1664

Eddie Morris stared morosely at his ale, while Dai Davis, with an equal measure of glumness, leaned on the table, resting his chin on his hand as he regarded the rain beating against the tiny window. It was early in the evening and the alehouse was deserted except for themselves and the landlord, busying himself in the back room.

The crowd, who usually livened the house up on a Saturday evening, had not yet arrived to fill it with the sound of working men's' rough talk and laughter. On some evenings there would be the sound of tunes played, inexpertly but enthusiastically, on fiddle or pipe, or someone may give them a song or two, but not tonight, not yet. That was the worst thing about arriving too early. There was no waiting for a drink, which was good, but neither was there much enjoyment in the drinking of it.

Eddie stirred on his seat and shifted his gaze from the window to look at his friend. "Is George coming to-night?" he asked, more to make conversation than because he wanted to know. George always met them there. Of course he would be coming tonight.

"I s'pose so." The reply did not invite further speculation. Both men returned to their private thoughts, although this time Edward directed his gaze at the rain-spattered window and Dai at his almost empty tankard.

Dai didn't think that George's presence would do a great deal to raise the spirits of the company anyway, the way he'd been lately. Quiet and bad-tempered. Not like himself at all. He was often a silent member of their trio, of course, but not usually surly. Usually he was quite a well-tempered man, very tolerant. So tolerant indeed, that he was often the butt of other men's' jokes and teasing. Even putting up with a certain amount of mild verbal bullying.

The three men, all of an age, had known one another as long as they could remember. Their mothers had been friends, going to each other's weddings and later enduring pregnancy together. Dai's and Edward's fathers had both worked as labourers on Master Chinnock's farm; the old Master Chinnock, that was, and each had followed in their father's footsteps. George too, had learned the wheelwright's trade from his father.

When George's wife had died leaving him with their little girl, the other two men's wives had helped him as much as they could, but only until he told them, as tactfully as he knew how, that he could care for his daughter himself. They knew that their concern was appreciated, but they also knew instinctively when to withdraw, although they were unsure about how he would fare without their help. They had always been good friends and neighbours.

Eddie broke the silence. "What d'ye think is the matter with old George?" He drank a mouthful of his ale. "'E's bin a bit into 'imself lately, aint 'e? He put his pot down on the table and leaned closer to Dai over the table. "I wonder if it's something to do with that daughter of 'is," he said in a low voice, which then became a conspiratorial whisper, "Yer don't think she's in the family way, do yer?"

Dai had been wondering this himself. Susan could not have expected that her alliance with John Taylor would go unnoticed by people in the village, especially her father's friends. She surely could not be that green. Despite these private opinions, he was reluctant to indulge in the sort of 'women's gossip' that seemed imminent. His son, Robert, like many other village boys, had lusted after Frances. Like them, he had been rebuffed in no uncertain manner.

Dai was unwilling to have the matter raised again.

"Oh, no, no," he said quickly, and truthfully. "She wouldn't get up to that sort of mischief. She's a good girl, that one. Won't allow anyone to take liberties with 'er. Oh, no. Got more self-respect, she 'as." He leaned a little further back on his bench. Edward was still leaning towards him, and his breath wasn't all that sweet. "No, no," he said again, and got up. "Ready for another one?"

There were more men and one or two women in the room, when, about a quarter of an hour later, George came in. Jack the fiddler had arrived earlier too and now struck up with 'Drive the Cold Winter Away', a cheerful jig, for which the alehouse keeper was grateful. 'It's been a mighty dull evening so far,' he'd thought, blaming the rain.

George removed his hat as he entered the alehouse and left it on one of the hooks on the wall just inside the door, but the shoulders of his jacket were very wet, so was his face, which he wiped with his hands. He bought his ale and looked around briefly before sitting down at the table with Edward and Dai. He smelt of the outdoors and wet leather.

Eddie and Dai were not going to show their concern for him yet. If they should feel that it was needed, they might offer to help, but not so that anyone would notice. By silent mutual consent they had decided that they were going to find out what was on his mind.

Any tactful sort of way to ask the question was a difficulty that Eddie was blithely unaware of. "What's bin the matter with you lately, George?" he asked. "You've bin a real misery. 'As there bin some mishap at 'ome."

George stared at him for a moment. He experienced an uncomfortable mixture of emotions more familiar to him with each passing day. Surprise, anger, indignation, disappointment, desolation and misery. Familiarity did not make dealing with these sensations any easier. In fact, it made them more unbearable. He felt a great surge of feeling yet his brain was working logically and methodically. He was deaf to the room humming with the sound of cheerful voices and the spitting of the fire when the occasional drops of rain fell down the chimney on to the smouldering embers.

Jack, the fiddler now struck up 'Goddesses' and the simple, repetitive tune, unheard by George who was more involved in what he was about to say, would for ever afterwards remind Dai of this rainy evening at the Green Man.

"George?"

Edward was regretting his enquiry. George's expression was murderous but his voice was silkily quiet. He did not rise from his seat and would have appeared to everyone else in the room that the men were having a normal conversation. As he spoke George glanced occasionally from one man to the other ensuring that they listened to every word he said.

"I have cared for that girl since she was no higher than my hip," he said. "I've fed and clothed 'er; I've bound up 'er scratched knees; I've taught her how to behave at 'ome, in company, in neighbours' 'ouses, in church; I've 'ad 'er educated more than me or 'er mother ever was. Everything I 'ave ever done 'as been done for 'er. Dai, you know 'ow awkward I felt about it, but I even asked your wife to tell 'er about women's things."

Dai, startled out of his spellbound concentration on George's words, jumped at the sound of his name, thinking simultaneously, 'She is in the family way', while the ominously quiet voice continued to be heard but only by the two men he was addressing.

"... One of those strange people who won't pay their taxes, or tithes, or church dues. They'd go to prison first. And she wants to marry one. Over my dead body, I've told 'er. I will not let 'er, and that's the truth of it. "His expression relaxed. "I know people are gossiping about what she's supposed to be doing. They're saying bad things about her which aint true. You two are as well, I know, and all along I've just kept quiet about it, like I've kept quiet about a lot of things. Well, I've 'ad enough of your teasing and mocking, not just about this business, but in lots of other ways too. So I'll thank you both to put an end to it now, and if you do then we'll stay friends."

He drained his tankard before rising from the table and saying in a more pleasant tone, "I'll bid you both good night, old friends, and hope to see you here again on Wednesday. "

Then, leaving them staring at his back, he walked to the door, took his hat off the peg, shook any remaining raindrops off it, put it on his head and walked out of the alehouse.

Eddie and Dai, dumbfounded, looked at one another and then through the window as George walked past in the still-pouring rain.

The alehouse-keeper's wife added more logs to the fire, which dulled its glow a little.

"Well," said Dai.

"Mm, "said Edward.

৪০ ৫৪

CHAPTER TWELVE

Thursday, November 3rd 1664

The day was cold and overcast. It had been foggy for most of the morning, but was clearing. A pale autumn sun cast a feeble light over the village and was thawing the ground frost a little.

Frances Palmer walked along the muddy road to her home past the stand of trees just before Ridge Farm where the Bowman family had been working hard to get back on their feet. Mistress Bowman was a lot better in her health and could often be seen working with her husband, their sons and the lad whom they'd taken in. She seemed to have recovered from her 'troubles'. Mistress Bowman was expecting again, too. She always had lovely babies.

Frances smiled to herself. She would like to have babies some day. Muffled up in her warm winter cloak, with her hood well up over her head and part of her face, she continued on her way. The uncomfortable and clumsy pattens on her feet were supposed to keep her shoes dry as she went about the morning errands, but despite them her feet were damp and cold. She cheered herself with thoughts of the warm fire at home.

There were other thoughts keeping her in excited high spirits, too. At this time of the day, just about the time workmen were taking a mid-day beak for bread and cheese and a drink of small beer, you never knew who you may meet on the road. It didn't always happen, but this was the place where she was most likely to meet one particular young carpenter, just by the bridge over the river.

They hadn't met for about a week and a half. Almost daily Frances, since then, had slipped out of the house to visit the village, doing errands which were mostly genuine, though always hoping to see John Taylor, but she hadn't seen him for all that time. He father, George Palmer, had forbidden her to see John ever again, which was the reason for her furtive behaviour. She didn't like deceiving her father and was unhappy that such measures had to be taken, but her mind was made up now. She had something special to tell John, which she knew would make him happy. Her heart started to beat just a little quicker than usual as his familiar figure rounded the corner, by the stand of beech trees. She started to walk faster although hampered by her heavy basket and her pattens. Once or twice she slipped a little on the frosty ground but they were soon face to face. His serious face to her excited, smiling one.

"What's wrong, John?" she asked. His unsmiling expression was making her nervous. Even when circumstances had been difficult over the last few months, their happiness in each others' company always conquered other anxieties, if only for the first few minutes after they met. The religious influences brought to bear on both of them by John's adoptive family, the Ockendens and Franny's father, each loving, each immoveable, pulled them in opposite directions. More recently the intervention of the Elders of the Meeting added its own strain. She had an apprehensive twisting feeling in her stomach that anticipated some, so far unknown, disaster.

Frances had decided to throw in her lot with the Quakers and the decision had relieved her of much anxiety. She was not and never would be, convinced that they were right, but it seemed the best solution to the problem. She had not yet told her father and when she did she knew it would make him unhappy, but she'd looked forward to giving John the good news. She'd even started dreaming of marrying John and the exciting business of putting their home together.

Now, in her heart, she knew that her cheerful optimism may have been a mistake. She could tell that what he was going to say would be troubling. He was so open and honest that virtually every emotion, happy or sad, was apparent in his expression.

As Frances came close to him and lifted her face up to him, John did not kiss her cheek as usual. He turned his head away and stood apart from her, shifting awkwardly from foot to foot. Telling her was going to be the hardest thing he had ever had to do and he needed all his reserves of emotional strength to say what he knew had to be said.

"The Elders asked me to carefully consider what would 'appen if I should marry out of the Meeting, Franny." He paused, thinking, 'I'm hurting the person I love more than anyone else in the world'. He managed to raise his head and, avoiding her eyes, looked over her left shoulder towards the beech trees, just visible through the clearing fog, as they guarded the little bridge over the stream. How could they look so normal when there was this turmoil in his life?

The words came out in a rush, "I'll 'ave to leave the Meeting, Franny." He was searching wildly for words which would be the truth but not hurt her too much.

"If anyone marries out of the meeting, they're cast out. If I marry thee, my family and Friends would disown me and neither family nor Friends would ever accept thee as my wife. I can't put you through that, it wouldn't be fair to thee. So, I'll 'ave to come to the steeple-house, at least thy father would be pleased."

Feeling humiliated and cowardly and knowing that his reasoning was flawed, his voice faltered and stopped. With an effort he forced himself, at last, to look into her beautiful face. She was smiling. She was about to do the most unselfish thing that she had ever done in all her life.

John's religion meant much more to him than Franny's did to her. The Law said that someone from every household had to go to church at least once a month if they were not to incur fines. For her it was a necessary duty, nothing more. She had no real desire to join a band of people whose every action seemed designed to provoke the wrath of the Constable, the Rector, Churchwardens and the neighbours. Her reasons for the decision were grounded in her love for John and a sincere desire that he should be happy.

"You don't have to be cast out, my love," she said. "And

you don't 'ave to come to the steeple-house. I've made up my mind to join you. I'll be your loving Friend and, even though you've never asked me, I'll also be your loving wife."

John reacted as Frances had hoped he would. His expression was of complete joy as he grasped both her hands in his, although his anxiety was clear as he asked, "What'll your father say, when I ask 'im if I can marry you?"

Frances was dismissive.

Secure in her love for John and with a vision of their future life together she felt an overpowering belief in her own invincibility. She had thought about everything and she saw no reason why her father should be angry when he heard the news. If there was any difficulty, she was confident that she could persuade him that what she was doing was right for her. Should her father still not be convinced she trusted her ability to get her own way. She was sure that in the end he would come to respect, even like, John for his principles, his kindness and his honesty.

"Don't worry my love," she said. "I'll have a little talk with 'im then I'll let you know when you can come to see 'im." She suddenly looked around her. The fog had cleared away completely now and the sun, though weak, warmed her a little. Facing him and smiling, she said, "Isn't it a lovely day, John?"

***

That night Frances lay awake in her narrow bed under the eaves of the cottage. Through the small window she could see, moon-lit, the fields and trees that she had known since she was born. The elation which had brightened her mid-day was gone in the middle of this night. She had tossed and turned for hours and still sleep would not come. She had cried for a long time, which had exhausted her but had not released all the tensions within her.

Her father had been in no mood to receive the news that Frances was about to join a group of mad men and women. He was still recovering from his outburst to Eddie and Dai of a few evenings ago. Usually a quiet, inoffensive man, he appeared to have put the incident behind him, as had his friends, but he was still angry with his daughter. Except for the religious differences, he would have been perfectly happy with the match. George had met John once or twice, around the village. As Frances had said, he seemed a good, honest and reliable young man; a hard worker who would make someone a son-in-law to be proud of.

It was just his religion.

Which was strange, because he didn't seem to be as mad as all that. He spoke in a way that many found disrespectful, particularly the gentry, who thought 'thee' and 'thou' was an over-familiar way to speak. His clothes were plain and sober and to be truthful, he didn't smile much. George had heard some of these 'Children of the Light', as they sometimes called themselves, preaching in the street, accosting passers by and making nuisances of themselves. John, on the other hand, seemed a quiet lad. With a shock George realised that he was not unlike himself at the same age.

But when Frances told him that she was going to leave the church, George lost his patience with her. This revelation, after what had happened that night at the alehouse, was the last straw. He dampened her excitement with one sentence.

"If you marry that lad, I'll not answer for the consequences," he stated quietly and firmly. "Now go to bed."

***

Frances's thoughts turned over and over again. This should have been one of the happiest days of her life, John's and her father's too. A problem she thought resolved had not gone away and there seemed to be no solution to it. Worn out, just before dawn, she slept. The last things she heard before her sore eyes closed were the ivy tapping against the window and her father in the next room saying her mother's name in his sleep.

***

A little further out of the village at the Ridge steading, Alice Bowman also lay awake in a house full of sleep. Hester lay in Henry's place beside her. Harry and Cornelius had been restored to their usual place in the loft. Hard-working Daniel slept soundly in a corner of the kitchen-place, with Meg the dog curled up at the back of his knees.

Alice had more than her present pregnancy on her mind tonight. After three months of comparatively tranquil life the world was once more turned upside down. Henry was in gaol again and likely to be for some time.

Oh, Alice. And you thought everything was getting a little better now. Now that you were back in your own home, with your mind in perfect health.

Alice, try to remember those early days following your release. In a strange way they seemed to be some of the happiest days of your life, didn't they? Do you remember the warm sense of being very weak in body and mind but surrounded by love and protection, as you grew stronger? You and your family learning to live together again?

Ah, Alice, you were happy then. You're only remembering the good times, aren't you?

But.

Sometimes.

It's good that, sometimes, you can't quite remember the bad times. Forgetting's a protection. Hold on to the good times. Try to look forward to the baby. Hold on to the happiness. You are going to need those gifts.

Of happiness.

Forgetfulness.

***

Henry with ten other Friends, all farmers, yeomen and husbandmen, had refused to pay tithes. The annual charge made by the church was based on the value of one tenth of every farm's produce. All had raised the same objections that they had raised on previous occasions. All accepted that their crops, animals, everything they had, were gifts from God the Creator, to whom thanks should be given. They agreed that giving voluntary tribute to the Lord in the form of charitable dues to the Church which were then distributed amongst the poor of the parish, was the right and proper duty of every Christian. However they did not agree that most of the dues should be diverted straight into the pockets of rectors in the parish, with vicars receiving a lesser sum.

Because they had all faced the same charge before, the Quakers knew that the penalty would be harsher this time. Their answers, given quietly, firmly and sincerely to the court, were not accepted. All of them were sentenced to terms of imprisonment.

80 03

CHAPTER THIRTEEN

November 4th 1664

Alice lay in bed feeling her kicking baby and looking out on to a misty autumn morning. She had an urgent call of nature. She must get up. Ellen and Cornelius were arguing again. Harry was going hedge cutting today and she herself had much work to do about the house and farm.

She thought, 'Henry will be waking up in prison this morning.'

God help you, Alice. Is it worth it? For the sake of refusing to pay tithes of a few shillings? Oh, Alice. Alice.

***

Frances Palmer performed her household duties with habitual ease. Though she, too, had slept little during the previous night. Earlier than usual she was out of bed and had breakfasted before her father rose and went out. His breakfast was ready for when he came in after a couple of hours' work. As was customary for the woman of the house she stood in attendance on him while he ate and drank the food she placed before him.

Her "Good morning, Dad," had received no reply, which was not out of the ordinary. George was not a very communicative man at any time, especially in the morning, but he usually grunted some sort of response to her greeting at this time of day or managed the trace of a smile.

"It's a cold morning, Dad," she said as she helped him back into his working coat before he left to go to his workshop in the yard. Once more there was no reply. She held the door open for him, "I'll have dinner ready for you at the usual time," she said. But he was already out in the foggy air, his back ignoring her.

Since the first emotional scene with her father, Frances tried hard to make her father change his mind about John. George remained firm in his decision. He even reiterated his threat that if his daughter joined the Quakers he would have nothing further to do with her. Despite all her frequent, tearful pleas to him to try to see John as she saw him, he was unmoved. In the end she had to admit defeat and raised the subject no more. The atmosphere in the house was very strained and uncomfortable, with both father and daughter, who loved each other dearly, avoiding physical or verbal contact as much as possible

Closing the door Frances turned to the table and began to clear the things away, although she found it difficult to concentrate on her work. She had drawn the water required for the day from the pump in the yard and now poured some of it, heated on the fire, into a bowl on the table and began to wash the pots.

After she had finished wiping the things to dry them she paused for a moment. She put her hands back into the water, reluctant to throw the warmth of it away on this cold morning, then tears began to trickle down her cheeks and onto her arms. She sniffed once or twice, refusing to give way to her hurt and disappointment, then tried to wipe her cheeks with the backs of her damp hands. It was an illogical thing to do and the idiocy of the action broke her resolve and she began to cry in earnest, standing with her hands over her face, as she wept.

After a while, when she could weep no more, she determined to get on with her domestic work, so she made herself bustle about, tidying, dusting furniture, sweeping. As the morning wore on the impetus for housework dropped increasingly until she could bear the tension no more. Throwing a shawl around her shoulders, she intended to fetch firewood from the outside store and bring it in to dry by the fire. Instead she made her way to her father's workshop which was separate to the house. He had never hurt her feelings so much as he had this morning and she wanted to make things right with him.

As she entered the workshop bringing a gust of wind and a few snowflakes in with her, George, humming tunelessly, was running his hands over a completed wheel. If asked, he would have said that he was checking for any roughness, but he, too, had found it difficult to concentrate on his work this morning and had not done a great deal. After thinking of nothing else so far this day he hated himself for how he had treated her at breakfast-time, but could not, in all conscience, forgive her for what she had said the previous evening. He did not look at his daughter as she came in and continued humming and handling the wood.

Frances closed the door behind her and stood there for a while. She loved the workshop with its smells of wood, glue and sawdust, but today she hardly noticed it.

"Dad," she said, hesitatingly.

He didn't stop what he was doing.

She repeated the word again, louder, "Dad."

George straightened, and turned to look at her. "Well, Frances?" he said, quietly, grimly. She moved nearer to him. "I'm sorry, Dad." She spoke in a low voice. Her father saw that she was trembling and for a moment his heart melted, but his resolve hardened.

Frances spoke again, more strongly this time. "I'm very sorry, dad, and I know I made you angry last night, but I really love John," her father made an impatient gesture, "I really love 'im, and he loves me. I know 'e does, and we want to get married. But there's this religion thing in the way."

George snorted. "'Religion thing!' What sort of talk is that? Religion is not a thing, to pick up or throw away like a toy. You say you want to turn to 'is religion. Well, I say as you won't and that's all there is to say." He turned back to his work.

Frances took a deep breath. She had spent most of the night tormented by her thoughts, only dropping to sleep a couple of hours before she was due to wake up. In the morning things seemed a little clearer and she had news for her father, if he was of a mind to receive it.

"I've decided not to go to 'is meeting," she spoke on a rush of breath and felt better for having said it out loud.

Her father showed little interest at first, then putting the finished wheel to one side, he turned to look at her and she could see plainly that he was not going to give way easily.

"So you've decided," he said.

"You've decided," his voice rose now,

"You can't 'decide' about this. The decision about religion was made for you by your godparents when you were christened and by yourself on the day you first took the Sacrament. The Church," he said emphatically, looking at her intensely, "The Church says that those meetings are blasphemous and irreligious. Also, it says, an' I say, too, you mustn't go to a meeting with them people."

"That's what I've been trying to tell you, Dad," Frances replied earnestly, "I'm going to ask John to leave the Meeting and come to Church with me, with us."

Even as she spoke, Frances, despite the strength of her feelings, was beginning to realise the improbability of such a thing happening. But having made the decision and hearing her voice pronouncing the words she resolved to continue with her plan, whatever the consequence may be.

George remained expressionless, keeping his feelings, a mixture of elation, scepticism and relief, to himself. For the time being he thought it best to allow himself little in the way of hope.

"Very well," he said, "Go to 'im tomorrow, tell 'im your plan. If 'e agrees tell 'im 'e can come and see me. After 'e's been to Church on Sunday."

Again his emphasis was on the word 'Church'. Then, the matter closed so far as he was concerned, he returned to his work, making no response when his delighted daughter kissed his cheek.

℘ଔ

CHAPTER FOURTEEN

Saturday, November 5th 1664

At The Grange the Chinnocks were preparing for the annual celebration of the deliverance in 1605 of King James, father of the present king, and Members of the Houses of Parliament, from murder by gunpowder, treason and plot. Ruth Chinnock intended that their festivities would be of a more restrained nature than those of other inhabitants of the area. Their house was a little outside the village in a prominent position, approached by a moderately long drive and it was unlikely that their party would be disturbed by the local rowdies, who, last year, had created such havoc.

As usual, crowds of young reprobates and their friends from other villages had rampaged around the countryside. They had been in search of anything combustible, stripping down gates, fences, stealing timber from innocent peoples' barns and generally making nuisances of themselves. Then they had built bonfires on any accessible patch of ground. Following this, leaving guards to make sure the fruits of their efforts were not themselves pillaged, they had removed themselves to other villages, to wreak the same kind of damage there.

No, Master Abel Chinnock and his wife, of The Grange, would hold an altogether more sedate and tasteful event. When Ruth had suggested the celebration, Abel had been doubtful of the wisdom of the proposition. His wife was the dearest treasure to him but she was liable to work herself into an attack of hysteria if the slightest thing upset her daily routine. Unlike himself, usually a placid, even stolid man, occasionally inclined to dry wit, Ruth was more volatile, especially when confronted with the unfamiliar.

She had made a list. Her widowed mother, Mistress Davies and Rebecca, her unmarried sister should come. There would also be Abel's son, Samuel, the eldest of four children from his first marriage, and Dorcas, his wife. The list also included half a dozen good friends and four others who were not so well known to either her or Abel. Ruth felt that these four could be of use, socially and professionally, to her husband.

Another list was of things she needed to do. She would have to supervise the setting-out of the room, including the seating arrangements at the supper table. Mistress Denny, the cook/housekeeper, must be told all her instructions for the day, including what was to be on the menu and see to the purchasing of necessary food and drink, which would be on another list.

Ruth put her plans for the evening to Abel, who protested once or twice, but gave up when he realised that she was set upon the idea and would become very upset if thwarted in any way. He knew that he was giving way to Ruth, which he had never done with his first wife but, for all her apparent vulnerability, his wife could sometimes be very wilful. He managed, however, to persuade her to reduce the number of guests. There would now be Mistress Davies and Rebecca, Samuel and Dorcas. The only friends to be invited were Mr Roland Atkins and his wife Florence and Master Nicholas Smart and his wife, Agnes, none of whom were chosen for any other reason than that they were friends of long-standing.

Today, when Abel returned from supervising his workers who were engaged in putting buildings in good order ready for winter, he was met by a more than usual fuss and commotion. Ruth, at nine o'clock in the morning, was already red-faced and flustered. As he entered the house he was halted in his tracks by the sight of his wife standing in the middle of the lobby, eyes closed, holding her face, which was screwed up as if in pain, between her two hands

"Whatever ails you?" he said, slightly alarmed, "Have you hurt yourself? Are you ill?" Her hands dropped to her sides as she opened her eyes and her face reverted to its customary endearing expression of slight anxiety. Wishing to reassure her husband she instantly came to him.

"Oh, my dear," she said, "I am perfectly well, but a little perplexed. I wanted to take out two pair of the best sheets my mother gave me on our Wedding Day but I fear I cannot find them."

Her hands went to her face again and she looked around as if expecting the missing sheets to appear from nowhere.

"I looked in the press where I keep all our linen and the dozen pair she gave me weren't there. I am so worried. Mother is coming this evening and will stay until tomorrow, or even the next day. She will be so disappointed if the best sheets, embroidered with her own hands, are not on her bed." Ruth clasped her hands in front of her and looked despairingly at Abel. "I wanted so much for everything to be just right for Samuel and Dorcas, too. It will be their first visit to us since their marriage."

Abel looked down at her. For once he had the solution. Household problems were not his usual strong point. "Do you remember Peter Littleton?" he asked.

Ruth looked puzzled. What was this man to do with her present predicament?

"Mistress Littleton's husband?"

Ruth remained mystified.

"The Quaker woman who asked you for work a year or two gone?"

Still no response. "She liked to read?"

"Oh yes," Ruth recalled. "Elizabeth Griffiths as was. Her husband works for people sometimes." Then she suddenly remembered. "He made the new cupboard!" The smile she gave him reminded Abel of the reason why he'd wanted to marry her, in addition to her marriage portion. "I've been looking in the wrong place! How silly of me!"

She whirled around and up the stairs, relieved and happy, leaving a smiling Abel nodding his head.

His wife was an April day; sunshine one minute, showers the next.

***

It was seven o'clock in the evening, and everything had gone well. The light supper, appropriate for the time of day, was clear evidence that the hostess was a lady of good breeding. Under Mistress Chinnock's instruction, Mistress Denny had surpassed herself and the sight of a well-appointed table greeted the guests entering the room where they were to eat. On it, in accordance with the fashion of the day, was the food for the entire meal, delighting the senses and tempting the appetite with glowing colours and enticing odours.

There were small chickens each roasted in a pastry case, one for each person. Most guests helped themselves to at least a couple of the small fish, called smelt. Garnished with fried parsley and cut lemon and having something of the delicate flavour of salmon, no-one noticed the slight oiliness of its flesh under its covering of fine breadcrumbs. There were various vegetables, although Ruth had been careful that not too many were served, as she knew that some people still regarded vegetables as food fit only for poor people. There were also sweet pies and puddings, which had tested Mistress Denny's ingenuity almost to breaking point for the variety of their flavour and artistic presentation.

Plate and china, glass and wine glowed in the firelight and in the light from what Ruth's mother regarded as an extravagant number of candles.

***

A portion of turf had been removed from one of the lawns, to save it from being damaged by the bonfire, which would be visible from the parlour windows. When the fire was lit and the fireworks set off the guests would be watching from comfort of The Grange's latest improvement, the parlour. The candles had been doused, to allow them to view the fire to the best effect and family and friends sat or stood, chatting quietly, around the windows. In the now deserted dining room Mistress Denny and Hannah, the maid who had once worked for the Bowmans, cleared the table. They would eat later; Mistress Denny had made sure that there would be enough food left over.

Abel, Samuel and one of the farm labourers each took a brand from the kitchen fire and carried them out into the garden to ignite the bonfire. The watchers in the house clapped and laughed as the flames and sparks rose into the cold night, while the silhouettes of the three men stood in dark contrast to the gold and orange blaze.

Ruth, standing in the darkness among her friends and relatives, felt herself to be the happiest of women and wept from it a little and from relief that all had gone well.

In due course, the novelty of the blaze having worn off, Abel and Samuel came in from the garden, the labourer being happy to sit in Mistress Denny's kitchen, eating his reward of a share of the left-over food. In the parlour the candles were re-lit, supplementing the glow from the fire in the hearth and the embers of the bonfire seen through the window.

As wine glasses were filled, Abel raised his in a toast.

"My dear family and friends," he announced. "Here's a health to His Majesty, King Charles the Second. May he live long and reign in peace." He sipped a little from his glass and then said, "Now, a small surprise for my wife, who thinks I am sometimes a dry old stick."

As she started to protest he continued, "Oh yes, you do, my dear. And you are quite right too. I spend more time with my labourers than you, do I not?"

He laughed at her embarrassment, but the laugh was kindly. He knew she had passed such a remark to her sister. "Today you deserve a little treat." Going to the door leading to the lobby, he called out, "Come along, everyone, we have some extra entertainment outside. It's a chilly night, but here are your cloaks, ladies."

The ladies were helped into warmer clothing by Ruth and Hannah, while Abel and Mistress Denny assisted the gentlemen. Mrs. Davies started to protest and Abel came over to her.

"Come along, mother-in-law," he encouraged, "I know you are comfortable by the fire, but do come, even if only for a few minutes. You'll enjoy the music." And he led her as she grumbled a little, out onto the lawn where a chair had been brought out for her and a blanket was arranged about her.

In front of the smouldering bonfire stood half a dozen musicians. They were the descendants of generations of local men and boys who had provided the music for every village event. Until the Commonwealth banned such entertainment, their presence was always available for public celebrations.

At Easter, Whitsuntide, Advent and Christmas time, they played. Not only in the streets, but in hall and cottage as required. They led the harvest home, and played for dancing at the Harvest supper which followed. Weddings, Saints' days celebrations, even funerals would be attended by their not always tuneful offerings. They also provided accompaniment for Morris dancing and occasional background effects for Mummers' plays. The 'rough music' played noisily and incessantly outside the homes to harass those thought to have been guilty of some minor misdemeanour was provided by this group. There was no village or local event that they and they forebears had not attended.

The country was getting back into the old ways, but gradually and with caution. Everyone knew that strong feeling remained among many non-conformists living in the area, who regretted the demise of strict Parliamentarian rule. The instruments the band were using, many of which were older than the players, had been secretly stored away during the Commonwealth and kept against the day when they could be played again.

They were led by Jack the fiddler. He had some experience of playing for the gentry and despite a desperate desire to pass water, didn't show any outward signs of the nervousness he felt.

The rest of the players were not yet accustomed to performing for any other than their own families and friends, or in the Green Man. To them the Grange was of a grandeur beyond their imagination and the Chinnocks were a class far above them. The five men and a small boy stood all, except Jack, unmoving. Clutching their instruments, their shield against unfamiliarity, they were trying to adjust themselves to the splendour facing them. They had glimpsed the furniture, carpets and paintings through the door. Now the beautifully dressed men and women who belonged to this other world, to which mere village musicians did not belong, were before them, waiting for them to play. The band, staring open-mouthed, would have remained longer in that state had not Jack called them to order. His nerves showed now in his manner and voice as he forced himself to address this new audience.

"Thank you very much, ladies and gentlemen," he said, a little shyly, "We 'ope you enjoy the tunes we are goin' to play. An' thankin' you kindly."

There were faint murmurs, mostly from the ladies, who, despite themselves, were slightly shocked at the rather raggle-taggle appearance of the musicians.

Then turning to his colleagues, Jack called the tunes, "'Drive The Cold Winter Away', then 'Friday Night and Saturday Morn'." And he and the other musicians struck up.

The first notes sent roosting pigeons flying into the starlit sky. There was another fiddler and a tenor cornet player who had to keep stopping to lick his dry lips. A young flute-player was equally dry-lipped and a hurdy-gurdy player provided an enthusiastic, though tuneless, drone. All through, a small boy kept time on a large drum, which was probably left over from the War. The old tunes sounded thinly in the cold night.

At first they were received politely though half-heartedly by their audience, but by the time they played their second tune the musicians were more relaxed and had warmed up, so that the listeners could not help but respond to the cheerful dance tunes.

Abel put a few more pieces of timber on the fire. He also brought out warming drinks for his guests and the players. This had good effect on them all; the players were more relaxed and the listeners a little more responsive. One or two of the ladies cooed over the sight of the little boy, manfully keeping the rhythm steady.

Abel looked around his family and friends. Rebecca was

clearly enjoying herself, clapping her hands in time to the music and singing, whether she knew the words or not. Even mother-in-law, sitting on her chair, was smiling now and tapping her feet to the cheerful tunes. Samuel, Dorcas, the Atkinses and the Smarts had formed themselves into a set and were improvising a dance between themselves, clumsily but cheerfully on the frosty grass. Ruth was smiling, her eyes sparkling in the firelight. Once again Abel thought of how happy he was with this woman.

His contented thoughts were broken, as wife, family and friends were scattered by a crowd of youths rampaging across the lawns, yelling and waving flaming brands above their heads. Lads from the village made brave by more liquor than they were used to, had broken down fences and hedges around fields, cottages and houses all over the area and now were making straight for the women among Abel's guests.

At the first sight and sound of the intruders the musicians stopped playing and without a moment's hesitation or consultation with one another, fled. They were all anxious not only for their own safety, but also that of their instruments, their next most important consideration. The flute-player not only made sure his own instrument was safe, but also took the drum from the little boy and left him to find his own way out of danger, as they all made for the nearest exit.

By this time a hefty village lad had already got hold of Rebecca and was attempting to kiss her. She was screaming and trying unsuccessfully to punch him, but she was pinioned in his arms. Roland Atkins went to her aid and succeeded in freeing her, while giving her attacker a sound whack on the side of his head with a piece of charred wood taken from the bonfire.

Two invaders had picked up Mistress Davies and her chair and were carrying her around and around the dying fire, swinging her about and threatening to throw her into the ashes. Nicholas Smart ran to help her as she shouted at them to stop, ineffectually beating at the air about them with her walking stick. A couple more youths were lighting fireworks with smouldering sticks from the bonfire and throwing them towards the frightened women. Nicholas Smart, torn between his duty to an elderly woman in danger of a painful fall, or protecting his shrieking wife, proved ineffectual in either.

At the first sight and sound of the interlopers Ruth fled into Abel's arms. He was hampered by Ruth clinging to him and in the absence of any weapon, attempted to rely on the loudness of his voice to repel attack. He was helped by an accompanying savage look. It was a look familiar to those who worked for him, having had power of which he was unaware. It proved alarmingly effective and two youths who had been chasing Ruth, swerved out of Abel's reach, resorting instead to insults and obscenities.

The whole skirmish lasted a few minutes only and ended when Nicholas, Agnes's husband, distracted at his inability to be of any use at all, remembered that he carried a small pistol for protection. Taking it out of his pocket, he fired it into the air. Suddenly, the fracas was over as the invaders took flight over hedges and fences, carrying smouldering brands taken from the fire.

Abel looked around at his family and guests, angry at the havoc which had been caused by the ruffians. Rebecca and Dorcas were weeping in each other's arms. His mother-in-law, safe now, was lying back in her chair gasping for breath, while Florence and Agnes tried to calm her, fanning her with their kerchiefs and patting her hands. Florence's husband, Roland and Nicholas set off with Samuel to chase after the miscreants. As Abel ushered Mistress Davies and her two supporters into the house, a fainting Ruth was being helped in by her sister, Rebecca, Mrs Denny and Hannah, who had come running out of the house when they heard the commotion.

The labourer, well satisfied with his tasty supper and something extra in a basket for his wife and children, had been on his way home when he heard the noise and ran back to the house to see if he could help. When he saw the situation he knew straight away what he should do.

"Shall I go for the Constable, Master?" he asked.

Abel nodded, taking the basket from him, "Run to Branslow and get him out of bed if necessary." The man glanced at his family's supper and Abel, pushing him in the direction of the village, shouted, "Run, man, run. Your basket will be here when you get back."

***

Later that evening the Atkinses and the Smarts, who were not staying the night, climbed gratefully into their carriages. Abel had assured them that all the miscreants would be arrested and punished and promised that business would be discussed in the very near future. Ruth, Mistress Davies, Samuel and Dorcas sat in the restored stillness of the parlour and tried to regain their composure.

While everyone was recovering the breathless labourer returned to the house with an equally breathless Constable, who was unable to offer any help regarding the identities of the interlopers. He told Abel that there had been many incidents during the evening and he and the other Law Officers had been hard-pressed to keep up with the complaints. Every time he'd arrived at a scene, he'd been just that little bit too late to apprehend them. He had his suspicions, but, until one or more of the miscreants were pointed out to him, there was little that he could do. Then, with an apology for his lack of success on this occasion, he bid Master Chinnock a good night and left the house and Abel returned to the rest of his family.

Once over her own shock and distress, Ruth's main concern was her mother. Mistress Davies had experienced a distressing assault upon her nerves. In truth, she had been in more physical danger than any one else that evening. The treatment she had received would have been frightening for a woman much younger than she. It was a measure of the lady's strength of character, body and soul, that she had not died of fright on the spot. Now, even though all those present had attempted to comfort and soothe her, she remained deeply upset.

Later, sitting in the chair nearest the fire, a medicinal glass of wine in her hand, Mistress Davies became calmer and a

95

little drowsy. Ruth, rising quickly from her own chair, caught the wine glass before it fell out of her mother's hand as the old lady finally gave up the fight and allowed herself to fall asleep. 'She's quite well, after all the excitement,' Ruth thought and looking around the room, she sighed more or less happily, despite her heart still thumping a little in her chest.

Abel looked up from his conversation with Samuel. "Are you feeling better, my dear?" "Oh yes," she answered, only a little shakily, "All's well now," but she could not completely keep the disappointment of a ruined evening out of her voice

Elsewhere in the room, Rebecca and Dorcas, fully recovered from their encounter with village youth, sat at a table playing checkers and giggling a little as they each recalled incidents from the evening.

"Wasn't the little boy with the drum an angel?" Rebecca recalled. "He was so beautiful, with his dark curls and big brown eyes. I wonder what his name is, he had such a lovely smile."

"Humphrey Yates." said Abel, half asleep. "His father is one of my labourers."

Dorcas, as a married lady, did not allow herself to dwell too much on the beauty of any adult member of the male sex besides her husband, but she did now confess, somewhat primly, "I will allow that Jack, the leader of the band, seemed a very personable young man." A sudden thought came into her head. What had happened to Jack, the little boy and the rest of the band? She turned to where her husband and his father were sitting, "Samuel, my love, where did the musicians go, when those dreadful boys rushed upon us?"

Nobody knew.

The truth was they were in the alehouse, bewailing the loss of their fee.

***

At the Ridge steading, two or three miles from The Grange, Alice, Harry, Ellen and Cornelius were sleeping, unaware of the young rowdies advancing along the lane after visiting the

Ockenden house. Despite the jeers and shouts of the rowdy group and the bangs and whizzes of the fireworks they lit, the Ockenden door remained closed, as Roger, Barbary and their adopted son, John Taylor, had gone to bed. Although wakened by the racket, they chose to ignore it. After only a few minutes of noise the boys moved on, disappointed by the lack of reaction.

Harry Bowman and Daniel Brass had all worked hard during the day and had gone to bed exhausted. Although it was early in the month they had decided to make a start on winter chores and since daybreak had been working on necessary repairs to outbuildings and barns. There would be more to do tomorrow and the next day, then it would be the stone walls surrounding their fields needing to be looked at and, should it be necessary, brought into good order.

Alice was the first to wake, disturbed by the sound of a firecracker. She had not been sleeping well and the slightest noise or movement would rouse her. During the busy day Henry's imprisonment could be put to the back of her mind, but at night her mind filled with appalling visions of his plight and the remembrance of her own earlier anguish. Alice's mental equilibrium, steadier though it was now after five months recovering in familiar surroundings, remained delicate and Harry was very protective of her.

As the geese and Meg, sounded their separate alarms the shouts outside grew louder and there were sounds of breaking gates. The poultry shut up for the night, were squawking and fluttering, banging themselves against the sides of their pens. There would be some broken legs and wings in the morning, Alice thought. Woken up by the noise the cattle, recently brought inside for the winter, became restless. Two donkeys, shut in another shed, began their melancholy braying.

Alice remembered previous experiences and was frightened that this was another attack on her home and her children. Within seconds, everybody was gathered in the house room, which was being intermittently lit by exploding fireworks. Harry and Cornelius were already hastily putting on some clothing before going out to attempt to send the attackers away. They too were unsure about the true nature of the disturbance.

"Thou stay inside, Mam, with Ellen. Daniel, look after them. Fasten the door," Harry ordered, looking at her so sternly that Alice was taken aback and shocked into obeying her son. But her heart beat so fast that she thought she would choke. Harry opened the door to go out. "Don't go!" Alice shouted, but her voice was drowned by the roars of the youths in the yard. As She ran to the door it was closed in her face. Shocked, she stood with her back to it for a moment listening to the roars of the youths in the yard as Harry and Cornelius emerged from the house.

"'Ere they come," one of the crowd shouted, exultantly. "'Ere they are. They'm mad people, they are." Another voice joined in, "Their dad's in prison for not paying 'is tithes and not goin' to church." Then someone else yelled, "They'm all 'eathens in that 'ouse." And the cry went up, "Eathens. 'Eathens."

At first the calls were fairly good-natured, if insulting and at first no harm was meant, just mischief. But, as with any highly excited, intoxicated crowd the mood quickly changed and became aggressive. One or two youths recalled real or imaginary offence caused by these nonconformists.

Geoffrey James had been with two or three young men setting up the maypole the previous year. They'd had a drink or two, to add to the enjoyment of a celebration which had been banned for so much time. Then two of these bloody Quakers, who had been walking through Branslow, went out of their way to cross the green and shouted at them, saying that the maypole was "licentious" and "gross indecency". The lads had retaliated by saying the maypole wasn't against the law any more, to which the two Quaker misery-guts had thundered in reply, "It's against God's Law!" Geoffrey and the other lads had just laughed and got on with their task and the two men, in their sober clothes, had walked away. Now Geoffrey, drunk and belligerent, was ready to take revenge for the undeserved shouting-at that he'd had.

"We don't want you 'ere," he shouted. "Go away and yer can take yer mad mam and dad with yer." His well-aimed stone hit Harry on his left shoulder and instinctively Harry's right hand went to it, but he stayed calm, as again he asked the gang to leave him and his family in peace. The answer was another rain of fireworks and stones, as another voice, Sam Stevens, joined the clamour. "Them meetings they 'old. They aint anythin' to do with religion. It's witchcraft." And the word was taken up. "Witchcraft, witchcraft."

Harry, trying to protect his brother, pulled Cornelius close and put an arm round him, while he entreated the noisy group to go home. Cornelius was trying hard not to cry. After all he was nine, nearly ten, almost a man now, or he wouldn't have been brought out into this confrontation, but his eyes were prickling and he just had to rub them. Seeing this delighted one of the gang, who shouted, "Look at the babby! 'E's cryin'. 'E's just a big babby!" At this Cornelius, unused to being the centre of attraction, gave way completely, broke away from Harry and ran towards the house. He only banged once with his fists and Alice opened the door to let him in, folding the weeping boy in her arms. Unnoticed, Ellen took her chance and slipped out into the yard

Outside the commotion continued for a little while longer although the supply of fireworks had run out, but the village lads were bewildered by Harry and Ellen's reactions. They offered neither defence nor retaliation and moved only to avoid missiles coming close to them. Ellen, aged eleven, a little older and braver than Cornelius, stood side-by-side with Harry. Although frightened by the noise, she felt strong because of Harry's presence. She remembered Harry looking after them that day at the Buxton's house. He'd known what to do; he would always know, no matter what the circumstances. In his father's absence Harry was the true support of the family.

Once, fleetingly nervous for a second, Ellen glanced at her brother for reassurance. Harry had been hit once or twice by flying stones but they hadn't seemed to bother him. He was standing, unmoved, his face, in profile, older, severe and beautiful.

***

Although the confrontation seemed longer, it only lasted about five or ten minutes and then the puzzled youths drifted away, grumbling that it was no good trying to have a bit of fun if the targets just stood there not fighting back. The brother and sister had earned the unwilling respect of one lad, at any rate. He was thinking to himself, 'They weren't cowardly, even if they didn't 'it back at us. It must've took some nerve to stand there and let us chuck stones at 'em, like that.' Then he realised the reason for the brothers' strange behaviour. 'I know why they did that,' he thought. 'They really are daft.'

***

Back in the house, the brothers relaxed. After the instinctive swift embrace, Alice had released Cornelius, wiped his face, rubbed his cold hands a little, told him to wipe his nose and gone into the kitchen place to heat up some broth. None of them would be able to sleep much for the rest of the night, but something warm in their bellies would be a comfort. Anyway keeping busy would stop her thinking too much about what might have happened.

Her children were all right, no harm there, other than the few bruises that Harry had got from the stones, but he said that it was no more than he sometimes came in with after a day's work. He'd fallen off the barn roof once and suffered more harm than he had suffered tonight.

Ellen was shaking a bit, but some of that might be the cold. She hadn't said much, none of them had, but that, too, was nothing out of the ordinary. Alice was proud of her, she was strong in mind and body, her mother's daughter.

Alice was proud of Harry too. The man of the house while his father was away, Harry had taken charge of the situation well. The rabble had dispersed and he had dealt with it without violence of deed or word.

He had been true to his conscience.

She poured the broth into four wooden bowls and smiled to herself. 'If the one I'm carrying is as brave a soul as these are, I shall be well pleased.'

"God be praised," she said out loud, "And thanks given to Him for this food. Thanks also for our deliverance and that the thatch wasn't fired." "Amen." came the reply.

Later, back in bed, Alice thought, 'I wish Henry was here.'

Alice, Alice. Watch out for the demons. Alice

༄ ༅

CHAPTER FIFTEEN

Sunday, November 6th 1664

The acrid smell of the previous night's bonfires and gunpowder hung over Branslow the following morning. The weather was dry, there was a clear sky and the wind was not too cold. Harry and Ellen were out collecting stones exposed during the previous year's wind and weather, which would later be used to repair damaged walls around the fields.

They were not the only ones working hard. Alice, household chores finished for the time being, was cutting heather to be used as insulation in some of the pens. It grew plentifully along the ridge which gave the farm its name and protected it from the worst excesses of the moorland weather. Cornelius, still a little shaken following the previous night's disturbance, was helping her. In Alice's opinion he was feeling more sorry for himself than was appropriate, which was why she was giving him the tedious job of carrying the heather bundles back and forth across the uneven ground to the handcart, which she'd left on the only slightly less uneven track.

"Work never hurt anyone and gives thee something to think about besides thyself," she said shortly, when, later in the afternoon her youngest broke the silence to complain that he was tired.

Four months into her pregnancy and not yet in full health following her release from imprisonment, she, too, was tired, but had no intention of giving in to it. She was also anxious about Henry.

She straightened up from the heather she was cutting and stood with her hands pressed into her back to ease it's aching a little. Then, to further demonstrate to Cornelius that, despite weariness, they must continue working, she turned back to her work and said, with an attempt at hearty encouragement, "There's another hour or so before the light goes. Enough time to get a few more bundles on the cart!"

With an exasperated "Mam!" under his breath, Cornelius resumed his trudging back and forth between his mother and the cart, as a few snowflakes fell from the darkening sky.

***

The short November day was coming to a close and, higher up the ridge than Alice and Cornelius, Harry and Ellen had laboured well together. Once they had collected a supply of stones sufficient to start the work they settled into a steady rhythm. Harry saw to the walling while Ellen continued to keep him supplied with stones of the right shape and size required. As the daylight diminished they stood looking across the moorland's soft evening green-greyness, lightened by the thin scattering of snow. Then they started to walk home, Henry's right arm across Ellen's shoulders. "Thee did well, Ellie," said Harry. "Mam'll be pleased with us."

***

Harry and Ellen arrived home later than Alice and Cornelius as they had further to walk and the road was rougher. Before entering the house they both paused to wash their hands and faces at the pump in the yard. Ellen was soon helping Alice at the fire, preparing their meal. Cornelius put bowls, spoons and tankards on the table.

Meg, the Bowman's dog, had slipped in from the yard as Harry and Ellen came in. She slunk across the floor in the direction of the hearth, looking neither left nor right, her head and back held low on creeping legs. A working dog, she should not have been in the house, but on this increasingly cold evening blind eyes were being turned. Keeping a watchful eye on his mother who was occupied in talking to Harry and Ellen as she tended the cooking pot, Cornelius opened the door quietly and slipped out of the house, returning a few moments later with a piece of sacking which he surreptitiously dropped on the floor to one side of the hearth. Meg gratefully made herself comfortable. Without a word, Alice stepped over her on her way to the table.

The meal ready, Alice called her family to their supper. Before they ate they sat for a few minutes in silence, broken only by Harry who, after a hard but successful day in the fields, felt moved to speak.

"My 'eart is very full," he said quietly, "It is full of peace after a troubled night when we came to no 'arm. Through 'Is grace, the Lord has seen fit to bless us with honest work on a fine day and good food and drink to fill our bellies. Blest be the Lord. "

"Blest be the Lord. Amen," came the response.

As was the custom, there was no further speech until the meal was over.

₧₨

CHAPTER SIXTEEN

Monday, November 7th 1664

Peter was up a ladder repairing part of the stone barn roof when he heard a shout. Looking towards the sound he saw a small group of Friends coming through the gate. Bob, having remained silent as usual when the visitors arrived, was now on his hind legs jumping joyously around them, uttering tiny yelps of delight.

The men were Richard and Simon Buxton, Robert Mellor, John Scott and Roger Ockenden. They looked even more serious than usual. The presence of Roger gave Peter an inkling of what this visit was about. The question of John Taylor and the girl not 'in the Light', but whom he wished to marry, had perplexed the Meeting for some time. Now, Peter thought, the time seemed to have come for decision.

Simon was the first to speak. He was finding it difficult to maintain a grave demeanour when the dog was behaving in such a silly fashion. "He gave no warning of our approach, Peter," he said, ruefully, "I'm surprised that thee still keeps him"

Peter, climbing down the ladder, smiled apologetically, "He is young yet. He will learn, I hope." Reaching the ground he welcomed each man with a handshake and led them into the house. Elizabeth, busy with her morning tasks, stayed long enough to welcome them in the same way then removed herself to the rooms above, not wishing to intrude on men's business. She too, had guessed its nature.

When they were all seated around the table Richard Buxton came straight to the point.

"Friend Roger Ockenden, has come to me, to us, seeking advice about his adopted son, John Taylor. We are all aware that the boy wishes to marry a girl not of our Meeting, or indeed any other Religious Society of Friends Meeting, and who, furthermore, has steadfastly refused to join a Meeting. John's action in engaging with this girl puts him in a serious and blameworthy position, the invariable outcome of which, is disownment by the Meeting. In spite of this grave consequence he seems determined to take this disgraceful step. In consequence, John may be persuaded by this girl to attend the Anglican Church, worship there, and marry there."

At this Peter, who had not heard of this latest development, stiffened and shook his head sadly. Disownment by the Meeting was an extreme reaction, which included not only religious denunciation, but also social rejection by all his Quaker associates including his adoptive parents. John's latest declaration, effectively forestalling expulsion from the Meeting by saying that he would attend Church even in the face of opposition, was a deep insult to the Friends.

"He must not be allowed to do such a thing," Peter said and all the men, including Roger Ockenden, nodded in agreement, "But what action must we take?"

"We have agreed that we will make every effort to make John see the error of his ways; help him to return to us, return to the Light. We intend to hold a Meeting for the purpose of persuading him on the third day of December. Will thee agree to be part of this Meeting, and take notes, Peter?"

Peter, knowing that such a Meeting would have to be called, had half anticipated that he might be expected to attend in the capacity of Clerk. He had dreaded the prospect. Despite his anxiety, he nodded in answer to the question saying grimly, "This is the most serious matter in which I have ever been involved. I hope that I will justify the Meeting's trust in me. With God's help, I shall not shrink from this most important task."

***

John Taylor was walking home in a state of bewilderment. He was thinking hard about the conversation he had just had with Frances. His own reaction to what she had said had surprised him.

They had met as usual, in the late afternoon by the bridge. As she rounded the bend in the lane John could see that Frances was upset and looked as if she had been crying. When she saw him waiting she started to run towards him and fell into his arms when she reached him. She began to cry again and John gently pushed her away from him so that he could to look into her face more easily.

"What's wrong?" he asked. He was alarmed because he had not seen her like this before and her tears unsettled him. "Now, now," he said, as she looked likely to lean against him again. She began to control herself, found her handkerchief and wiped her eyes before beginning to speak.

"You 'ave to see the Elders soon, don't you, John?" The word, 'Elders' in her voice sounded strange to her as she spoke it. John answered the question with a nod.

"Yes?" he asked.

"Well," she said, nervous about what she was going to request from him. "I wanted to ask you if you would leave the Meeting and join the church."

He was silent and she said quickly, "You said you would when we talked about it once before, and I could see you didn't want to, but I thought I could bring my Dad round, and 'e wouldn't mind if I came in with you."

The words were easier now, rushing out. The relief was immense. "But I couldn't make 'im change his mind, and 'e more or less told me that 'e wouldn't have anything to do with me if I joined. Oh John, please say you will come to church, then we can be together. We can get married, and everything - with me and me Dad - everything will be all right."

She paused for breath and waited for his response.

There was none. John stood looking, not at her anymore, but past her, down the lane and into the trees where the autumn fog was being held. He had no words at present to explain to her how he felt. Already shaken by her weeping and clinging to him he was bewildered by the change in events, nervous about the meeting with the Elders and completely at a loss about what action he should now take.

"I'll 'ave to think about it," was all he could manage when, at last he did speak. Sensing her feelings of disappointment, he knew his reply had been inadequate, but there was nothing he could do about it. He would really have to think about what she was asking him to do and he couldn't do that immediately. He wanted to be on his own, to be quiet, to be clear in his mind.

"John?" Frances's eyes were searching his face for some sort of reassurance that all would be well. It wasn't there.

"What?" He started, looking at her as if he had never seen her before, which hurt her to her heart, then pulled himself together. He couldn't just leave her now, telling her that he wanted to be on his own to think. That would be cruel. He loved her. She deserved an answer. He decided on compromise.

"Let's walk a bit," he said. "Just down the lane to thy house. While I 'ave a think. Come on," he took her hand and together, without talking, they walked past the stand of trees and the Ridge steading and past the scrubby field where the Bowman's donkeys were kept. Here they stopped. His decision, made under pressure, but made, must now be voiced. He took her other hand in his and said, "I'll come to Saint James's Church on Sunday."

With a kiss and a promise that they would see each other the following day, Frances left him, running round the corner and into the wheelwright's house to tell her father the news.

John was to remember her smile and her joy for the rest of his life.

***

He turned and continued with his homeward walk back towards the bridge and Branslow where he lodgèd with his adoptive father, Roger Ockendon and his wife Barbary. His heart should have been lighter, his head higher, his step fleeter, but he was to see the elders in ten days time.

There was a wood pigeon cooing somewhere. He remembered how his father, Walter, knew birds as much by their song as by sight and taught him so much about the natural world. His father knew the places where the first primroses would be and always took John's mother a posy of them on her April birthday. Both were dead and buried in unmarked Quaker graves twenty miles away. Orphaned by the age of eleven, John wished they were with him, helping him, now.

***

John's father, Walter Taylor, carpenter, had converted to Quakerism at one of the large open air Meetings held in the moorlands very soon after its beginnings in the early 1650s.

George Fox, the founder of the Society of Friends, visited Staffordshire after being released from Derby gaol in 1651 . He'd walked south, pausing to preach at Burton-on-Trent, before arriving on the outskirts of Lichfield. Standing on the brow of a hill and looking down on the city in the valley, he'd had a vision of blood flowing down its streets, into the market-place and gathering into a pool. Aware of the local legend that hundreds of Christian martyrs were killed by Roman soldiers in this region, the vision was, for him, symbolic of the blood of all Christian martyrs.

Arriving in the city he'd walked in his stockinged feet through the snowy streets shouting loudly and prophesying, "Woe to the bloody city of Lichfield." He'd preached there, but his message, calling for dismissal of the clergy and simplicity in Christian worship, was, predictably, not received well in the Cathedral city. Leaving, he'd continued the walking and preaching which had had been his reason for leaving home a year or so earlier.

Arriving in the Moorlands some months later, he'd preached out of doors near the village of Cauldon in the Moorlands, where the same message of simplicity was better-received by a large number of people. He'd continued with his travelling and was followed during the next five years by many other missionaries preaching the same ideas. In common with communities in other counties, a large number of the people of North Staffordshire were receptive, even enthusiastic. Anyone could speak at these Meetings for

109

Worship, and because of the excitement generated by the need to voice what they felt God was directing them to say, they trembled and shook. In consequence they were called by the derogatory name of 'Quakers'. The numbers at these Meetings were always at least one or two hundred and many became willing converts to a religious sect which did away with ritual and the clergy.

It had been at such a Meeting that Walter Taylor, his wife Eleanor and their small son John met Roger Ockenden who was to become one of the little family's greatest friends. So good a friend that when Eleanor died of a fever soon after John's eighth birthday, Walter, suddenly aware of his own mortality, asked Roger to take care of John, should the boy be left an orphan. The promise was made and the trust was so great that it was only ever mentioned once more in Walter Taylor's life.

For the next two years father and son lived happily together. They were helped to some extent by Roger's wife Barbary, who, without encroaching excessively on this male province, made sure that as far as possible the house and occupants were kept clean, tidy and in good order.

In the winter of 1655 Walter contracted a chest infection which despite all the efforts of Barbary and the local apothecary, persisted until January the following year. John would never forget the wintry afternoon, sparkling with frost, that Roger and Barbary came to stand with him at his father's bedside, just in time to say farewell. Walter was sitting up in bed supported with pillows, every breath a chest-ripping effort. He asked his son to come closer and John bent over and embraced his father as best he could. The dying man kissed his son's tear-damp cheeks, saying, "Thou art Roger Ockenden's son, now, lad. Be thee a help to him and a credit to me."

***

When his daughter burst through the door, pink-faced, breathless and looking so beautiful, George knew that decisions had been made that he was not going to like. Frances was so obviously happy and excited, but all he could feel was foreboding. Tensions, in the air for so long, couldn't continue but wouldn't be removed easily. It was impossible for him to share in her elation right away. All he could do was listen to her, silently.

"John says 'e will come to Saint James's Church," was the first thing Frances managed to say once she had regained her breath. She danced around the room. "'E'll come to our church. 'E just said so. Everything'll be all right now. 'E's going to leave that Meeting he goes to an' come over to our side."

Exultant, she threw her arms around her startled father and kissed his cheek. "Oh Dad," she said, "We'll be able to get married now, and I won't 'ave to join those people". She stood back from George searching his face for signs of approval or pleasure. Her mood quickly lost some of its gaiety when she realised that her father was experiencing neither. She looked up, searching his expressionless face and her elation drained away into anxiety. "What's the matter, Dad?" Her voice was quieter now and not as strong as before.

Frances was torn between disappointment and anger. Why couldn't he be happy for her? John had done a wonderful thing by saying that he would leave the Meeting. Because he had done that, her father should realise that he was a good man. He would have known that anyway if he had allowed himself to meet John and get to know him better. What was the difficulty now?

"Are you sure that's what 'e wants to do, child?" her father asked, gravely. "Are you sure that 'e'll really change?" She started to assure him that John had really said he would leave the Meeting but he didn't let her finish.

"It's a big thing, is religion," he said quietly, "It's not to be held lightly. We may not think that what these people believe is the truth, but they do, just as we believe that what we think is the truth. They're just as strong in their beliefs as we are in ours. People will say anything sometimes, to try to solve a problem easily. Sometimes a problem can only be solved by saying a hard thing."

George paused, looking down at his hands. There was a tiny black splinter in one of his fingers. He looked into Frances's eyes. "For you and John the hard thing would be to say goodbye."

"Dad!" Frances cried out and moved away from her father.

This wasn't at all how she thought it would be when she gave him the news. She wanted him to be happy for her and he was clearly not.

George was silent, grieving, unsure of what to say or do. He felt he didn't know this young woman who minutes ago had been so joyful, bursting with her good news. She was now looking at him as if he too were a stranger. He knew that he had hurt her terribly but was unable to think of anything to say to console her or salve his own conscience. He couldn't be anything but true to himself. He wanted Frances to be true to herself, too, even if the truth was painful and difficult; even if it meant carrying a hurt which would last all her life.

He suddenly thought of Margaret, his wife, who had died so many years before. What would she have said or done? He realised that their time together had been so short that he had no idea. For all the love that he had felt for her, he realised that he hadn't known her well at all. He couldn't even remember what she looked like. He could remember when he had laughed at some dryly witty comment she had made, but couldn't remember the sound of her voice. The thoughts tore at his heart. He shook himself a little and pulled himself back into the present. Such thoughts were best put to the back of his mind and not drawn upon again. Life must go on.

He made an attempt to console Frances for the pain she was suffering. Moving towards her he held out his hands and attempted to take hers but she pulled away.

"I'll get supper," she said, and went into the kitchen place. George sat down by the fire and listened to the sound of his daughter preparing food and quietly weeping.

Tuesday, November 8th 1664

By morning father and daughter had benefited from a few hours reflection. Now that he'd warned his daughter, George had been thinking that he should be less prickly. He would try to show a little more interest in her future marriage, since he felt sure it would take place whether he consented or not. He could not risk losing his beloved daughter because of his own stubbornness.

112

Frances woke determined to look to the future. Her father's words the previous evening had disappointed her, but this morning she had regained her buoyancy. She would not let his forebodings stop her from thinking about and planning her wedding. In the years to come her married life with John would prove to everyone that he was the perfect match for her.

When George came in for his breakfast the atmosphere was less charged than during the previous evening. Remnants of anxiety in his mind and resentment in his daughter's were still hanging, quivering, in the air. During the meal Frances served her father his food as was the custom and each spoke only when it was necessary. Neither was happy but both truly desired a return to their former ordered and contented life. Both were prepared to make allowances.

The meal ended. Both spoke at the same time. "Dad? " "Franny?"

George said, "Yes Franny?"

Frances said, "No, you first." She thought, 'It's ages since he called me Franny'.

George continued. "Will you be seeing that John today? If so, you can tell 'im he can walk out with you - "Frances's eyes widened as her mouth opened, but he continued. "'E can walk out with you, and mebbe later you can get the Banns called."

Frances squeaked her delight.

"You can get the banns called," he continued, "But not yet. I want you to wait a year at least. Then, if you still want, you can marry the lad."

He rose from his place at the table. "I'm back to the workshop now. I'll be in for me bread and cheese an' beer at dinner time." He reached for his jacket, kissed Frances briefly and went out.

Frances, still astonished by her father's change of mind about her proposed marriage, stood in the open doorway for a few minutes watching her father walk to his workshop before she turned back into the house. Closing the door behind her she sat for a while as she tried to remember what her household duties were for the day but she found it difficult to concentrate. Eventually she managed to compose herself and carry on with the morning's work, fetching more water, tending the fire, washing the pots; but her 'insides' lurched with excitement and there was a permanent smile on her face.

***

As he learnt his trade, measured and sawed, planed and sanded, alone in Roger Ockenden's carpenters' shop that day, John's thoughts returned time and again to Frances. He knew that he loved her and that she loved him, that it was the dearest wish of each of them that they should marry. But under such circumstances? Was the change he was about to make the right thing one? While he had given serious thought to his intention to attend church, had he thought enough about it? Was he proposing to make this change in his religion because he wanted, really wanted to? Or was it because it would be the only way to remove an obstacle to marriage?

Doubts filled his thoughts all morning, until, at some point, he realised that the more he thought about his uncertainties, the more they seemed to increase. He tried to see things more clearly, to look at both sides of the question - Meeting House or Steeple-House?

For a while he even succeeded in convincing himself that things weren't so bad after all, but anxiety had returned by late in the afternoon. He was sitting disconsolately on his saw-bench when Roger came in.

"Well, young 'un. How's it goin'?" was his adoptive father's cheery greeting.

***

The promise made to Walter Taylor had been well kept by the Ockendens. They had continued to look after John, as they would have their own son, ever since Walter died. At the start there had been a slight difficulty about what John should call Roger and Barbary. The boy felt uncomfortable calling them

'Dad' and 'Mam'. The couple understood although it made them a little sad. So far they had no children of their own and it seemed unlikely that there ever would be any. Privately and regretfully they accepted that John would take some time to settle to his new home, probably never regarding himself as their son and eventually 'Uncle' and 'Aunt' were settled on

When John was about twelve Roger inherited property from a bachelor uncle. It consisted of a house twenty miles away at Branslow and the piece of land that went with it. Having spent all his previous working life renting both home and workshop, it was the chance of a lifetime to own property and in due course, the move was made. A year later, it was agreed that John should begin to learn the carpenter's trade at Roger's side, as he would have done with his real father.

***

"John?" Roger's voice was gentle, now, less jocular. Seeing that the boy seemed worried, he guessed what was causing it. He and Barbary knew of John's growing love for, and wish to marry, the girl they had previously only regarded as one of his friends. They knew that she was not 'In the Light', which was a cause of alarm for all the Friends. Everyone in the Meeting knew that the Elders had questioned John and that his answers had not been satisfactory. Everyone knew also that he would soon be returning to be questioned by the Elders again, when he would have to give a definite answer about his intentions.

"Sorry, Uncle," John replied, attempting a smile, "I'd better get on with my work."

"Leave it," Roger answered. "It's getting late, the light's going and it's cold. Come on, we'll go in."

***

Roger, Barbary and John were sitting in the firelight. It was almost time to go to bed. Roger was dozing in his chair and Barbary was sewing.

John was working on a small piece of wood he had found

lying about in the workshop a few days earlier. Only about three inches in length and of an irregular curved shape, it had suggested some sort of animal to him and he had been working on it with a small knife in any spare minute. Every so often he stopped and raised the shaped wood in front of him, squinting at it, turning it in order to view it from every angle. In his mind's eye he could see it finished although he didn't know what animal it was. It was a work of his imagination, occupying his mind as well as his hands. For these few minutes he was free of anxiety. For a brief few moments his declaration to Frances, the forthcoming meeting with the Elders and lingering remnants of grief for the loss of his father, were forgotten.

But it couldn't last. The present invaded his mind, forcing his conscience to challenge him. While he carved, the memory of the day's conversation with Franny retreated, but now it rushed out from its hiding place. He kept thinking of her open, happy face earlier in the day. At the same time he was mocked by his own inability to reach a decision about the marriage; a decision that he could be truly comfortable with. He stood up, the little carved animal falling to the floor in a small shower of shavings. Suddenly he had to be on his own, to think and pray. Anything to clear his mind of its shameful wavering.

He said, "Good night," to the other two people who loved him and climbed the steps to his bed under the eaves.

80 ○3

CHAPTER SEVENTEEN

Saturday, November 12th 1664

Hannah Wilson, Mistress Chinnock's maid, was enjoying a few hours off. This special treat had been awarded to her because the master and mistress were visiting Master Chinnock's son and his wife in their fine new residence and the maid's services would not be required until candle-lighting time. She was sitting at the table in the Palmer's kitchen with Frances and two other friends, listening open-mouthed as Frances related to them the news that she and John Taylor were to be married.

"But 'e's one of those people," Jane Mason breathed, fascinated. "'E's a good-looking lad, but aren't they all a bit funny?" And she shuddered with a tiny burst of delighted fear. Small and energetic like the rest of her family she had so far, like them, greeted every experience of life as a challenge to be dealt with, but not too seriously.

"I worked for some of them once." Hannah was suddenly regarded with more interest than she had ever known before. "They were strange in some ways and quite ordinary in another. But she -" She looked around. All the girls were leaning forward across the table towards her, waiting for every morsel of gossip. They all knew all about the Bowmans, "Mistress Bowman. Alice, she likes to be called. She was really mad."

"She's better now." Mary Johnson, a shyer girl than Hannah and Jane and less inclined to gossip, spoke quietly. "She's been working in the fields again, even though she's expecting soon." Mary lived near the Bowmans and had some sympathy with them. Sometimes, secretly, she admired their strong faith and respected their loyalty to it.

Jane, for the most part unfettered by serious thoughts of any kind, ignored the comment, saying quickly, "My dad says they're like 'eathen animals, only lookin' out for themselves." Warming to the subject she slid forward on the bench so as to bend closer over the table and, making sure that all three girls heard the pronouncement, said in a voice which managed to combine both drama and scandal, "They work on a Sunday and don't go to Church, and I've 'eard as Master Bowman's in gaol. Again!" Laughing, she said, "What d'you think of that?" as she slid back into her former position having delivered, she thought, her best bit of news.

Frances, fearing that she had lost control of what should have been her own triumphal moment, endeavoured to bring attention back to herself.

"That's nothing," she said in a louder, defiant tone, "That's nothing to those people. What's something," and all eyes were turned towards her, "What's something is that my John is not going to have nothing to do with them no more.' E's going to leave them." She straightened her back, her chin was high.

"For me!" The note of triumph in her voice left no one unsure of the truth of the statement.

There was a chorus of girlish expressions of amazement and pleasure as Frances' three friends digested the information. Hannah was the first to express herself with something more than gasps and delighted giggles. "When you getting married then? Will it be proper? At Saint James's? "

"'E'll have to go to Church. " Jane butted in. "'E's never bin before. 'E won't know what to do." She suddenly dissolved into laughter, "'E'll wear 'is 'at in church!"

Frances was indignant, "'E won't," she snapped. "I'll show 'im how to do things and what to say. 'E'll be coming to church with me a few times before the wedding." Less confidently, she continued, "'Course 'e won't wear 'is hat." Suddenly deflated, she said quietly, "I 'ope."

The mood of the little party changed, all four young women silent and serious. Even Jane sensed that something wasn't quite right, but none of them knew how to react to the bride-to-be's abrupt change of mood.

Hannah was the first to speak. The autumn light was fading and she had to be back at the Grange well before dark. Grateful for the reprieve she rose from the bench and took her cloak off the hook on the back of the door. "I'll 'ave to go," she said to Frances, "Master and Missis will be 'ome soon, and woe betide me if the candles aren't lit, and the fires tended." They all said their goodbyes as she kissed her friends lightly on their cheeks and pulling her hood over her head, she went out into an afternoon turned grey and drizzling with rain.

It was not long before boisterous Jane left, departing in a flurry of kisses, hugs and a cloak billowing in the gust of wind, which blew through the door as she opened it. "What a night!" she laughed, "I'll be blown 'ome to Branslow!"

***

Mary sat in silence for a few moments after Jane had left, while the fire crackled and a few drops of rain dropped down the chimney and sizzled. Frances was upset about something, all three girls had sensed it, but Mary, the most thoughtful of the trio, was reluctant to leave while her friend was troubled. She ought really to go soon to help her mother with the evening meal, but she hesitated. A meal would also have to be made ready for Master Palmer, busy in his workshop and he would be in soon when the light faded into nightfall and then all chance to talk quietly about what was on Frances' mind would have gone, perhaps forever.

Frances, close to tears, got up and went over to the fire, supposedly to replenish it, in reality to hide her distress. When she saw the girl's shoulders shaking, Mary quietly joined her by the hearth and, placing an arm around her friend, said, "Tell me, Franny. I won't tell anyone else."

At first reluctant to speak, Frances shook her head, but the strain which had been gradually developing for the previous few days, coupled with Mary's sympathetic approach, proved too much too bear.

"Oh Mary," the cry burst from her, "I don't think 'e really wants to marry me at all!" Tears rained down her face as she turned towards her friend. "I've only seen 'im once since we decided, and that was only because I waited for him by the bridge. I wanted to tell 'im what my dad said, about the banns and everything, and it was just like 'e didn't want to talk to me, really, and 'e's not been there since, even when I've waited ages and ages for 'im. 'E's changed in just a week, and I don't know why."

Frances was sobbing as Mary led her back to the bench by the table and sat her down. "I can't understand it. I can't understand 'im." She calmed down a little, realising that she must have her emotions under control when her father came in. Then another thought occurred to her and she was agitated again. "Do you think I've upset 'im, Mary? I can't think of anything I've said or done that would hurt 'im, but do you think I could've? How could I 'ave?"

Mary had quietly allowed Frances to talk as much as she needed to, but now that she was faced with direct questions, she felt she must offer more than sympathy.

"My Auntie 'ad the same problem." she said, "She was going to marry a man who lived in the same village, everybody thought it was a real love-match, but after a bit 'e seemed like 'e didn't want to talk about the wedding or anything. She was ever so worried, and she came to see me mother, who's her oldest sister. Mam told me about it after, because she said it was something I ought to know. And that was, that men often stop being so keen about marriage when their girls start talking about the actual wedding. She said it's because they're uncomfortable about the fuss, and the dressing-up, and the rude jokes from their friends. They're keen enough to get married...and everything..." Mary blushed a little, but bravely continued, "They just get a bit nervous beforehand, that's all, and they worry a bit about the responsibility and that sort of thing."

Frances was calmer now; fascinated by the longest speech she had ever heard Mary deliver and interested to hear the outcome of this other bride-to-be's problem. "Did they get married?" she asked. "Oh yes," replied Mary, "They've been married years and got four children - " Frances interrupted her, worried again, "Maybe that's it," she said, "Maybe 'e don't like children!"

At this point Mary thought the matter had gone a bit too far and it was getting late. As she reached for her cloak, she said, "I don't know about that, but I've got to go now." She kissed Frances' cheek, said kindly, "Don't worry any more," and left the house.

If she had left a moment earlier, she would have seen George standing outside the door, where he had been stopped in his tracks when he heard his daughter crying as she confided in her friend. He'd not wished to go into the house, interrupting any girlish confidences that might be being exchanged and he had been equally reluctant to eavesdrop, but Frances' distress was real; his own concern was real.

He had resolved to make every effort to change his view of John, even grudgingly admired the boy's bravery in consenting to go to the Anglican Church, but overhearing now about John's recent coolness towards Frances caused him to think again. Mary's explanation was reasonable. Perhaps John was nervous about the wedding and would, like George had himself, make a good husband when the ceremonials were over. He justified his eavesdropping with the thought that, though he would not tell his daughter that he had heard the conversation, he would keep it in his heart. If necessary later, he would be able to understand and console her.

When he heard Mary saying she had to go he had slipped around the corner of the house. Now he emerged, passing her on her way down the path to the road. "Good night, Mary," he called, "Good night Master Palmer," came the cheerful reply.

***

The Littletons had just finished their evening meal. Elizabeth was clearing things away and Peter was setting the table with cobbler's last, hammer, nails and a piece of leather, ready to mend the hole in the sole of one of his wife's shoes. This was one of the little jobs, which had been neglected until this quieter part of the year, but with the winter coming on strong shoes were necessary and the little job now became more important.

Bob, the Littletons' silly dog, had once more sidled his way from the simple shelter of the kennel into the comfort of the house and was under the table. From this position he could decide whether to lie near the fire, from where he may find herself driven back out of the house by Elizabeth, or to stay under the table, unseen. He made his decision and stayed under the table, lying down and leaning contentedly against the warmth of Peter's ankles. A hand stretched down and scratched behind his ear.

Elizabeth finished her tidying and came over to stand behind Peter at the table. She put an arm across his shoulder, leaning down to kiss his cheek. He looked up at her and smiled.

"This won't take long," he said. "And then thee will be able to wear them again. It doesn't seem so long since last autumn. With God's help and Friends' we are prospering a little now, aren't we?"

Elizabeth patted his shoulder in agreement, moved to her seat by the fire and took up her mending.

Not a minute to be wasted, even in the evening.

They each bent to their work until a reluctant Bob was put out into the yard and it was time to go to bed.

&&

CHAPTER EIGHTEEN

Saturday, December 3rd 1664

A pale sun was forcing its light through lowering clouds over Branslow. It gave a strange light to the village, its surrounding fields and trees, the hovering hills to the east and the ridge that protected the Bowman's farm in the southwest. John Taylor, walking purposefully along the road to the wheelwright's cottage, head down against a blustery wind, thought, 'If it was raining, there would be a rainbow. A sign of hope to Noah in the Ark. There's no sign of hope for me.' He hunched his shoulders a little higher, trying to keep his neck warm. He regretted that he had not accepted the muffler offered by Barbary Ockenden as he prepared to go out into the late autumn morning. John's leave-taking had been hurried, with few words from him and tears from his adoptive mother, who understood his anguish.

Roger had already left the house to go to work which he claimed was urgent, although the previous evening he'd told John that he could take the following day off. He'd slipped out early while Barbary was busy fetching water and mending the fire before breakfast. Roger knew his leaving was a cowardly avoidance of unpleasantness at home.

In their separate ways both men were suffering in the aftermath of the previous day's Meeting about John's proposed marriage. It had started badly, despite all efforts to exercise control over strong feelings.

***

As was customary the Meeting at Simon Buxton's house started in silence, broken only by the distant sound of a farm

123

cart trundling along the road to Branslow. It was a time for each man to centre down to his spiritual being. This period could have lasted for hours, without speech of any kind, but today everyone, John in particular, was spared this. The silence lasted for only about an hour.

It was broken by Joshua Dale, the most respected and experienced elder at this special Meeting, who rose to his feet and said, "Friends we are here to question John Taylor in regard to his intransigence in the matter of a female, not in the Light, whom he intends to marry. In silence we have come to the Lord to seek for His help and blessing on this special Meeting. In particular we now ask for His guidance as we attempt the solution of this significant problem".

John was sitting bolt upright on the bench, every muscle and fibre tense with fear and anticipation, when Joshua turned to him and motioned him to stand up.

Joshua continued, "There is no doubt that our first question to John must be as follows: Friend, does thee intend to marry?"

"Yes, Friend." John's reply was sharp and swift.

"Friend, does thee intend to marry one who does not belong to this Meeting?"

"Yes, Friend." Again John's answer was unequivocal.

"Thee knows that thee will be cast out of this and any other Quaker Meeting? That thee will be a pariah in our eyes, and excluded from our society?"

The question rang in the cold air of the Meeting room like a series of gunshots. The silence, broken by this brief examination, resumed. John's accusers, for that is what they seemed to him, were waiting for his reply. The room was soundless except for the occasional creak of a stool or bench when its occupant surreptitiously changed position slightly. An immediate answer was not expected. John would be expected to speak after he had earnestly considered what his reply would be.

Roger's thoughts were troubled. Try though he would, he could not calm himself in order to receive inspiration of a divine nature. It was the son his wife had never been able to have standing abjectly before the Elders, eyes closed and head bowed, his hands clasped together behind his back. Roger had listened to all of the elders' discourses over the previous weeks. His religious beliefs had prompted him to sympathise, even with their almost hostile attitude to John, but increasingly he found that he could not. He was too close to the one who, to all intents and purposes, was on trial.

He had also been asking himself in his own private devotions, what he would do if he were in John's shoes? There were no easy answers. For weeks the Meeting had been in turn discussing, silently considering and praying about the matter of his adopted son's marrying out. They already appeared to be treating John like the outcast he would be if he proceeded with his marriage plans. Roger too, had misgivings, but this young man was his friend's son, whom he and his wife had promised to care for. It seemed to him that little or no consideration was being given to John's feelings.

Sitting silently in this Meeting, Roger realised he was faltering in his loyalty to the Quaker cause. He knew that John's situation was being dealt with at this Meeting as it would be at any other, but the harshness had never been brought home to him so strongly before. Opening his eyes he looked at John who still stood deep in his own thoughts.

John was, in fact, fighting off strong impulses to break up this Meeting, violently and noisily. He wanted to shout and wave his arms about; he wanted to kick and punch the Elders and everyone else sitting there in judgement on him. Even his uncle Roger. He opened his eyes and saw Roger looking at him, saw the love and pity in his face, saw the tears in his eyes and knew what he had to say.

"Friends," he said, his voice high and loud, louder than anyone there had ever heard him speak before, "There is no human kindness in you, though you preach it in your sermons and in your testimony at Meeting. You worship God in the name of the Loving Shepherd, but 'ave no idea of the true nature of charity, which I'm not afraid to call love. I've found it in the simple girl who has no other wish than that we should spend all our life together as man and wife. She, more than you, knows what love is. Read your Bibles again. Friends" - and the John spat the word 'Friends' now and at every following repetition of it. "Read it well, Friends." He looked around the room with rage on his face before reciting.

"'Though I speak with the tongues of men and of angels, and 'ave not charity' - The Apostle speaks of love. Friends." Again the word was emphasised - "'I am become as sounding brass or tinkling cymbal.' and again, 'Though I bestow all my goods to feed the poor, and though I give my body to be burned, and have not charity, it profiteth nothing."

Here John picked up the heavy Bible and held it in both hands above his head. "Paul the apostle was writing to the Corinthians - and us - about love. Friends." And with that word he threw the heavy Bible at the whitewashed wall with such force that the leather binding left a dark stain there. He continued, "About which you know nothing!" His fury expressed, he sat down heavily.

He had no other option, his legs refused to support him.

While he sat there, panting slightly, Friends had listened to his outburst without any outward sign of surprise, outrage, or any other emotion, other than concerned glancing at each other at the start of John's answer. They now looked to Joshua for his reaction, which was unusually swift.

He rose and walked over to where John sat. Joshua was one of the most revered Friends in the area. An elderly man, a little stooped, he had been among those one hundred and eighty Quakers who had suffered severe punishment and imprisonment following the mass arrests in the winter of 1660/61. While the silent room waited, he put his hands on the young man's shoulders, at which John raised his head and looked up into his eyes. He saw no sympathy in Joshua's face and felt his anger subside, subdued by the lack of response. He could not hold the Elder's gaze and bowed his head.

Joshua removed his hands from John's shoulders, stepped back and, still looking sternly at him said, "The apostle Paul also wrote, in his second epistle to the Corinthians, 'Be ye not unequally yoked together with unbelievers for what fellowship hath righteousness with unrighteousness? And what

126

communion hath light with darkness?' Thee quotes the Holy Book without full knowledge, and at thy peril, Friend John." So saying Joshua returned to the Elders' bench and sat down.

Silence was resumed and continued for a further quarter of an hour after which Joshua again rose to once more ask John the question "Does thee still intend to marry this woman, Friend?"

John, who had been weeping in his heart during the silence, only waited for a short while before giving his answer. Bereft of any more emotional energy following his outburst and unable to summon any thoughts other than wishing to bring this tension to an end, John rose to his feet. He felt enormously tired as if he had been physically beaten. Slowly he looked around the room.

Joshua's eyes were closed. Roger was the only man present who met John's gaze and the look in his eyes was of deep sorrow. He opened his mouth as if he was going to speak to John, but, for emotion, was unable to out loud, so silently mouthed, 'Go on. Son'.

"Friends," John's voice was surprisingly deep now, after the shrillness of his rage. He was calm now, and suddenly strong. "I will not marry Frances Palmer," he said. "I will 'ave no further association with 'er and will put 'er out of my mind. I beg the Meeting's pardon for my disobedience to it and pray that God will forgive my sinfulness."

Joshua Dale walked over to him and shook his hand saying only, "God be with thee, John and bless thee," before returning to the bench.

Pale-faced and dignified John also resumed his seat and silence once more descended on the Meeting.

Monday, December 5th 1664

John was on his way to face the Palmers. He hoped that Frances would not be at home and that he would only have her father to face. Strangely he felt that George Palmer would be the lesser of two evils. The talk would be man-to-man and likely to be over quickly. John would not have been surprised if it ended in violence.

George had always been opposed to John's association with Frances, saying little to him if they met, his surliness emphasising that John's presence was not welcome. John knew it was because of his Quaker principles and the danger they represented for anyone who followed them, including his daughter. In this respect John was partly right, although he was intelligent enough to sense that there was another reason, unconnected with religion, or with himself in particular. For now, the religious differences between himself and the Palmers, so recently reinforced by yesterday's meeting with the Elders, had assumed greater importance today than ever before. He had not given much thought to any other reason for George's antagonism.

For all his firmness the previous day when he had announced his change of mind about the marriage, as he approached the Palmer's house and workshop today, he was less sure of himself. When he had woken this morning he had resolved to keep his word to the Meeting. It would be his sacrifice for his religion and he determined to make it, hoping to be made strong by it.

Opening the gate into the yard, he faltered a little. If Frances were to be present John dreaded that he would be persuaded again by the lovely girl. He was ashamed of his weakness and determined to conquer it.

When he knocked on the door Frances opened it.

She was smiling and flushed with happiness to see him. As she reached to kiss him and be kissed he put her to one side, unintentionally a little roughly and stepped inside the house. He had to be strong.

"Where's thy father?" he asked, looking around.

She was relieved. It was all right. He wanted to speak to her father about marrying her and he was nervous. That's why he was so sharp. He was worried. She loved him the more for it.

"'E's workin' my love," The words hung in the air.

"It doesn't matter," John said dourly, "I may as well talk to thee." Frances realised then that John had not come to see her father about a wedding. Paler now, she stood in the doorway waiting for the sentence which would end the dream.

"I can't marry thee, Francis Palmer,"

The words wounded Francis like a flash of lightning in her brain and her heart thumped terrifyingly in her chest. She managed to stammer, "Why not?" before the tears came.

John ignored them. He was amazed by his own strength. His voice rose slightly, "I can't marry thee because my conscience will not allow it. The Elders have guided me back onto the right path." He seemed oblivious of the effect he was having on the girl who loved him so much.

At first she had tried to take him in her arms but had been pushed out of the doorway into the yard where he faced her as she stood, her face covered by her hands and weeping hysterically. Hearing the sound of her crying, George came running out of his workshop in time to hear John, carried away with religious fervour, saying, "I can not marry thee, because thee are not in the Light. Thee are not blessed. Thee are not chosen."

Frances, unaware of anything other than her own distress, once again tried to embrace John, shrieking, "I'll change. I'll change. I'll come with you - thee!"

But she was pushed away again, this time into her father's arms. George struggled to control his daughter's efforts to escape from his arms to John's. Half-choking with rage, he shouted, "No you won't, Frances. No you won't. I'll see you dead first!" Her struggling lessened, then ceased and was replaced with weeping. George turned his attention from Frances to John, by now heading for the yard gate. "Not so fast, young man," he roared, as he let Frances go and ran to catch up with him.

John felt a strong hand grasp his shoulder. He stopped, turned towards the older man and immediately felt the punch on the left side of his face and the trickle of blood down his cheek.

He had never been struck before in the whole of his life and the blow brought him to his senses. For the briefest, fleeting moment he regretted everything that he had said in the last few minutes; everything that he had done and said that had hurt Frances and offended her father. He wanted more than ever to join his life with hers. Then he saw, with shining clarity, that it would never be possible. The differences between the three of them were too strong and deep. The sweetness of their love was too frail, too delicate, to withstand any future conflict, whether it be in family or community.

"I am very sorry, George Palmer," he said. "I have done thee and thy daughter great wrong, which I will regret for the rest of my life. I will trouble thee no longer, if I may be allowed to leave peaceably."

The young man's answer, so contrite, so gentle and quietly spoken in such sharp contrast to his earlier outbursts, took George by surprise. He had expected to have the blow he had given returned. It was difficult for him to maintain his anger in the face of this calm opposition but he needed to have his say, even if most of the fire had gone out of his anger. Flustered, he replied, "You can go, you heathen. You can go, and never come back here again. You will never see Frances again, you can be sure of that."

There was nothing else to say or do. John held out his hand to shake George's, the usual Friends' leave-taking gesture. It was ignored. John walked out through the gate and George turned to attend to his daughter, still standing, alone, in the yard.

"Father?" she said.

"You'll stay in the house until I say you can go out," he answered.

***

As he walked through the door at home, Roger and Barbary Ockenden greeted John with gentle words and open arms.

℘℘

CHAPTER NINETEEN

Monday, December 12th 1664

The Advent wreath of holly and ivy hung in the sanctuary of Saint James's church at Branslow. The second candle had been lit during the day's services, but was snuffed out now like the first one. They both looked strangely forlorn in contrast to the waxy whiteness of the two remaining candles. For its three hundred and forty-second year, the little church was in waiting for Christmas.

***

At the Grange Abel and Ruth Chinnock sat in their customary positions on opposite sides of the fireplace. They had enjoyed supper after which Abel had spent some time going over his books. At this time of year it was too dark after supper to walk his fields with the dog, his usual daily habit in other seasons. In addition to the income from his land he had taken up one or two small business speculations, which at present were performing very satisfactorily. The drawings made of the improvements he wished to make to the house had passed his inspection and building would begin in the springtime.

This late in the evening conversation had lapsed and in the loose woollen gown and embroidered cap he wore in the hour before bedtime, snug and warm in his comfortable chair, Abel was close to sleep. Occasionally, in the companionable silence, to prove that he was awake, he glanced at his wife and if she caught his eye, gave her a fond smile, which she returned in kind.

Abel had no idea of the turmoil in Ruth's breast. She sat, head bent over the inevitable piece of embroidery; the epitome of all the wifely virtues: serene, modest and quiet. One of Abel's sleepy glances had noticed nothing more untoward about his wife than the wisp of curly golden brown hair which peeped out from beneath the edge of her cap and lay on her bent neck. He contemplated the curve of her neck happily. What an angel she was. A pearl without price.

Unaware that Ruth was looking at him he was startled when she said, "Abel, I have something I wish to ask you." Her voice broke slightly with the words, because she was a little nervous. She gave a small cough, put down her embroidery and came over to his side of the fireplace, where she knelt at his feet looking up into his eyes.

"We are very happy, are we not, Abel?"

"Of course, my love."

"I only ever wish to be a good wife to you, husband."

"And in that you succeed, my dear wife."

She was finding it difficult to come to the point. Although she loved Abel she was sometimes a little over-awed by him. He had been brought up in a much grander way than she and she quite often worried that she would let him down in some way. She was quite wrong in these anxious assumptions, but it would take a few more years of marriage to Abel before she gained the confidence she was now finding it so hard to achieve. She coughed again and wriggled a little on her knees.

"Get up, Mistress Chinnock," Abel said encouragingly, and not too impatiently, "Bring that stool nearer and tell me what is on your mind."

Obediently Ruth carried the small stool with its embroidered cover, over to the side of her husband's chair.

Sitting down, she turned to look at him and said, in a rush," Abel, dear, don't be angry, will you? You have four beloved sons whom I love too." She struggled for words. "Would you be very angry to have another?" She looked down at her hands, twisting in her lap. "After he is born, if you don't want him, I will make sure that he never bothers you, and you won't even have to look at him." She forced herself to look up at him, anxiously searching her husband's face for signs of approval or displeasure. Blushing, she looked ten years younger than her thirty-two.

Abel sat upright, wide-awake now, emotions of surprise, pleasure, tenderness, obvious in his expression. In fact his cup of happiness could not have been more full. Of course he would not have told Ruth this secret, but his happiest times with the first Mistress Chinnock, when not working, had been spent in the company of his four boys. Especially when he could abandon his role as master of the household and estate and frolic with his youngest, Benjamin.

Ben was twelve years old now and to Abel's regret, had long outgrown toddler playtimes. He had joined Leonard, thirteen, away at school. Peter at fourteen years old, to his father's alarm, had set his mind on joining the Navy. He was now seventeen and away at sea. Abel consoled himself by thinking that at least it was better than joining the clergy. Now, at his age of fifty and his wife's of thirty-whatever-it-was, there would be another one, to brighten the house and his parents' lives, even if those parents were a little elderly.

Made nervous by his silence, Ruth spoke again, "Are you pleased, Abel?"

Roused out of his happy reverie Abel rose, turned to his wife and raising her from her stool, held her to him, kissed her firmly and fondly, then, holding her a little space from him so that he could see her properly, said, "Of course I am pleased, you goose. Another little Chinnock! What could be better? And what a clever little wife you are."

He leaned over and pulled her onto his lap then, suddenly solicitous, he began to caution her, "You must be very careful about your health, my dear. Nothing but the best for you at table, and nothing heavier than your dear embroidery to occupy your hand or mind. We will get you a maid to look after all your needs and employ a good midwife and a kind nurse when the time comes." he thought for a second, before thinking out loud, "For midwife, shall it be Mistress Jackson or Greenlow? - "

Ruth smiled with relief and allowed herself the pleasant luxury of snuggling in her husband's arms. They were sitting quietly in the firelight when her pleasure and his ponderings were interrupted by a loud noise from outside the house. Voices were raised in more or less tuneful song:

"Call up the master of this house,
Wearing his golden ring.
Let him bring us a piece of beef,
And better we shall sing"

"It's the Wassailers," Ruth breathed, "It's that time of year again." Releasing herself from his embrace she ran to the window, opened the curtain and called to Abel, "Come and see. They're out in the yard." She beckoned to him excitedly as he hesitated. "Abel, come here. Look!"

There were about a dozen and a half fantastically dressed young men and women and a small boy making the yard bright with burning torches, which illuminated their blackened faces. They sang to the accompaniment of Jack on fiddle while the small boy, Humphrey Yates, beat the drum in time. In this new role, he occasionally took a whistle from his pocket and blew a few ear splitting single notes on it.

Centre front of the group was the Captain of the Wassailers, distinguished from his fellows as much by his great height and breadth as his dress. Like all the Wassailers, he wore a quantity of green holly, fir and ivy branches hanging down from his shoulders to his knees. Both men's' and women's' costumes left only their black faces, lower legs and feet, mostly shod in working boots, visible. Under the greenery the women's' skirts were hitched up into their apron waistbands to ensure their anonymity and protection from the scandal of appearing bare-legged and with such vagabonds.

On the Captain's head, over a mass of dark curly hair, was a circlet of holly and ivy intertwined with brightly coloured ribbons, which lifted, twisting and rustling in the chilly evening breeze. In his two hands he held a large wooden bowl, decorated with more ribbons and winter greenery. Baked apples floated in beer which slopped about, catching the light in its ripples. For some reason lost in antiquity,

Humphrey was dressed to represent a bird and was referred to as the Pippit.

The Wassailers, seeing no movement to open the door of the house, sang the song again, louder this time and possibly a semitone or two higher. The fiddler quickly adjusted to their voices and increased his volume as much as he could while Humphrey banged his drum louder between shrieking blasts from the whistle. Abel, roused from his paternal musings, had no choice but to follow Ruth as she grabbed his hand and led him to the house door. He protested a little that this activity was too energetic for her in her present condition, but she only laughed at his concern, and hurried on enthusiastically towards the excitement waiting outside.

The Captain, controlling the weight and instability of the bowl and its contents with some difficulty, approached the door as it opened, framing the Chinnocks. At his signal the Wassailers, who had sung previously because the door was closed, now sang, louder and less tunefully, because it was opened.

All members of the Chinnock household were familiar with the form and tradition of Branslow Wassailers. They had been suppressed during the Commonwealth but were now revived. The Chinnocks were joined by Mistress Denny, carrying a tray of minced meat pies taken from a stock made for Christmas and Hannah with a pint tankard in her hand.

All joined in the ritual, clapping hands and tapping feet in time to the music until it ended. Then the Captain, bowing precariously as the liquid slopped about, offered the bowl to Abel, saying with ritual solemnity, "Will you take a drink from our Wassail bowl, my lord?" Whereupon Hannah pushed forward by Mistress Denny, offered Abel the tankard, which he dipped into the bowl and stood for a moment, looking around him. He had forgotten what had happened in previous years, but was aware that a form should be followed. Unsure of what he should do next he wavered a little until Ruth whispered, "With all good will, Captain," and waited while he spoke the words. Once started he remembered them from earlier times, and said more confidently,

"For it's your Wassail
And our Wassail,
And joy to us all
In the name of Lord,"
then drank deeply from the pot. Mistress Denny then stepped forward with the pies, which were grabbed eagerly by the Wassailers. After that the pot was dipped repeatedly into the bowl and passed from hand to hand all round until it came back into Abel's.

Finally it was time for them to go. "Come Wassailers, come Pippit," shouted the Captain, and the ritual was completed. Then everybody cheered and the Wassailers left with out-of-tune music, singing, drumming, blowing deafening whistle-blasts and shouting good wishes for the Christmas time to come. As they walked out of the yard Mistress Denny and Hannah returned to their duties leaving the Chinnocks standing side by side on their doorstep, watching the lights from the flames move away down the road. Abel turned to his wife, saying, "Such a Christmas as we are going to have, my dear."

***

The Wassailers' reception had been very different on the other side of Branslow. Starting at the village green, their usual practise was to perambulate the district calling on as many neighbours as they could. The Grange was their last stop before they ended the ritual at the Green Man. They had performed before a small but enthusiastic audience of people in Branslow, who either partook of the Wassail bowl or contributed to it with more beer. They then moved on to the lane which led them south west out of the village, stopping at individual cottages on the way to offer Advent good tidings and drink before they arrived at George Palmer, the wheelwright's, house.

Earlier in the day George's two friends, Edward Morris and David Davis, had tried to get him to take part again this year, but he had seemed even more morose than usual and refused. It hadn't been the first time that this had happened, but the two men were suspicious when they'd gone to see George, as Frances had not been about in the house or the yard. She could have been off seeing her sweetheart or one of her friends of course, but the house didn't look as tidy as usual and George looked unkempt and unhappy. For once, Eddie and Dai, not usually the most observant of men, realised that something untoward had happened in the Palmer household.

Dressed in greenery with their faces blackened, Eddie, Dai and the rest of the Wassailers approached George's cottage. They were surprised to see that there were candles visible in each room and to hear the sound of George's voice raised in noisy song. The rest of the company took this to mean a receptive audience inside but Eddie and Dai were not so sure, and looked at one another anxiously.

As the green-clad performers moved nearer the cottage Eddie cautioned them. "There's summat wrong 'ere," he said nervously. "One of us'll go in first, eh, Dai?" Dai, relieved, saw his chance to hang back, saying, " Oh, ah. I'll stay 'ere then, but call me if you need me." Eddie gave his treacherous friend a long look then, suppressing his own urge to avoid trouble, he walked up to the door closely followed by Tap, George's dog, betraying his part-terrier ancestry yapping and nipping at his heels.

Through the window he saw George walking around the kitchen, still singing and banging a metal spoon against a pewter plate in time to his wordless tune. Eddie hesitated and then drawing on bravery he hadn't known he'd got, he knocked on the door. George didn't hear him. Eddie turned to see if Dai and the other Wassailers were still in the yard. They'd all retreated nearer to the gate. Dai, who had deserted his post immediately behind Eddie at the first sight and sound of George's strange behaviour, was now unrecognisable in the green crowd.

Eddie shrugged his shoulders and grunted to himself before knocking on the door again, louder. George fell silent, then, delighted, shouted, "Franny?" The door opened framing the wheelwright's tall figure silhouetted against the candlelight. His arms were spread wide and there was a welcoming smile on his face.

The smile disappeared when he realized who his visitor was. "I thought you were Franny," he said, going back into the house. Then he turned, saying, "Oo are you anyway?" Dai, illogically, removed his leafy headdress. It did nothing to prove his identity as his black face was made darker still in the half-light. In the excitement of the moment he had forgotten his disguise.

"It's me, George," he explained. "Come wi' the Wassailers. To bring you good tidings for the coming of Christmas." Turning, he beckoned to the Wassailers, who, immediately back in character, marched and capered up to the door. The Captain moved to the front, to begin the opening lines of the ritual:

"Call up the master of this house,
Wearing his golden ring.
Let him bring us -

The words were interrupted by a loud cry of "Damn you all to 'ell!" from George and the crash of the door being slammed shut.

The Wassailers were used to this sort of reception on the few occasions when their entertainment was unwelcome. In particular, Puritans and Quakers found the Wassailers offensive, and sometimes castigated them, but their language wouldn't have been quite so forthright.

From George, who usually took part in the festivities even if in a more subdued way than some of the younger folk, the reaction was startling. For a few seconds they stood looking at each other wondering whether to try again, but George's voice settled the matter for them. "Clear off! Get off my land, before I set the dog on you!" and the company turned about, making for the gate. Dai, baffled, replaced his headdress and joined them.

***

Later, as they all walked across the moor to Thomas Hickock's house, heads down against a strengthening wind, Eddie and Dai reviewed the incident.

"It's that daughter of 'is," said Eddie.

"Ah," said Dai.

"And that dog's no bigger'n a rat!" said Eddie, sulkily.

"No," Dai replied.

***

Lying alone in her bed, the only place where she had time to think, Alice Bowman heard the music as the revellers approached. She knew at once what it signified.

Wassail, the start of the vile heathen celebrations surrounding the birth of Christ. It would soon be time for the villages to begin garlanding of houses with greenery inside and out. There would be the Mummers' pagan play-acting, with men dressing in strange costumes, even animal skins, capering about and mouthing heathenish words. There would be general shameless drunkenness and licence. She had heard that that most pagan of symbols, mistletoe, was hung in the porch or even placed on the altar in some churches in the county, to stay there for the whole twelve appalling days.

Restlessly, she turned over. Her baby, due in the spring, had become lively and she was glad about that. It would be a strong, healthy child. Perhaps a little girl.

A replacement for Susan, Alice? Oh, Alice! A little girl to teach the womanly things to. Henry would like a daughter to feel protective of, wouldn't he?

'No, not a replacement.' Alice countered to herself. 'A daughter!'

The music was outside the house now. Alice pulled the covers over her head and put her fingers in her ears.

You can shut out the devil's music, Alice, but it's there, all the same. Closing your ears to the sound will not destroy it. Beating at its drums, blowing its whistles, singing its pagan songs. Sinful men and women dressed in devilish greenery, showing their true wicked selves and disregarding the wrath which will fall upon them one day.

139

They caper about like savages, these heathen men and immodest women.

Alice! Did you know there is a child with them? An innocent at birth, but already tainted with sin?

***

Henry Bowman, lying on the floor of the cell, tries to hold on to sleep. It is a way of escaping from his present situation. He is very cold and his chest hurts. Few of the prisoners have anything to lie upon. Some have not quite enough straw between themselves and the stone. Some have none at all. No one has a cover other than his coat, or a pillow other than his shoes.

Heartless city Wassailers have made their loudest music and sung their crudest song the loudest outside the walls. They know many religious dissenters are incarcerated inside the castle being used as a gaol. Their city song, newly re-worded for this visit, was ribald, was deliberately offensive to religious sensitivities and those not used to the uncouthness of crowded streets. Instead of offerings of beer and baked apples, the prisoners received clods of earth, rotten vegetables, fruit and eggs; even a dead rat was flung through the barred windows. All accompanied by shouts and catcalls. Oaths and excrement.

Henry tries to think of Alice. It is two weeks he thinks, since Alice came to see him. One or other of the boys have seen him supplied with food, clean clothes, straw. Harry cut his hair for him the other day. He felt a little better for it. His cough troubles him sometimes but he tries not to worry about it. He tries to remember happier times but it is difficult under present conditions. He tries to pray but that is difficult, too and he manages only the prayer learnt in his Anglican childhood. 'Thy Will be done...Deliver us from Evil...For ever and ever. Amen'.

Frosty stars decorate the midnight moonlit sky. The rough-throated night watch makes his wheezy call "Twelve o'clock, and all's well!"

***

Cautiously, Alice removed her fingers from her ears and turned the covers down to her chin. The music had faded away. She relaxed, offering up a prayer of thanksgiving for its passing. As a counter to the evil sounds which she had just borne, she began to think about the good things in her life now.

Except for the absence of Henry, in gaol since early November, all was going well with the farm. The boys worked well together, even eleven-year-old Cornelius. He seemed more willing to take on some of the more heavy work now that he knew he wasn't always to be the youngest one.

Henry could be in gaol for months, years, even. When he was released he would be pleased to come home to a farm that was prospering so well. Pleased that all the hard work the whole family had put into it was proving successful. Alice smiled to herself. She looked forward to his approval, which was important to her.

The strong support given by Friends, trading chiefly between themselves, was of much help to Alice in building up Ridge Farm. Unusually for the time, men and women were treated equally in the Society of Friends and the level of respect Alice received was equal to that of her husband, whether in matters of religion or business.

Non-Quaker traders, originally suspicious of the non-conformist sect to which she belonged, were at first reluctant to do business with her and found the idea of a woman taking on her husband's business dealings difficult to accept. They were, however, to learn that Quaker integrity made for reliable business dealings

All Quakers were barred from corporate office in any trade by their refusal to swear the Oath of Allegiance. They responded to this restriction by operating between themselves, practising a collectively recognised level of honesty and integrity, buying and selling at prices which were not haggled over. They did not confine their straight-forward business practices exclusively to Friends and many non-Quaker traders who ventured to approach them found advantage in dealing with people of increasingly acknowledged uprightness.

There were disadvantages. Some businessmen, traders and

merchants were envious of increasing Quaker prosperity. Others, who were glad to take the opportunity to trade with them, did so despite finding it difficult to understand Friends' refusal to haggle over prices, either as buyers or vendors.

Alice traded successfully in her husband's absence. Initially non-Quakers found it difficult to understand how she, a woman not of independent means, was able to conduct business in Henry's absence, while following her strictly religious principles and adhering to such unusual trading practices. Eventually it became known that Alice could drive a hard bargain, using acknowledged Quaker methods, such as selling only for a stated price and when buying, never asking the vendor to lower his price.

Yes, the family had all worked together, Friends had supported them in many practical and financial ways, and perhaps it would not be too long before Henry was released.

God bless you, Henry. Amen

She turned over onto her side while she still could and pulled the covers closer around her. Tucking the pillow into her neck she slept. Tomorrow she would go to see him. They hadn't let her see him for a month but she could go now. She would tell him not to be anxious about the farm. The boys were doing well. She was doing well. All was well

All is well? Are you sure, Alice?

***

John Taylor had seen the Wassailers as they passed through Branslow earlier in the evening. He'd slowed down on his walk home, to watch the rituals being carried out at various houses and cottages in the village to the amusement of the inhabitants. He regarded the celebrations with a mixture of reluctant amusement and moral disquiet. Brought up to regard these rituals as pagan, therefore offensive and hateful, at the same time he found that he could understand how the simple repetitive music and deliberately clumsy dancing could cause amusement among the onlookers. He knew that they had few diversions their lives and these interludes, when most people in Branslow came out to watch, were a small relief from the hard effort it took to live from day to day. Their smiles and laughter seemed very innocent to him.

Horrified, he mentally tried to shake himself free of the evil trap into which he had almost plunged. Such thoughts had been put into his head by the Devil and must be cast aside. He must pray for God's forgiveness; must pray long and hard to expurgate the wickedness into which he had nearly fallen. He quickened his step. The sooner he was home the better.

Hearing footsteps behind him he turned round and saw there was a girl following him. His heart leapt in his chest. Franny! He almost stopped walking but thought of the promises he had made to the Meeting and his family and instead he walked on faster. As he quickened his pace the girl started to run after him, "John! John! Stop!" she shouted. He stopped, turned around; but it wasn't Franny.

***

Mary Johnson had been visiting her friend Jane Mason, who lived with her parents and her brothers and sisters at the baker's shop in Branslow. She had intended to go home earlier but had lost track of the time. The Wassailers would be visiting her parents' house some time during the evening and she wanted to be there when they arrived.

Her father always enjoyed taking part in the ritual and she and her mother enjoyed the joke of pretending not to recognise him in it. Her mother, particularly, made a great show of outrage when her disguised husband took her in his greenery-festooned arms and kissed her leaving black marks on her face. There were always ribald comments about new babbies next year. Any baby born around September was teased for the rest of his or her life, as being the result of a "Sooty Kiss" in Advent.

This time she and Jane had been so engrossed in their talk

about Frances Palmer, that it wasn't until they heard the approaching music that Mary realised how late it would be when she got home and she left the house after wishing Jane a hurried "Good night."

Only a few minutes after she had left the shop Mary caught sight of John walking a little distance in front of her. Even from behind he looked so dejected she instantly felt sorry for him. His head and shoulders were bowed as he trudged, hands thrust in his pockets, along the road to his home on the outskirts of Branslow. 'Poor lad,' she thought. ' It'll take 'im ages to get over what's just 'appened to Franny.' And she called his name. He seemed to hear her, as his step faltered a little, but he carried on, not speaking. When she shouted again, he stopped and turned around, a half-smile on his face.

The smile disappeared when he recognised Mary. She instantly noticed the change and realising that he had been expecting to see Frances, her own smile faded. "Good evenin', John," she said, a little breathless after running. He did not reply and walked on, as she half-walked, half ran to keep up with his long strides. This curtness, caused by his Quaker lack of conventional greetings perplexed many who thought it impolite, but Mary, used to the down-to-earth attitudes of country people, was not unduly offended. She was even more sure that he must be brooding over the latest news about Frances.

A few more steps and the impulse to express her sympathy for his trouble became too strong, and perhaps foolishly, she said, "I'm ever so sorry about Franny, John. I think what 'er dad 'as done is very 'ard." He stopped walking and turned to look at her. "What does thee mean?" he said, puzzled, then an angry note in his voice, "What has 'e done? - If 'e's hurt her... "The words 'I'll kill him' came into his head, to be instantly suppressed in deference to his Quaker conscience, leaving him without any expression of retaliation or revenge.

Mary was horrified. It was clear that John knew nothing about George Palmer's solution to his problem with his daughter. On the one hand she was reluctant to tell him, on the other she knew that he should be told. She decided that the news would be better from her than from some others. There was little doubt that the Branslow boys would count it a great game to taunt him cruelly next time they met him. They were probably looking forward to the sport. And if they were to be the ones to pass on the news they would be brutal in their gleeful telling him of it. They would give him no rest for months or at least until the next poor soul came to their notice.

Mary took a deep breath. There was only one way to tell him. It would be hard on him and she didn't know what his reaction to herself would be, but the poor lad should know.

"Master Palmer has sent Franny to Dorset, to live with her Aunt, John," she said quietly. Then courage failing her, she removed her gaze from his while she waited for his response. The silence was unnerving. Eventually she had to look up at him. He was staring over her head, pale with grief and shock. For a moment or two they stood unspeaking, then Mary said his name once or twice in an attempt to pierce the wall of stillness which was surrounding him. Then with a suddenness which startled her, he seemed to come out of his waking trance and said one word.

"Dorset?"

For him it could have been America or the Algiers, the two furthest places he had ever heard of.

"Yes, John," Mary answered, then "John. Would you like me to walk to your house with you if you are not feeling well?"

"No." The answer was short, and without any further word or look, John walked the last hundred yards home thinking 'I loved her, more than anyone else in the world. Now she's gone, as if she had never been.'

Watching him turn into the carpenter's yard Mary thought, 'E did love 'er. Truly he did love 'er,' and walked along the road past the house until she turned off to the left, to go to her own home.

❧

CHAPTER TWENTY

Friday, February 3rd 1664/5

On a bitterly cold day Alice Bowman was making an unusual visit to Branslow. She had been helping to get the in-lamb ewes under cover, or at least closer to the steading before lambing time. In the usual way pregnancy gave her little trouble, but today she irritable and not feeling too well.

She'd had a frustrating morning. While she was adding a few more vegetables to the stew-pot bubbling over the fire, she'd heard the telltale sizzle of liquid falling on the flames. The old iron pot had sprung another leak. It had been second-hand three years earlier, when it had been given to her after the bailiffs took away her best copper pot. Since then Henry had repaired it many times and it had, until now, served well. Alice was uncharacteristically fond of the old thing but Grace Wells, Tom's wife, had given it to her. Grace, too, had few household goods at the time, but gave it to her anyway, so ever since Alice had regarded the pot as a token of Friends helping each other.

But today she decided she should buy a new cooking-pot. She hadn't had a new one since her marriage, so it was about time. In the normal way she would have walked the three miles to Branslow, but the ground was icy to walk on; to carry a heavy iron pot in such weather was unwise. The horse and cart would be quicker and she could be home sooner than if she walked.

At first she'd been offended, assuming that it was because of her religion that the ironmonger had waited until the shop was empty before serving her. So she was surprised and unsure of how to respond when, after she had chosen and paid for a fine new pot, he'd said quietly, "I do not approve of my son's behaviour towards you Quakers. I have no quarrel with you. What he did was wrong."

He said no more to her and she stood open mouthed as Master William Jenkins Senior, the ironmonger and father of Will Jenkins the informer, carried the pot out to the cart for her.

"Good day, Master Jenkins!" A cheerful female voice called out. "And a good day to you, Mistress!" Alice, who had been preparing to climb up into the driving seat, turned round involuntarily to see who it was speaking to her. She saw a woman, pretty, though not young, fashionably dressed and smiling straight into Alice's eyes.

"You must be careful my dear," Ruth Chinnock continued, "In your condition you must be very, very careful." Alice's response was little more than a grunt but Ruth was insistent. "When is your little one due, mistress? Is it your first?"

Alice restrained herself. She felt inclined to ask this over-bearing woman if she looked young enough for it to be her first but didn't, attempting again to get up onto the cart. "Oh, please, mistress, let me help." And Ruth moved to assist Alice, who froze, one foot on the footboard, embarrassed and unused to gentleness from a stranger. Suddenly the horse shifted position, jolting the cart and Alice lost her footing and fell on the icy ground.

Within a few minutes she was back in the ironmonger's shop. Master Jenkins made a discreet withdrawal to fetch his wife after finding a stool for Alice, while Ruth murmured soothing sounds to her. Alice, previously anxious to get onto the cart and drive home as fast as possible, could do nothing but submit herself to being taken care of. It only took a short time for her to recover, then, thanking Ruth and Mistress Jenkins, she assured them both that she was perfectly well but must get home, as her husband would be concerned about her. Will Jenkins helped her up onto the cart and she headed for the security of the Ridge steading.

After she had gone Ruth Chinnock asked Sarah Jenkins, "Who was she? She appears a little unsettled in her mind."

Sarah shrugged, "Mistress Bowman is very shy and quiet

in the normal way of things. It is after a child is born that she suffers more disquiet."

Not wishing to expand more on Alice's state of mind Sarah brought the subject to a close, with assurances to Mistress Chinnock that the Bowmans and their children were not troublesome if left to themselves. Sarah had become accustomed to Henry and Alice Bowmans' unconventional behaviour over the years. Henry used her husband's shop sometimes, though Alice not so often. William knew about the consequences of the Bowmans' actions, but at this establishment, as in every other business used by the couple, there were no complaints about their honesty and integrity.

But Ruth's curiosity was aroused and she determined not to lose touch with the enigmatic Mistress Bowman.

℘ ℭ

CHAPTER TWENTY-ONE

Monday, July 17th 1665

It had happened to Abel Chinnock four times before, but that didn't make it any easier. He was older now and his patience was wearing extremely thin. It was particularly hot today and he was never comfortable in hot weather. For coolness he'd removed his wig as he walked up and down the saloon on the ground floor of the recently built new wing of the house. Should anyone enter the saloon he would put his wig back on again, so as not to forfeit his dignity. Walking was making him hot too, but he had spent a lot of money on this long, elegant room and was determined to use it, since Ruth's pregnancy had prevented much of the entertaining for which the room had been built.

He paused at one of the windows. The grassy slope around the house was soon to be made into formal gardens, a waste of good growing space in his opinion, but it was what Ruth wanted. Beyond the proposed gardens he could see more of his land under useful cultivation and earning him money. The weather was perfect for haymaking, which was well under way. Abel could remember how hard he had worked in the fields as a young man and in his heart he pitied the men working today. It was warm work and the sun was still high in the sky. It was much cooler inside the house.

He had been advised by the midwife, Mistress Jackson, that his presence would not be required anywhere near the room where his wife was at present in labour. In fact his being there would be both unnecessary and unseemly. This was definitely women's work and a husband's attendance was neither welcome nor expected. Mistress Jackson was a round, cheerful woman, well known in Branslow and the surrounding district as an expert in the art of midwifery. She fully understood Abel's desire to have the best care at his wife's bedside and she knew that Master Chinnock was, naturally, deeply concerned for his wife in her travail.

Abel continued with his walk along the new oak floorboards. His footsteps sounded loud in the quietness of the room. Suddenly aware of it, the sound began to irritate him. He must calm himself. These things take time. He must be patient. Things could not be rushed. Again he paused to look out of the window. Near it was an armchair with coverings embroidered by Ruth. He stroked the padded armrest. What must the poor dear be suffering at this moment? He pushed that thought out of his head. He must wait a little longer. He sat down and waited to be informed when he was to visit his wife and new son.

There was a sudden flurry of noise and activity upstairs, with sounds of running feet and raised voices. Once he thought he heard the well-remembered sound of a new baby protesting at leaving it's warm haven and being thrust into a colder, brighter place. He thought, 'At last,' and put his wig back on. And now it was happening. There was a knock on the door and in came Eliza Bailey, the nurse Abel had engaged for the three months leading up to and three months following the time of Ruth's confinement. Eliza was the daughter of the midwife who was at present upstairs attending to her patient in the aftermath of giving birth.

Eliza was twenty-three years old, recently married and therefore an appropriate person to learn the craft. She still found the arrival of new babies exhilarating and was smiling broadly as she entered, "Congratulations, sir," she said shyly. "You have a beautiful baby daughter." She would have said more but Abel was pushing past her through the door.

As Abel walked quickly towards the stairs, with Eliza following, a perspiring, though smiling, Mistress Denny came down to meet him. "You'll be able to see the little darling in good time, sir." she said.

"Yes, yes," replied Abel, breathlessly, "How is she?"

"A sweet rose of a child," Mistress Denny replied, "The

midwife said she came out with no trouble at all. Healthy and with every one of her fingers and toes." All the time she spoke she had been patting her damp, flushed face with her handkerchief. She stopped to take off her spectacles with one hand, while with the other she mopped her brow with the already soaked piece of cloth. Putting it away in the pocket of her apron, she adjusted her white cotton cap strings before replacing her spectacles

Abel was about to reply that his enquiry had been about his wife, rather than the girl-child, when there were more sounds of commotion coming from the floor above and Mistress Jackson appeared at the top of the stairs. She looked very agitated. "Eliza!" she shouted, "Come up here. Quickly, girl!" and Eliza ran to the top of the stairs, where her mother pushed her into Ruth's room.

The sudden appearance of an obviously concerned midwife made Abel very worried and he turned to the housekeeper for some sort of explanation or assurance. Mistress Denny was secretly fairly alarmed herself but she tried to remain outwardly sanguine. "Nothing to distress yourself about, I'm sure, sir. It's women's matters, really, sir, women's matters. If I was you I would keep myself away from them as much as possible. Mistress Jackson knows all there is to know about things at a time like this."

They both reached the top of the stairs and although Abel got to the door of his wife's room first he stopped, reluctant to intrude on 'women's matters' and waited for Mistress Denny to catch him up.

"Please do not be troubled, sir," Mistress Denny said. "I will go and find out what the matter is." As she opened the door she whispered reassuringly to Abel, "Women's matters," again before she entered the bedroom, closing the door and leaving Abel outside waiting for news.

He didn't have to wait long. The sounds of commotion continued for a few minutes then there were sounds of surprised laughter. Moments later the door opened and Mistress Denny came out. She was beaming. "Another one!" she said, clasping her hands together and gazing at the ceiling as if appealing to the gods to help her survive this thrilling surprise. She looked back again at Abel. "Another one, sir. Another one. A handsome lad this time." She removed her spectacles and mopped her face once more. "Hot. Such hot weather we're having, sir," she said breathlessly, before bustling off towards the kitchen.

Abel had to wait a little longer before Mistress Jackson at last allowed him into the bedroom. Ruth was sitting up against a pile of pillows, looking hot, tired and a little tearful, but very happy. A swaddled baby lay at each side of in her in the curve of her arms.

As soon as Abel came in she started to apologise. "I was so sorry, Abel, when they told me it was a girl. I knew you wanted a boy and I tried all the remedies. I ate all the right food but I thought that none of them had worked. I even tried..." Abel put his index finger to his lips and then to hers to stop her apologies.

"Hush," he said. "Let me see them." He leaned forward to look at the one nearest him. "Which one is this, my dear?" On being told it was the girl he kissed the forehead of his sleeping daughter. To him this baby looked like every other baby he had ever seen. Babies, boys or girls, they were all the same until they could run about and chatter and be interesting.

At that point the baby opened her eyes and with her first vague, blue, unfocused look, gazed at her father. Abel changed his mind and everything became clear.

This was a most remarkable daughter. She would grow up to be beautiful, well behaved and accomplished. He would buy her pretty clothes. He would let her have her own pony and the best puppy that he could find. She would learn to play a musical instrument. He didn't know what sort. He didn't know anything about music, but she would learn to play something. She hadn't got any hair at the moment but he knew that when it grew it would be dark. That was the fashionable thing for ladies to be at the moment. Her hair would be curly and long and tied in ringlets on each side of her face.

Abel was in love.

Ruth said, "Are you pleased, after all, Abel?"

Abel came out of his rapture.

"Oh, yes," he breathed. "I am very pleased. Mistress Denny was right. She said it was a sweet rose of a child and she is, she is. You may choose for her any name that you like my dear, but to me she will always be my Rose." He went round to the other side of the bed to meet his son. "I shall chose this boy's name," he said. "He will be called Joseph. Joseph Chinnock. Joseph James Chinnock." He looked at his tired wife. She was finding it difficult to keep her eyes open, but before she fell asleep she said, "And our little girl's name shall be Rosabella.

***

In the kitchen Mistress Denny, Mistress Jackson and Eliza enjoyed pigeon pie and small beer, while they related every moment of Ruth's confinement to an enthralled Hannah Wilson, who listened, alternately thrilled and appalled, to every word. After each detail had been discussed at least twice, laughed and cried over, Mistress Jackson prepared to go home leaving her daughter behind to continue her daily care of the new mother.

Before she left the house, she returned to the room where the happy parents were and, putting her head around the door, beckoned to Abel to leave his wife for a moment.

"All is well with your wife," she said, "I shall be going now, but will come back tomorrow, just to make sure. that she and the babes continue in good health."

After telling Ruth where he was going, Abel escorted the midwife downstairs and into the lobby. After congratulating Abel, Mistress Jackson discreetly cautioned him concerning certain husbandly considerations which would be appreciated by his wife. Then she took her leave and left the house, dignified by her expert conduct of a confinement in which sure danger had been successfully overcome. "Twins, twins," she said to herself, shaking her head and wondering at the miracle of it all, as she drove her little skewbald pony and cart home.

೮೦ ೦೪

CHAPTER TWENTY-TWO

Saturday, December 8th 1666

Many townspeople attracted by the crowd joined Quakers from all over the county who were gathered outside Court House. More people were crowded inside. About thirty Friends were being tried for not attending church, non-payment of tithes and refusal to pay the fines due for committing the offences. This state of affairs had become familiar to Justices, officers of the law and the general public all over the country.

The Courtroom was noisy with raised voices shouting insults and abuse at the Quakers. The accused, mostly men, stood silent and stony-faced amid the tumult. Many of them had appeared in court at least once before and knew what to expect. A few hid their fearful thoughts behind masks of rigid self-discipline.

Henry Bowman was among those facing trial. Alice and their oldest son Harry, had been unable to get inside and were waiting outside with other Quakers, to hear what the verdicts were. Everybody knew what to expect. Like the accused inside the court, they stood; quiet, still, centred down in a silent religious Meeting in support of the Friends inside.

As the doors closed on the overcrowded courthouse, the silent worshippers were quickly surrounded by the town's constables and the local militia, all intent on breaking up the unlawful Meeting.

This time there was little violence. The militia used their firearms to force people away from the courthouse as many Quakers protested at the intrusion into the Meeting. Harry was among them and received a blow from a Constable's staff on the side of his head which knocked him on to his knees.

Alice, momentarily separated from him by the crowd, but recognising his voice when he cried out, rushed to his side. "I'm all right, Mam," he said as he got to his feet.

On the other side of the square elderly Joshua Dale, who had only recently recovered from the pleurisy, was trying to explain the peaceable nature of the people being treated so badly. The militiamen pretended to listen carefully but as Joshua warmed to his message, he realised they were making fun of him, copying his head and hand movements. He paused for a moment then took a deep breath before starting to speak again, which made him start to cough uncontrollably. The militiamen, laughing, imitated his wheezing breath and shaking shoulders. Then, suddenly, their mood changed and they started to beat him with the butts of their muskets, leaving him lying on the ground.

Joshua, protesting that there was no need, was soon carried to a safer place by Friends, but the conflict continued. About eight or nine Friends had resumed the silent Meeting on the steps of the Courthouse and gradually others were joining them. They were trying to take the heat out of the situation in the square, by emphasising their peaceful intentions. The action only caused Friends further trouble. There were a few more blows to heads and bodies as they attempted to reason with their attackers, but the majority of Quakers were old campaigners in this war of conscience. They realised that they would be of more use after accused Friends had appeared at Court, by visiting them in prison and helping them with food, bedding and money.

Alice and Harry among them, they moved away without further argument. Disappointed that they could not stay, but relieved that there had been no arrests, the Friends remained philosophical as they walked to their nearby homes or prepared for longer journeys back to the moorlands and other distant parts of the county. They would all know the verdict eventually.

"Good morning, Mistress Bowman!" came a clear call through the general clamour of people, horses and carts starting to move along the road. Alice, unused to be being addressed in this way was unaware that she was being spoken to, but when the greeting was repeated, Harry drew her attention to Ruth Chinnock trotting towards her. Alice's first thought was of instant flight but it was too late, Ruth had caught up with them.

"I am Mistress Chinnock, D'you remember?" she said, breathless, "Baby is at home and well, I trust?"

When Alice, dumbfounded, did not reply, Ruth went on, "We all had such a surprise at The Grange in July. When I saw you last I had no time to tell you of my expected happy event, as you, in your condition, took such a tumble." She paused for breath again. Alice, still poised to make her escape but held down by Harry's firm hand holding hers, still said nothing.

Ruth continued, "We had such a surprise, as I say. In fact we had two!" The word exploded from her lips with such force that now she started to cough. Alice, her natural concern for others beating her desire to get away, went forward to help her by gently patting Ruth's back.

"Thank you, thank you, mistress." Ruth said, recovering. "Please do visit us at the Grange when you are able. Our babies, Joseph James and Rosabella, are so endearing, you will love them."

Five months of motherhood had convinced Ruth that all women felt the same way as she did about her own darlings, but Alice returned to her former frostiness.

"I rarely go along that road," she said, abruptly.

Ruth, a little hurt, was immediately subdued. "I am so sorry if I have offended you, Mistress," she stammered. Then she remembered Mistress Jenkins' words, that day outside the ironmonger's shop. Mistress Bowman was shy and likely to be agitated, especially after her baby was born. Trying to make amends, Ruth decided to ask about the Bowman's baby.

"How is your little one, Mistress?" she enquired, only to find that once again she had said the wrong thing.

"My name is Alice Bowman. We do not use such titles as 'Mistress'. Our given names are sufficient."

The reply was curt, made as Alice was walking away, but Harry did not go with her.

Realising this, Alice stopped and turned round. Harry was

talking to Ruth, and as she came up to her son and the now weeping woman, Alice was overcome with regret at her sharp tongue and put her arm around the shaking shoulders.

"I am sorry," she said stiffly, "I should not have spoken to thee in such an unfeeling way. I was not expecting friendship from one who is not one of us and it made me unkind. Thank you for your enquiry about my babe. It is a little girl-child and we call her Hester." Ruth, all sunshine after the tears, as ever, smiled into Alice's concerned face and forgiving blue eyes met apologetic brown.

Harry began to move towards their waiting horse. His mother was to ride pillion behind him. "We must hurry home, now, mother," he said.

Ruth, smiling, said, "Good day, Mistress - er - Alice." And Alice shook Ruth's hand briefly, saying, "Good day -?" Alice realised she didn't know this woman's name.

"Ruth," she replied.

"Ruth," said Alice.

***

In Court most of the accused, including Henry Bowman and Peter Littleton were sentenced to varying terms of imprisonment for refusing to pay tithes which Thomas Fletcher, the parish priest, had demanded. This wasn't the first time that either of the men had been punished for the crime which they didn't recognise in any way as an offence. Previous refusal to pay tithes or the fines imposed for non-payment, had resulted in a visits from the bailiffs and goods to the value of both being taken from their houses, but Peter, unlike Henry, hadn't been sentenced to gaol before. Because of the frequency of his offences he'd expected imprisonment as an inevitable consequence of listening to the promptings of his conscience.

Always bearing in mind the sufferings of Christ his Saviour and taking comfort from His teachings, Peter now prepared to accept any hardship as cheerfully as he could.

***

With about fifty Quakers and other prisoners Peter, Henry Bowman and other Friends were confined in the day cell, which amounted to nothing more than a high, wide corridor, lit by three small windows too high to see out of. Every day each prisoner made a small place for him or herself in this area and defended it from all comers. Leading off the day cell were heavy studded doors leading into four windowless cells, two each for men and women, in which they were locked at night. Sometimes straw protected them from the cold stone floor; it depended on whether they had the money to buy bedding from the guards. Sick and dying prisoners were carried in to the night cells and took their chances with the rest.

Peter forced himself to tolerate the disgusting leftovers of other prisoners' food. It was all that was available if Elizabeth hadn't been able to visit him with food, or the money to buy it. He accepted the presence of vermin, both insect and animal and attempted to make of his incarceration an opportunity to try to convince his fellow prisoners that they, too, could share in the Quaker vision and walk in the Light.

There were other Friends who had been in the gaol for months, years, even. Peter, Henry Bowman and other Friends arrested at the same time, attempted to persuade non-Quaker to 'join them in the Light', but with little effect. At first some of the other prisoners, men and women with whom they shared the degrading circumstances, were drawn to the Quaker message. At first many inmates were drawn to Peter's strong and affirmative presence and tried to clutch at the straw of hope which Quakers offered, but most fell away for want of the passionate faith that sustained Friends. The total darkness of the windowless cells, when the door was closed, took away the only light they knew.

Despite his own religious strength there were many times when Peter's resolve weakened. Then he had to bear his imprisonment with as much fortitude as he could find within himself. It was very difficult to rise above the despair to which, from time to time, he descended. Should he be visited by his wife at such times he was careful to conceal from her the depths to which his soul had sunk.

"Why, Elizabeth," he said, with a smile, on one such occasion, "What I have here is the perfect chance to worship God without the distractions of the world." He waved a hand in the direction of the window, which showed a glimpse of grey March sky. "His Light shines. Even here!"

***

Elizabeth Littleton was not so sanguine. Before Peter's imprisonment the Littleton house had become a haven for Friends who had suffered in many ways for their religion. All of them were made welcome to stay for as long as they pleased. If they could help with finances such help, however small, was accepted. If they could offer nothing but their labour on the farm, that too was received gratefully, but often the recipients of Littleton hospitality were old or infirm or both.

Peter's imprisonment put great strains on Elizabeth, a situation she shared with many other wives of men held prisoner, whatever their crime, Quaker or non-Quaker. She was left with the responsibilities of running a farm as well as caring for a crowded household. Whenever he could Peter's cousin, Thomas Hickock gave help, but he had his own farm to care for and could only spare a short time away from it.

It was hard for Elizabeth to live without the simple pleasure of her husband's loving presence, harder still when she went to see him in the gaol. The filthy, smelly conditions were horrifying enough, but the crowding together of men and women at such close quarters filled her with revulsion. Many of the women were pregnant or had babies at their breasts and she tried to help them, but more often than not there was little that she could do.

ഓരു

CHAPTER TWENTY-THREE

The first and second candles which had illuminated the Advent wreath during the service were snuffed out now, their waxy scent lingering in the air. A memory of their flickering light. Christmas, the time of good will to all men, was getting nearer. Preparations for twelve days of celebration were being made in most houses and cottages in Branslow and the surrounding homesteads. Jack practised a new tune on his fiddle. His wife sighed and got on with her sewing. The Pippit adjusted the straps of the drum. It didn't seem so heavy today.

***

Friday, December 14th 1666

Part of the town's medieval castle was being used as the gaol, because the local building used to house petty criminals and debtors had become overcrowded. It was not unusual that prisons were regularly filled with more inmates than they were designed to hold.

Alice approached on foot. She hated visiting the gaol. It always stirred unwanted fears in her. Harry, sometimes with Cornelius, visited their father more often than she did. She had forced herself to come today. She would have walked the whole ten miles from Branslow, but Harry, had persuaded her not to and brought her to town riding pillion behind him. He was not visiting his father today as he had business to attend to, but he would be waiting for her when she came out.

It had rained the previous day, but the morning was crisp and cold, dry and sunny. Alice took little notice of her surroundings. She was too intent on conquering her fear and making sure that she trod in as little as possible of the muck and filth that littered the muddy streets. She only looked up when she needed to make sure that she was walking in the right direction. She had wanted to bring little Hester, now about eighteen months old, for her father to see and to keep her company, but was glad now that she hadn't. The town was no place to bring a baby.

She had been watching the regular movement of her feet in their pattens, left, right, left, right, as they appeared from under her tucked-up skirt. There were things she wanted to discuss with Henry and as she walked she rehearsed them in her mind so that she wouldn't forget even the smallest item. She looked forward to seeing his face when he saw the small chicken pie she had made for him and she had brought a little money for him too. She was absorbed in her thoughts when, lifting her head, suddenly she saw the great stony heights of the castle, towering above her, silhouetted darkly against the bright sky.

Suddenly she felt small, insignificant and of no consequence. The massive walls seemed to her like a giant brooding beast, waiting, silent and patient, for her to fall once more into its clutches. She had been its victim five years ago and for an instant she experienced again her feelings of helplessness and fear. Impatiently, she forced herself to regain her self-possession, and reinforcing her hold on the bundle she was carrying, she kept her head high as she walked through the great doors.

When Henry was taken ill, Alice had brought medicines and poultices of her own making for his painful chesty cough, or sent them with Harry when he visited. Henry's present illness had at first been mistaken for plague, which was always a danger in crowded situations. There were often small occurrences of the disease all over the country but news of the recent terrible outbreak in London had alarmed many, whether or not they lived near to the capital.

There had been much anxiety before, when Henry became ill shortly after being imprisoned the previous year. There had been news of plague being brought to the village of Eyam in Derbyshire, where there had been many deaths since the first one in September. Alice was convinced that her husband had contracted the dreadful disease, but he did not show the incriminating plague spots in groin or armpit. The family was relieved that he had been spared the awful disease and although he had never regained his former robustness, he did not die.

Today she had brought a remedy she had made of honey mixed with pepper, sage, rue and other herbs. Henry was to take a spoonful of it night and morning and she was sure that this time she had found the cure for him. 'He usually gets over illness.' she thought, 'He'll recover this time too. It's taking a long time because he's not at home, where he belongs.'

Following other friends and relatives of prisoners into the noisy and crowded cell, she searched in vain for Henry but could not see him. She saw Peter Littleton and waved briefly before continuing her search. After a short while she became frightened, thinking that Henry had died and nobody had told her. Noticing her distress, Peter came over to her. "I'll take thee to him," he said, understanding her anxiety and inventing a reason for her difficulty. "We are more crowded than ever since the last time thee came."

The man who Peter took her to was not her Henry; the absent Henry she carried in her mind and memory.

The change in him was terrible. She'd forgotten how bad he'd looked when she last seen him. The memory of how he'd looked at that time had been cleaned from her mind, defending her, temporarily, from distress.

This man was gaunt. His breath wheezed in and out of his chest and a rattling cough shook his whole body every few minutes. After about a year in gaol, where he had endured whippings, become weakened by an acute chest infection and hadn't had the strength to fight off other prisoners who stole his food, Henry, like others about him, was seriously ill. Nevertheless he looked up at his wife and smiled, his eyes and teeth looking enormous in his thin, unshaven face.

"Alice," he said, seeing her bewildered expression, "Dost thee not know me?"

Disregarding the foetid straw Alice fell to her knees beside him as he half lay, half sat on the floor. Her entire attention was concentrated on her husband as she knelt at his side. She'd dropped her bundle in her surprise and anguish, so was unaware of Peter as he picked it up and placed it close to the couple, away from thieving hands, before returning to his corner.

"Henry! Oh, Henry!" She cradled him in her arms, rocking him as she would a small child. "What have they done to thee?" Her question wasn't answered. Henry, his eyes closed, was content to stay as he was, quietly in her embrace. He had fallen asleep.

***

As arranged, Harry was waiting for his mother outside the gaol when she came out. He knew immediately that all had not gone well. The anxious expression on her face and her tense posture, with her cloak held tightly around her, told their story. He leaned down from the saddle and grasping her forearm, pulled her up on to the pillion.

Almost before she was properly seated she was berating him. "Why did thee not tell me how bad thy father is? How long has he been this way? What have they done to him?"

The questions poured out of her, releasing some of her tension, but not allowing Harry time to answer even if he'd been ready to. He thought it best to wait for a pause in the flow. There could be no consolation in anything that he said, but remaining silent for a while gave him a chance to think of what to say. His silence quieted her so that she too fell silent. There was just the sound of the horse's hooves squelching in the mud and the occasional flurrying of birds disturbed in their roosting on this late, darkening, winter afternoon.

Alice repeated just one of her questions, "How long as he been like this?"

Harry shook his head. The beatings when his father had first been imprisoned had weakened him. That, and prolonged exposure to cold, dampness and the close company of other prisoners who were sick, even dying, had affected

Henry after only a few days, but he wouldn't tell his mother that. It would be too troubling for her, to tell her something that she already knew about, but was unable to put right.

"Since just after the last time thee saw him," he said. He could offer no comfort to her. Recognising this, Alice made no reply. She thought, 'I must go to see him more often. I have been selfish and disloyal to my husband. I will mend my ways. Whenever I can, I will go to him."

Harry was desperately trying to think of words which would calm his mother and raise her spirits. "Perhaps he will soon be released," he said. Alice murmured her agreement. Neither of them believed that what Harry said could be true.

Sunday, December 23rd 1666

Alice attempted to visit Henry again but was refused admission. The gaoler reminded her, implying by his manner that he found her behaviour improper and beneath contempt, that it was Sunday, the day of rest and that travelling was an ungodly thing to do on the Sabbath. He said he would give Henry the food, medicines and money she had brought, so she handed them over. She didn't trust the gaoler to hand them over, but she couldn't risk that he wouldn't, so, with little argument, she had to give in. Alice left the castle feeling frustrated and sick at heart.

This time she'd ridden to the gaol alone own in spite of her fears. But now, as she left the town boundaries behind her and came once more into the countryside, the familiar surroundings made her feel more comfortable and she relaxed a little. She was homeward bound, smiling to herself as she thought of her sons and how they spoilt their little sister.

***

Cornelius had been angry when Hester was born in May 1665. He'd been looking forward to getting a new brother. He'd known that this would happen because his mother had said so. Harry and Richard were always leaving him out of things. A younger brother would be his own friend. They would do

164

everything together. Now he felt that his mother had broken a promise to him. Both Alice and Henry, who had been released from prison shortly before the baby was born, tried to explain to him that he must be mistaken. Neither of them would ever have said that the new baby would be a boy, as nobody, not even Mam, ever knew that until a baby was born. Alice reminded him of the family's speculations about the sex of unborn calves, lambs and foals, but this did not console him. Cornelius had made no further comment about baby Hester and decided to have as little contact with her as possible.

For the next few months despite, or because of his older brother and sister's affection for the girl-child, Cornelius became more distant from them as well as the baby. He watched Ellen and Henry, in between farm and housework and in the evenings, getting to know Hester, playing with her, tickling her to make her laugh, dandling her on their knees and making little playthings for her. After a while, envious of the happy times they seemed to be having, he found that he wanted to join in but he couldn't. He felt stiff and self-conscious, which made him withdraw further into himself.

Alice thought fleetingly, as she watched his awkwardness, 'He was the youngest for too long.' A miscarriage and a stillbirth between Cornelius and Hester had seen to that. She was unable to think of any way to cure him of his unease or the sullenness which he seemed to be developing. There was little time to dwell on such matters anyway; he would have to find his own solution.

Alice's smile broadened as she rode along the lanes, bordered with leafless trees. She was remembering that morning in the spring of this year. She had been laying the fire in the bread oven. Hester, clean, fed and chattering to herself, was propelling herself around the kitchen place in the wheeled wooden walker, which had been made for Alice when she was a baby. Henry was out in the fields and Ellen was fetching water.

Cornelius was sitting at the table, chin cradled in his hands, dreaming. Alice was about to remind him of his work for the day and turned to speak to him just in time to see him lift his legs over the bench, so that he sat with his back to the table. He was looking directly at Hester for the first time since her birth. Alice moved a little so that she could observe him without his realising and watched as he quietly, almost furtively, stood up and walked over to the little girl.

She watched, wonderingly pleased and deeply moved, as he leaned over and very gently put out a finger to the child, as if about to touch her cheek. As he did Hester grasped hold of his fingers and laughed at him. He looked quickly towards his mother, who smiled and nodded encouragingly in Hester's direction. Cornelius carefully picked the baby up.

"Good morning to thee, Hester," he said, a little stiffly, before quickly putting her back. That was all. It was enough.

***

Alice was nearly home by the time she emerged from her recollections. Before her she saw the flickering candlelight in the windows of the house and the dark shapes of the outbuildings, showing greyly against the greater darkness of the ridge. Henry would not be in the house and farm for a long time, if ever. She gasped at the unbidden thought that her husband might die in gaol. With an effort of will, she drove it from her mind. He would be coming home. He would. He would. Then she would make him better. She and the boys and Hester would help him to get better.

***

But the thought kept returning to her for the rest of the evening. She fought it as she prepared the evening meal; as she fed Hester; as she supervised her sons' securing the animals for the night and then while she and the family settled down to sleep. But in the night the demons came again.

After all this time.

The faces, mocking, grinning, swirled about her, twittering. They advanced and retreated as if in some grotesque dance.

166

They shone with eerie light in their dark habitation somewhere in her brain.

Henry looked so ill, didn't he, Alice? As he lay there on the dirty straw when you left him the other day. You couldn't tell whether he was dead or alive, except for that tiny pulse in his neck, could you Alice?

What if the gaoler doesn't give him the money, Alice? If he does, what if someone steals it off him? What if the gaoler uses the money for his own self? He could do, Alice. Then what would happen to Henry?

Oh, Alice!

₮℞

CHAPTER TWENTY-FOUR

Tuesday, February 12th 1666/67

Peter was sitting with Henry Bowman, reading to him from a book which Elizabeth had brought in, and was surprised to be hauled to his feet by the guard. He was told to pick up his belongings, which he did, few though they were, then he was taken to the governor's room. He was further surprised to see his cousin, Thomas Hickock, there.

"What misdemeanours has thee committed, Tom?" he asked, with an ironic smile, assuming that his cousin must be joining him in gaol. His attention was drawn from Tom to the sound of the governor's growling, "He's paid your tithes to the reverend Master Fletcher. You don't deserve such good fortune. Now get out."

Two months into an expected three-month sentence for refusal to pay tithes, rather than being pleased to be released, Peter was outraged. Even as he was led, or rather pulled away from the gaol, blinking in the wintry sunshine, he was protesting. "Thee should not have paid the tithes, Thomas. They were my tithes to pay if I wanted, not thine! There are people in there who need me. Henry Bowman's very ill. He needs me."

Thomas ignored him, holding firmly onto Peter's hand, dragging him towards the cart, as he said, "How can I make my point if you step in and destroy it?"

His cousin, irritated said. "Be quiet Peter. Elizabeth, your wife, Peter, is suffering. There is too much to do. She needs your help. You're needed at home. For the Love of God, man - the house is full of old and sick people. And it's lambing time!"

The gates clanged behind the two men as Peter, shading his eyes from the glare of the light of day, countered his cousin's exasperation with, "Take not the name of the Lord thy God in vain." The grumbling went on, "It's my fine, Tom, not thine!"

Tom didn't answer him, but with a firm shove with both hands on Peter's behind, pushed him up onto the cart before climbing into the seat himself and clucking the horse into movement.

Saturday, April 27th 1667

Under a clear, blue sky, two months after his unexpected and unappreciated liberation, Peter was closing off a meadow from sheep and cattle. The grass would be left uncut until haymaking later in the summer. From somewhere across the moors came the call of a cuckoo and the echoing sound of mate or rival, some distance away. Elizabeth Littleton smiling despite the effort involved, was drawing water from the well. It was good to be alive on such a morning.

When it was full she lifted the heavy pail over the edge and placed it on the ground beside her, before attaching the other pail to the chain and lowering it into the water. Glancing up she saw two men approaching the house. Ignoring them, she leaned forward and continued with the business of filling the second pail. Straightening up and looking at them for the second time, she recognised them as the Churchwardens. Thomas Bott, serving his third term of office, was walking, heavy with importance, towards to her accompanied by a younger Warden she didn't recognise.

Elizabeth's heart fell. 'This is the time,' she thought, 'God be with us all'. She placed the wooden yoke on her shoulders, crouched down to attach the two pails to the ropes and straightening up as well as she could, she walked towards the men.

There were no salutations. As the senior of the two Wardens, Tom Bott got straight to business.

"Where's your husband?" he asked.

"He's in Near Field." Elizabeth replied courteously. It was no use being otherwise. Tom had been a friend of the Littletons. Now he and they occupied different areas of religious thought.

"Get him for us," was the curt order, "And quickly."

The other Warden, William Preston, newly appointed to the post, stayed silent.

"And no tricks." The more experienced man snapped. "No helping him to get away."

"May I carry my pails into the house first?" Elizabeth enquired. She knew as she asked the question, that the answer would not be 'yes'.

"Leave them where they are," Tom ordered. "Go and get your man!" The last words were bellowed and as Elizabeth relieved of her burden but nervous, began to walk hurriedly towards the field gate, he shouted, "Be quick about it!" and kicked over the pails.

Elizabeth's first thought was 'All that back ache for nothing.' Her second was to run as fast as she could across the yard to the far end of the Near Field. There was no sense in antagonising the men. Silently Peter accepted the news that the Wardens had arrived. Robert Davis, a non-Quaker, had been taken on to help as a farmhand during Peter's recent imprisonment, remaining after his release. Peter gave him and a couple of labourers a few quick instructions before he returned to the farmyard with his wife. Robert shrugged his shoulders, exchanging wordless looks with the labourers. They all knew what the outcome of this visit was likely to be. Peter and Elizabeth walked across the field side by side, hand in hand, talking quietly. Strengthened by each other's presence, they refused to be rushed by the shouts of the Wardens. Both knew that it could be some time before they had this freedom together once more.

***

Peter was taken to the church Vestry, where he stood quietly before the Wardens as they sat at a small table. Will Preston, made uncomfortable by Peter's tall, strong figure and commanding presence, stared at a paper placed on the table before them. It was a list of Peter's previous misdemeanours in regard to his refusal to pay tithes or attend church.

Glancing at it only occasionally Tom Bott recited Peter's offences.

"You have persisted in refusing to pay tithes or attend Divine Service. You have also refused to pay any fines, despite being distrained of many household goods and private belongings. You have even been imprisoned. Yet you now come before us having continued with your recalcitrance, being absent from Divine Service for many months. The fine for this crime is twenty pounds or you will go to gaol."

Peter expressed no surprise, regret or penitence. "I will not pay a fine when I have committed no offence." he said. "Tom, I will pay towards the poor of this parish, you must know that, but I will not put money into the pocket of an evil parson. I worship God in the silence of our Meeting, but I will not be preached to, or prayed for in a church full of idolatry, sinfulness and pagan ritual.

"You must do as the Law says!" Tom's voice was more angry. He knew that he would not be able to break Peter's stubborn will.

"I will not. I obey only God's Law." was Peter's only response and they took him away.

***

That night Tom Bott knelt with his Jane at the foot of their bed. Together they confessed their own sins and frailties. They prayed for the well being of every member of both their own and other peoples' families. They prayed for the sick and the dying in the parish and country. when they finished they rose to their feet and went to get into their respective sides of the bed. Jane was surprised when Tom dropped upon his knees again and, hands together and eyes closed, he prayed, "Please, God, give me strength to deal with these Quakers. Amen." He felt rather as he had as a child, when he had prayed for some fervently desired plaything.

***

Peter was imprisoned once more. This time no cousin would be able to come to his aid.

***

Quakers were not the only people who found the Law not to their liking. There were many men and women to whom religion was not that important. For them church services were a waste of valuable time which could be spent more usefully working, especially at busy times on the land. In small, isolated communities it was not unusual for the authorities to conveniently ignore such absences sins of omission.

But Quakers were another matter. Their refusal to attend was unlawful and persistent. They would not give way. The custom was that when the Churchwardens visited a non-Quaker to warn him that his absences had been noted, there would be a general acceptance that nothing official would be said for the moment. Of course, the wrongdoer would be sure to attend the next service, wouldn't he? Of course, Warden. Quakers, on the other hand, were adamant that no matter how lenient the Wardens were willing to be in regard to fines, they would not attend Divine Service and were prepared to accept the consequences, even when that involved imprisonment or even transportation overseas.

***

When arrested by the constable for absence from Divine Service Peter had offered no resistance. It was compulsory for everyone over the age of 16 to attend church at least once a week. A fine of one shilling for every missed attendance could be extracted from the offender by the Churchwardens, who could confiscate the miscreant's household goods to the value of the fine, should payment be refused. Absence from Church for over a month attracted a fine of twenty pounds, or the forfeit of two thirds of his property to the Crown. Peter hadn't attended church for many months, even years.

He knew what the penalties were and knew what he should do. He had to make a stand. He was not alone. Besides Henry Bowman, still imprisoned since the previous year, Thomas Woolrich, Edward Scotson, John Till and James Kendall had all been charged at around about the same time in their respective towns and villages. All were Friends known to him through Meetings held at Friends' houses in other parts of the county.

கூ௧

CHAPTER TWENTY-FIVE

Monday, June 24th 1667

The Quarter Sessions were a demanding time for the Judiciary, as they travelled around the county's court houses. As well as crowded courtrooms every day, sometimes for weeks, the presence of the judges was always seen as a prime opportunity for a busy round of social gatherings of one sort or another. The higher social classes of the town were as anxious as any to include their Lordships in their activities.

Peter, chained at his ankles and with his wrists manacled behind him, hoped for the best, but anticipated the worst, as he entered the Court Room . He knew that most Judges were unsympathetic to Quakers, frequently to the point of undisguised hostility, but took little hope from recent news that some local Justices of the Peace could be more open-minded than others.

After the Easter Sessions a Quaker named John Baddeley had appealed against a fine of ten shillings on the grounds that he had been wrongly accused. In this instance, the Justice was persuaded by him that he had indeed been treated unjustly and allowed him the refund of his fine. Peter was aware that he was probably going to be viewed as a serious threat to law and order by this Higher Court and was not expecting any such degree of leniency.

There had already been an altercation with a Court official concerning the removal of his hat. Peter had offered no resistance when it appeared that it would be forcibly removed from his head. He considered that there was no good reason to keep it on and he removed it because it was not needed on such a warm day. To make his position clear he further stated that practicality was the reason he removed his hat, not deference to a polite convention which he did not acknowledge.

*****

Today His Lordship had a headache, his stomach was upset and to make things worse there was this raving lunatic to deal with. They were all raving lunatics, these Quakers. He'd dealt with them in other places as well as here. When Peter was brought into the dock before him, The Judge regarded him without interest for a second or two then made a show of writing something down. In reality he was making him wait, showing who had the power in this stuffy room with its uncomfortable seats and smelly onlookers. Settling his robes more comfortably around himself, he nodded to the Constable and returned to his writing while the charges against Peter, refusal to swear the Oath of Allegiance and refusal to attend church, were read out.

The manacles securing his hands were removed from his wrists.

"Place your hand on the Bible and swear the Oath of Allegiance," said the Clerk.

"No," replied Peter calmly.

The order was repeated and so was the response. The Judge, still writing, intervened in the wearying tone of a man who'd already made up his mind. "I order you to place your hand on the Bible, and swear the Oath."

He shifted his position again, slightly, but his chair remained just slightly uncomfortable. He was anxious to get this case over. If this nuisance of a man would just agree to the Oath, a short trial would take place and time and patience would be saved. The absence of an Oath meant that a proper trial could not take place, the accused could not give evidence and no witnesses could be called. It would make no difference to the verdict, anyway.

Peter remained silent, looking steadily at the Judge who, unconsciously responding to Peter's quiet presence, stopped writing and fidgeting. Looking up, he found himself confronted by blue eyes that held no fear or cringing respect, simply intelligence and strength of spirit. The silence was broken only by the sound of the Clerk's scratchy quill recording the morning's events on the Court Roll.

Having got the Judge's attention, Peter gave his reply. "I will not swear this oath. It is against Christ's teaching, when he said 'Swear not at all, neither by heaven, for it is God's throne; nor by the earth, for it is his foot-stool; neither by Jerusalem; for it is the -'

"Silence," shouted the Constable, while the Judge waved a languid hand in Peter's direction.

"I've heard all this before, Littleton. All four verses of the Gospel according to St. Matthew, five." He assumed a sneering expression and a higher-pitched tone of voice to quote a few more words from the scripture. "Let your yea be yea and your nay, nay." He reverted to his normal voice. "I've heard it before. Every Justice in the country has heard it before and none will accept your excuse for refusing to swear on oath. Place your hand on the Book and swear the Oath of Allegiance to his Majesty."

"I will not," said Peter.

"For the last time. Will you place your hand on the Book and swear to tell the truth? If not will you swear to the supremacy of the Crown, and reject Papacy?"

"No," said Peter.

At this point, when it was obvious that Peter was not going to co-operate, the Judge barked, "Make him!" In response to the order a court officer took hold of Peter's right hand in an attempt to press it on to the Bible, but Peter was too strong for him and raised his arm away from the book with such force that, although that had not been Peter's intention, the officer almost fell to the ground. Another officer came to add his strength to the struggle but Peter, fired with indignation and religious fervour still managed to resist.

In desperation one of the men took hold of the book and pressed it to Peter's mouth in an attempt to make him give the effect of kissing it, which was at that time the usual confirmation of swearing to tell the truth. It was a part of the hated oath-taking rite which Quakers found particularly objectionable. Peter turned his head to one side with an involuntary expression of disgust while all those watching the tussle, except the Judge and the court officials, gave way to raucous laughter.

The two officers stepped away and turned to the Judge for further instructions. They knew the scene had been enacted many times before in many other courts, with the same lack of success in making Quakers swear on oath. The Judge, irritated, gestured to the officers to return to their places.

His Lordship sighed inwardly. He wished it were a thief, a fraudster, a murderer, even, rather than this irksome Quaker standing before him. Other, normal, criminals were straightforward. He knew where he was with a thief or a murderer. These misguided religious zealots were impenetrable. They baffled him. Other Judges, wishing to be reasonable, had allowed Quakers to leave court after refusal to swear, to return the following day when the order to take the oath would be repeated. In some cases this course of action had been repeated over many days before the last resort, of force, had been used to make hands and lips touch the Bible and still such men and women remained stubborn.

The Judge saw before him a strong man; physically strong, as well as strong in his religious faith. Being forced to go through the procedure of having the book thrust against his mouth had disgusted Littleton profoundly, but he was strong enough to resist and remain true to his misguided beliefs. His Lordship sighed inwardly. He had no stomach for enduring repeated appearances by a man who obviously would not give way. There was no point in prolonging a case which was going to come to the same end anyway.

At this stage the Judge decided to move on to the subject of the defendant's refusal to attend the Anglican Church. He knew what the answers to his questions would be, but decided that since they had to be asked anyway, he would make the most of this opportunity to bait one more of these exasperating people. A moment passed during which the Judge again adjusted his robes before he looked towards Peter and said, "You refuse to attend Divine Service in the Anglican

Church, which you are obliged to do by Law. Do you deny this? If not, be so good as to give us the usual heathen Quaker reasons for your obstinacy." There was a short burst of laughter from one of the people watching, instantly halted by a reprimand from the Constable.

Peter, his hands once more bound, took a deep breath and squared his shoulders. He looked fearlessly at the Judge, who, uninterested in what the answer the accused would make, continued with his writing while Peter began his explanation. He knew that there was little likelihood of being able to complete it without interruption. Despite this he spoke quietly and firmly.

"As a member of the Religious Society of Friends, I do not believe that the form of worship practised in Steeplehouses is in any way that which our Saviour and Redeemer, Jesus Christ, intended His followers to observe. For that reason it is against my conscience to attend its services." The Judge remained intent upon his writing, but the crowd in the courtroom was beginning to stir while the court officers looked at one another nervously.

Ignoring what was happening around him and intent upon the matter in hand, Peter went on against a continuous background of increasingly angry murmuring. Incongruously, under the circumstances, he was reminded of his bees in the hives at home, emerging from their winter sleep. Elizabeth was nervous of them, as bee-stings made her very ill. Would she take care of them while he was away? She had done before, but reluctantly. The uninvited thoughts skipped into his brain and as quickly flew out again. Because of this sudden interruption to his train of thought he hesitated a little in his explanation, but quickly picked up where he had faltered.

"Rituals, such as the wearing of vestments and the use of gold and silver plates and cups are contradictory to Christ's teaching, which is to put away such things and worship God with simple reverence and in poverty. We believe that we can worship God without a priest's intervention."

There was a cry of "Blasphemer" from one or two of the onlookers but Peter would not falter again. His heart was beating rapidly. The feeling was one he had experienced many times while sitting quietly at Meeting. It was the fluttering, literally quaking, feeling which preceded the sensation of being pushed up off his seat in order to stand and answer, fearlessly, the Spirit's call to give Testimony. He felt that strength of the Spirit now. He continued.

"Using no written order of service, our Testimony of Truth can be expressed at our religious Meetings by any person, man, woman or child, when moved by the Spirit in the Light of Truth. Friends do not need the rites of eating bread off golden plates and drinking wine from golden cups in a Steeplehouse to commune with God. Ours is the true, purer religion." The murmuring of the crowd increased. His voice rose. "We do not need idolatrous pictures and statues to remind us of the presence of God. We are in His presence in the company of any human being."

At this uproar broke out. There were cries of "Blasphemy!" "Anti-Christ!" even "Witchcraft!" Somewhere someone shouted, "They started the Great Fire in London, last year, you know!" The Constable struck his staff against the floor, and shouted for silence. The crowd, anxious to hear the Judge's pronouncement, quietened.

The Judge carefully placed his pen in his inkstand. His long, thin, very clean hands tidied the papers on which he had been writing and moved them slightly to one side. A shaft of late afternoon sunlight pierced the gloomy room. He still had a slight headache but his stomach was grumbling with hunger now. He would feel much better when he had eaten something. Without doubt, the criminal before him had, with his own words condemned himself. There was no question of Littleton's guilt; this case was almost over, and His Lordship would soon be enjoying good food and wine at the Angel Ascending. He rose slightly from his seat in order to rearrange his robes once more, then sat down again before addressing the accused and the interested public, who had been enjoying the spectacle being enacted below them.

Twelve men, seated in two rows of six, had been called for service as Jurors. The majority of them were either minor gentry or yeomen of the same class as Peter but more financially successful. One or two of them were known to him and he would have called them his friends, but today their verdict would not be heard. With his refusal to swear to tell the truth Peter had lost his right to Trial by Jury. His Lordship would deliver the verdict. It took only a few seconds for him to prepare himself for the coup de grâce.

He began, "I have listened to your blasphemous outpourings and for your repeated refusal to attend the Anglican Church you will be fined twenty pounds, which I have no doubt you will refuse to pay." As his lordship paused, Peter interposed with a single firm statement,

"No. I will not attend the Steeplehouse."

The Judge, with an air of inevitability, continued, "In that case you will be distrained of goods to the value of twenty pounds. In addition to this you will also forfeit two thirds of your property to the Crown.

"I further sentence you to forty days imprisonment, during which you will have time to repent of your refusal to swear the Oath of Allegiance. If you remain obstinate, you will serve a further forty days, at the end of which you will again be given the choice to take the oath or serve another forty days in gaol. If you come to your senses now, and take the oath, you will be released at once; if not the forty days will be repeated for as long as it is necessary to achieve the end of the matter required by Law."

The Judge had pronounced a sentence which meant a living death to those whose lives were commanded by their consciences to disagree with the swearing of an oath. He bent forward a little to ease his aching back and folding his arms, leaned on his desk. He was tired, hungry and somewhat bored now, but he hadn't finished with this irritating man.

"As you will also be excommunicated and therefore deprived of the protection of the Established Church which you so heartily despise, you will be unable to call upon its help, which would be more merciful to you than that of the Law of this land. Have you anything to say?"

Peter's response was immediate. "I will swear no oath. I will attend no Steeplehouse."

***

Peter knew that his sentence could be shortened if he agreed to take the oath. If he didn't he would be kept there for months, even years. Other Quakers, under this Sentence of Excommunicato Capiendo, had died in gaol rather than commit an act contrary to their consciences. Every fortieth day a Bible would be brought into the stinking cell which he occupied with varying numbers of other men and women and he would be ordered to swear an oath of Supremacy to the King upon it. On every occasion that he refused he would be sentenced to a further forty days imprisonment.

***

Later that day, sitting in the Angel Ascending, discussing the day's business over their ale, one of the superfluous jurors confessed to the others, "I would have let Peter off, just this once. He's a strange fellow, I know him well, or as well as any one can, but his heart is good and he will always help anyone if he can." He shook his head, sorrowfully, "Such a good man."

"But not worth finishing up in gaol for," put in another, after taking a mouthful from his tankard, "I heard of a jury. In London, I admit." His voice reflected his own poor opinion and that of his fellows, of southerners in general and Londoners in particular.

"They didn't agree with what the Judge said about one of these Quakers. There was a lot of trouble about it. The Judge said they must convict the man, but the jury wouldn't. The argument lasted a week and in the end they all finished up in gaol with the daft Quaker."

He took another draught of his ale and wiped his mouth on his sleeve. "And that's the truth, that is," he said to the incredulous faces around him.

ഇ ൪

CHAPTER TWENTY-FIVE

Monday, September 23rd 1667

John Taylor leaned on the parapet of the bridge. He'd so often met Frances Palmer here, until three years previously. The last rays of the sun, sparkling on the rippling water were so bright that it was difficult to see under the river's surface to the lower level, where fish were sheltering under streaming weeds. As his eyes became focused on the river's depths he could see shoals of small fish keeping steady in the water's flow. Suddenly there was a flurry as silver bodies fled to the safety of stone and weed and the long slender snout of a grey-striped pike shot out from the shadow of the bridge.

'Big fish eating little fish,' John thought, 'Little fish eat smaller fish and so it goes'.

He straightened up and, picking up his tool-bag, made to continue his walk home. At first, after Frances had gone to live in Dorset, he'd avoided the lane and the bridge, but quickly realised that it was impractical to further the distance between his home and wherever he was working, just for the sake of sentimentality. Now he found that he could follow the route without the emotional heart-leaping which he had formerly experienced. But he had to admit to himself that he thought of her, even if only for a moment, every time he crossed the bridge.

He resolved to try not to think any more about what her life may be like now. Such thoughts had stopped hurting him, they could easily be discarded.

***

A hundred yards down the lane was the Johnson's cottage. In the warmer weather he would often pass the time of day with Mistress Johnson and Mary, as they sat, one each side of the door, spinning by the fading light of the setting sun. The sight of mother and daughter lost in the rhythm of their whirring wheels seemed to John a peaceful, even beautiful picture. They would always call a greeting to him, which he would clumsily acknowledge with a raised hand.

As a Quaker, John did not use terms such as 'Good day' or 'Good morning,' which were considered unnecessary and superfluous. The phrases were also against the Testimony for Truth, as a non-Quaker could never in their view, have a 'good' morning. John, used to dealing with non-Quaker customers, had learned not to be offended by a well meant greeting but could not yet bring himself to return them. For this reason many people now accepted his raised hand and the quick nod of his head which sometimes accompanied it.

At this time of year the early evenings retained a little of the daytime's heat but were cooler than earlier in the summer; it was also darkening, so John was not too surprised that the Johnson women were nowhere to be seen. There were, however, sounds of laughter and singing coming from inside the cottage and as he walked towards it he was overtaken by Jack the fiddler, with Humphrey the small boy known as the Pippit, now ten years old, grown taller and carrying the drum with no effort at all.

"Evenin', my friend," Jack shouted cordially as he and Humphrey, not wearing his Pippit costume today, but carrying the drum, turned to go inside. Before he went in Jack turned back, "Too shy to come in John?" he said, smiling. Then Mary appeared in the doorway and Jack went inside to sit with Eddie Morris and Dai Davis, already comfortably seated and supplied with ale.

Mary stayed by the open door, "Come in John," she called, "Come in and wish me 'appy birthday." She would have brought him in, but her attention was drawn away, back into the cottage and John was left standing in the lane.

He felt strangely bereft. The sounds from inside Mary's home sounded so cheerful. Both Mary and the fiddler had been so welcoming that he had felt truly invited. Since Frances had gone there had been many times when had had been both attracted and repelled by the sight and sound of people enjoying themselves.

The anniversary of his own birthday in May, elicited much less enthusiasm. It was usually a time for his foster-parents to review his previous year's misbehaviour and shortcomings. After which followed their appeals to him to improve his ways. So far as he could remember, his birthdays had always been almost sad occasions rather than happy ones. He had a sudden, faint memory of his much younger self being given a small gift by a woman; perhaps it had been his mother. The memory, recalled so unexpectedly, now so precious, must have been of a time before his parents' conversion to Quakerism. He smiled to himself thinking that he must have been about four years old at the most.

Hitching his tool-bag more comfortably on his shoulder he was preparing to walk the last mile or so home when Mary's mother called out to him, "You're not going, are you, John?" She came out on to the lane and caught up with him, "Mary would be right disappointed with you if you went after she asked you to come in." As he hesitated Mistress Johnson took his hand firmly in hers and led him into the cottage.

Inside were a dozen or so of the Johnsons' friends sitting on benches around the table, or on the floor, talking and laughing while they and Humphrey waited for Jack to tune up. As John walked in silence fell, broken only by the sounds of two or three children playing in a corner of the room, where the now still spinning wheels stood. After a while even the children quietened guiltily as they realised that their elders had become silent.

John had done carpentry work for one or two of the men and these greeted him awkwardly while others, after staring at him for a moment or two, made embarrassed attempts to restart their interrupted conversations.

Mistress Johnson and Mary immediately regretted the uncomfortable situation which had risen because of their bringing John into their home and came over to him. Mary was close to tears as her mother attempted to smooth over the incident. "Don't take any notice, John," Mistress Johnson said, quietly. "They don't know you like we do." She turned to the men and women at the table. "Come on everyone, move up and make a place for one of the two best carpenters in Branslow!" There was a hasty shuffling about in order to create a space as most people there were anxious to make amends and there were calls of "Come 'ere, John. Sit down by us!"

But the damage had been done.

John turned to Mary, shook her hand and said self-consciously, "Happy birthday, Mary." He then shook Mistress Johnson's hand, saying, "Thank thee for thy kindness." Then he went out of the door, through the now moonlit garden and continued his walk home.

***

John wasn't the only one to leave the birthday celebration feeling unhappy. Later in the evening a dispirited Humphrey, carrying the drum, walked home behind his mother. He had been to the Johnson's house in his capacity as the Pippit, to accompany the fiddler. His mother, Widow Yates, a friend of Mistress Johnson, had come along to keep an eye on her son and to make sure he behaved himself while in someone else's house. Her two younger children, a son and a daughter, she had left with a neighbour for an hour or two.

Both Mistress Johnson and Widow Yates had enjoyed their evening's socialising. Such events were few and welcome breaks in a hard-working life. The two women had caught up on the village gossip and after John's departure, had shared their sympathy for him. He was a likeable young man even if a bit surly sometimes. They agreed that he couldn't help the way he had been brought and he would have made a perfect husband for young Frances Palmer, if it hadn't been for his religion. And her Dad. John was a hard worker, honest and reliable.

Their chattering while washing the pots had been interrupted by raised voices in another part of the room. Jack the fiddler, Eddie, Dai and, to his mother's astonishment,

Humphrey, were all shouting at each other and all seemed about ready for a fight.

Widow Yates, hands dripping, rushed over to separate her son from what she'd assumed was a grown man's quarrel not a child's and adding her voice to the tumult, snapped, "You ought to be ashamed of yourselves. You especially, Dai." She rounded on him, " What do you think you're doing?" And then, with one hand, she grasped her son by the neck of his thick woollen jerkin and lifted him clear off the floor and out of range of any fists that seemed likely to fly at any moment. Dai, who true to form had said and done very little during the quarrel, sat, open-mouthed and baffled at Widow Yates' attack.

The reason for the scuffle and for which Humphrey was mainly responsible, was professional pride. Jack, Eddie and Dai, as members of the wassailers had taken the opportunity to talk, quietly, but not quietly enough, about Humphrey's position in the ceremony.

The Pippit's prime function was to be so disarming that onlookers couldn't refuse him when he proffered them the collecting bag. His musical prowess was secondary to his youth and pretty face. Struggling with a big drum only added to his appeal. They all agreed that Humphrey was getting too big to be the Pippit and should be replaced by another smaller, more beguiling, child.

Unfortunately Humphrey, thought to be fully occupied with taking the opportunity to shovel as much food as he could into his thin, wiry body, had overheard the conversation and been bitterly upset. He liked being the Pippit. He was the pet, the littlest one. As the oldest of the widow's children it was a novelty for him to be the youngest of a group. He had flown at Jack, usually his hero, pummelling him with his fists shouting, "I want to do it. I'm the Pippit. Nobody can do it better than me!"

The three men had tried to placate him but Humphrey was deaf to their explanations. He refused to accept that he was almost grown up now, that he was certainly too big to be the Pippit, "I'm not, I'm not," he shouted.

They tried to make him understand that although he was very good, the best Pippit they'd ever had, he just couldn't do it now. A smaller, younger child would have to be found. At this Humphrey grew even more incensed.

He knew what was going to happen.

His little brother, Billy, would be the new Pippit. That little pest with his big brown eyes and his curly hair and his smile like a girl's.

"No!" he bawled and started to lay about the three men, who were just raising their arms to fend him off when Widow Yates caught sight of them, thought her son was in danger of damage to life or limb and pounced.

As he shuffled along the lane behind his mother, the drum he'd thought was getting lighter becoming heavier with every step, he plotted what he would do to Billy when he got home.

He'd never smile his girl's smile again.

He, Humphrey, would knock all his teeth out for him.

***

A safe hundred yards behind, the widow and Humphrey, Jack, Eddie and Dai were also walking back to the village.

"Spirited little chap, that 'Umphrey," said Jack.

"Ah," chorused Eddie and Dai.

Walking behind the other two, Dai thought, "And that widder woman is lively too. Big arms on 'er. Comes from bein' a washerwoman."

He shivered a little in the autumnal cold and looked up at the bright moon in a clear sky and thought. 'Nice woman, though. Warm.'

෴

CHAPTER TWENTY-SIX

Wednesday, March 11th 1668

After sixteen months Henry was released from gaol. Peter shook his hand and wished him well before he was taken out of the cell by the gaolers. Henry was still in very poor health. Only help given to him by his family and Quaker friends had kept him alive. Elizabeth Littleton, who was visiting Peter at the time, shook hands too, saying that she would be coming to see him and Alice and the family very soon.

During Peter's imprisonment, although tired and ill-looking, Elizabeth had become much calmer, less inclined to panic; was stoical even and stronger-willed. She walked with Henry to the great metal-studded gates, supporting him as he clung to her. Speaking quietly and gently, she gave him brief messages to pass on from other Quaker prisoners to their families and friends, all the while ignoring the gaolers' impatient demands for them to get a move on. At last the gates were opened and she released his arm from hers and handed him over to Harry and Alice.

Alice, happy, relieved, excited, shocked, suppressed her tears. She must be the strong one now; stronger than she had ever been. But Henry looked so fragile. In the gaol, even though he had gradually overcome his illness, he'd still appeared to be in a slightly worse state than the others, who were all dirty, ill and uncared-for. From being close to death at one time early in his sentence, with the help of his own strong will, he'd improved a little and very slowly. Not completely recovered, he was, praise God, alive.

On the cart they made Henry as comfortable as they could then, as Harry slapped the reins and urged the horse on, Henry and Alice looked at one another. Apart from saying each other's names when they embraced, briefly, outside the gates, they were silent. There was so much to say that neither of them could speak. Harry drove for a quarter of an hour or so then turned round to make some remark to them. They were sitting on opposite sides of the cart, simply looking at each other. Harry, too, understanding, remained silent.

Monday, May 18th 1668

Although the Bowman farm now mainly consisted of cattle they still kept a few sheep. Today, lambing over, their somewhat odd selection of various breeds, soon to be sheared, had been turned out onto the hills bordering the ridge. Although Henry was still not in full health he was stronger all the same but not yet fully involved in the work of the farm, Alice, Harry, faithful Tom Wells the labourer and the boy, Daniel Brass managed to cover the daily field and yard work between them. Ellen saw to the workings of the house with the help of Hannah's successor, Kate Watson, a Quaker friend's daughter who now lived in at the farm and helped to look after the younger children.

It was a bright, mild day. The clouds blown by a warm wind from the south were moving gently, high in the sky. Alice and the men their work finished for the moment, sat on the grass relishing the moment, while Meg, the dog lay, chewing a stick and growling at it. Henry had spent the morning hoeing turnips in the lower field near the house but now Harry, looking down towards the house, saw him beginning the climb up the side of the ridge. "Look, Mam," he said, "Dad's coming up to see us."

Alice, immediately anxious about her husband's ability to manage the climb, got to her feet and started to walk down to him followed by Meg. Waving to him, she called, "Henry, Henry, what are thee doing? Thee's not well enough for such a climb as this!" He had heard her, because as she shouted he raised his head and looked up at her. Now he ignored her, looking where he put his feet as he continued with his walk.

While he'd been hoeing he'd been thinking hard about his

and Alice's present and future life. First of all he was determined to recover his full health and one way would be to stop allowing Alice to pamper him. He would work towards becoming the man he once had been by simply walking to the top of that ridge. It sometimes seemed to hang over the steading like a sheltering arm, but at other times it hovered like a giant animal waiting to pounce. Today. This very day. Now. He would conquer it.

Halfway along the line of turnips he'd thrown down his hoe and headed for the rising path, which would take him up the ridge. He'd seen Alice waving, heard her shouting and guessed the substance of words he couldn't quite make out and resolved to take no notice.

When they met a few minutes later Alice immediately began scolding him for putting himself to such trouble, "What is so important that thee put thyself at risk?" she asked. "Thee's done enough this morning with the hoeing."

Henry put his hands on her shoulders, looked deeply into her eyes and said, teasing her, "Be quiet, woman!" Then continuing his uphill walk, he took her hand and led her back towards the top of the ridge while Meg trotted behind.

Harry, Tom and Daniel met them on the way but were directed back down the ridge, with directions from Henry to tasks in other areas of the farmyard and fields. Meg, unsure of which group to follow, barked and raced back and forth once or twice then decided to follow at Henry's heels.

The climb to the top hadn't been easy for Henry. But eventually they stood, looking out over the farm; it's buildings and surrounding fields. Henry was a little breathless but pleased with himself. Alice was also pleased but speechless, surprised by this sign of the return of her husband's more robust self.

"Well, Alice," Henry said when he had got his breath back. "What was it thee was saying about putting myself at risk?" She opened her mouth to speak but he silenced her once more with a mock stern expression and a raised forefinger pressed against her lips. Alice felt a surge of annoyance. It was unfair. He had asked her a question, then not let her reply. She looked up at him ready to try to respond to his enquiry again. In doing so, she looked into his face. He was smiling at her and she realised that he had been poking gentle fun at her. He was letting her know that she could leave the main responsibilities to him once more. She smiled back and relaxed.

Henry continued. "I haven't brought thee to the top of this dangerously 'igh mountain without reason," he said. "There is much I wish to talk to thee about, away from anyone else." He sat down on the grass and she sat beside him. Meg found another stick and flopped down to chew it. Alice suddenly felt like she had as a small child, when her father was about to tell her a story; interested to hear what he had to say. "Go on, Henry," she said.

"We've suffered great troubles for the last few years," he said, "And've come through them well. The farm's prospering, our living children are well and growing into honest upright people." Alice nodded. She was remembering the children who had not lived. But Henry was continuing.

"We 'ave our religion, which has kept us in good heart. The Lord's been good to us and looked after us."

He paused, looked at the sky briefly and thought, 'There'll be rain before nightfall'. Alice, sitting on the grass in front of him, waited for him to continue.   "Alice," he said, "Are thee still strong in thy faith?"

She moved to answer him, but he stopped her with his next question.

"Will thee always be as strong? Dost thee wish for us to carry on in the Society of Friends that we've both belonged to for so many years?"

Alice was beginning to think that her husband was going to suggest that they deserted the Friends, yield to the Anglican Church and attend the steeple-house. She knew that she would not, could not do such a thing and opened her mouth to protest. Henry, seeing her agitation, guessed the reason and hastened to put her mind at rest.

"I know we'll always belong to the Society of Friends," he said, "But I 'ave a proposition to put to thee". He shifted his position slightly before going on. "We'll always be strong in our faith. Of that I'm very sure, but I'm tired, Alice. I 'aven't lost my faith, but 'ave lost my fight." He laughed, wryly. "I'm like an old soldier. I believe in the battle, but I can't be in the forefront of the struggle any more."

There were tears in his eyes now and Alice suddenly felt her own fatigue. She could see now that his sufferings in prison had destroyed much of his strength. She also realised that should he have to bear another gaol term it could kill him and his death would be hers too.

"What shall we do, Henry?" Not having considered such questions before she had no idea what his reply would be and was apprehensive.

"We'll carry on living the way we believe in. We'll look after our family and the farm. Our children will be brought up in the Light. We'll adhere to the principles of our religion as before, but we'll do so discreetly. We'll make every effort to live quietly and peaceably with our neighbours, avoiding conflict. We'll even hold Meetings for Worship in our house, if Friends wish."

Objections were forming in Alice's mind as he spoke but she knew that what Henry was saying was sensible. Since Hester's birth and her tenuous friendship with Ruth Chinnock she'd noticed some of their neighbours seemed to be more sympathetic towards her and her family. Other Friends, too, had noticed that non-Quakers were adopting a different approach to them.

People now understood that the activities of Quakers were harmless enough, despite their strange behaviour and appearance. Their business practices were well known to be of the highest integrity and they were in all ways to be trusted. In addition, it had to be said, though secretly of course, that if, say, carpenter was needed urgently on a Sunday, or even on Christmas Day, Roger Ockenden or John Taylor had no qualms about working on such a day and would charge no more than on any other day.

Henry waited for her reply which he knew would be difficult for her to voice just now. He understood that what he had said had been a shock to her. When she did speak Alice, surprisingly, raised the question of informers. Such men were dangerous. Being paid by the Crown, some of them were making a lot of money out of their hatred of Quakers and many had suffered because of their activities.

"Informers will always be with us," he said. "But if we are quiet and discreet in our own 'ome we may not be of interest to them."

He began to rise to his feet, stretching his limbs as he did so.

"And some of our neighbours may warn us. They're becoming better disposed towards us than in the past. It won't be easy, but then, neither is being in gaol, being whipped, or even only suffering the taunts and insult of unbelievers."

He held a hand out to Alice and pulled her to her feet. The air was cooler now; the day was coming to a close. Ellen would be ready with the evening meal. "Come, Alice," he said. "Let's go 'ome."

80 CR

CHAPTER TWENTY-SEVEN

Friday, July 15th 1669

Abel Chinnock was now a respected and prosperous yeoman with financial securities well over fifty pounds a year in land, goods and property. This level of income carried with it certain duties and responsibilities, which is why for the last week he'd been serving on the Jury at the Magistrates Court.

The cases tried were mostly concerned with theft from houses, but there were also other petty thieves, such as pickpockets and highway robbers to deal with. Each day there had also been at least one or two Quakers, some returning for the third or fourth time, who held up proceedings by refusing to swear to tell the truth or to swear the Oath of Allegiance. There had been a case yesterday. A Quaker father and son, Vincent and William Haywood. The bailiffs were going to take some of their household goods away, just because they would not pay the fine for not going to church. They should be ashamed. What madmen they are!

Now he almost leapt off his horse outside the Grange door and trotted as fast as he could into the house. John Denny, Mistress Denny's oldest son, recently appointed stable hand shook his head and muttered to himself, "Silly old fool," as he led the horse away, assuming that his master was anxious to see the missus and the little twins. He was mistaken. Today there had been a variation in Quakerly misdeeds and Abel couldn't wait to tell his wife about it. He had even taken less time than usual over his convivial drink with the other jurors at the end of the day's Session, in his haste to get home.

"You will not believe what happened today, my dear," he

told Ruth, as she poured him a glass of wine. He took a sip. "Excellent," he said then continued with his story.

"Today a most odd case. Everybody in the Court remarked upon it. The parson from the village had charged two of those Quaker people, men, where they live, with disturbing the peace. " He took another sip. "They'd been at a funeral. Some draper from Shepstones. Not a Quaker, but did business with 'em, so they went to his funeral as a mark of respect, I suppose."

He raised the glass to his lips once more. "Where did you get this from, my dear? No matter." He replaced the glass on the small table by the side of his chair.

"The parson brought the case to court and when the Judge asked him -," He took another sip of the wine. It really was quite good. "- He asked the parson what exactly was the breach of the peace? It all seemed to have proceeded quietly enough. And the parson said -"

Abel started to laugh and the rest of the sentence was gasped through his mirth. "- The parson said they'd disturbed him because they'd kept their hats on while the corpse was being buried!"

Abel mopped his eyes and blew his nose to calm himself before continuing with his story.

"Then the Judge said that there was no case to answer, and that the parson should be ashamed of himself for making the two Quaker men - who seemed perfectly sensible and respectable to me - making them have to travel so far for no reason." He sat back in his chair, still panting slightly.

Ruth had found his story less amusing than he, but loyally laughed heartily at his telling of it. As she went out of the room to supervise the preparation of their supper, she wondered if her husband had remembered that it was Joe and Rosabella's fourth birthday in two days' time.

ℰℛ

CHAPTER TWENTY-EIGHT

Wednesday, March 20th 1672

Just over six years since his cousin had, against Peter's will, liberated him from a previous gaol sentence, he looked up to the window, high in the wall of the same gaol. All he could see was a grey March sky. He was older, thinner and grey was dulling his fair hair but his eyes could still burn with the passion of his convincement. Earlier in the morning he'd been asked once more to swear the Oath of Supremacy and once more he had refused.

For the five years since his imprisonment, Peter Littleton had resisted all efforts to make him swear the Oath of Allegiance. His captors maintained that his obstinacy, which his friends would have called his strength of character, had only increased with time. Determined to stand by his principles, so far as he was concerned he could be imprisoned for the rest of his life but never, never would he swear an oath.

He'd just listened to the governor sentencing him to another forty days in gaol and now, back in the dank and gloomy day cell, he sat on his patch of floor, a wry smile on his face.

Six years measured in periods of forty days. He knew that all he needed to do to be released from this sordid place was to swear an oath acknowledging the supremacy of the King and his opposition to Roman Catholicism. The authorities would not accept his personal declaration that he was loyal subject of King Charles, acknowledged His Majesty's governance of the realm and that, in common with most Protestants, he did not recognise the authority of the Pope. In spite of his declarations his word alone was not enough. Every forty days the same ritual was performed.

He stood up to ease his limbs. The stone floor was cold and damp. Condensation from the prisoners' breath ran down the walls. He shivered and pulled his jerkin closer across his chest in an attempt to get warmer. He was hungry. If he could walk about a little it might warm him up but there was not enough room. He resumed his uncomfortable position on the floor and resorted to 'centring down', the Quaker practice used in Meetings for Worship, of emptying the mind and waiting for the Spirit to enter it. In this way he could separate himself from his surroundings and achieve a little relief from his discomfort. He prepared himself for the next forty days.

***

An hour or so later he was roused from his inner silence by the sound of excitement among the prisoners. He stood up and looked around him. Most of the Quaker prisoners were gathered around one of the gaolers who was reading from a piece of paper. Peter could only catch occasional words and phrases and what he did hear filled him with equal measures of reluctant relief and conscientious indignation.

The gaoler withdrew and Peter found himself surrounded by Quaker men. They were all in such various states of excitement that he could only pick out scraps of information. The words "Declaration of Indulgence" were uttered more often than any other, then "Freedom of Worship" and "Cancelling all penal legislation against non-conforming Protestants and Roman Catholics."

***

Once more Peter had been interrupted in his personal crusade against the Oath of Allegiance and compulsory church attendance. This time he had suffered five years imprisonment, not two months out of three. This time it wasn't his cousin who was securing his reluctant release, it was King Charles the Second himself. Throughout his realm, all Quakers and others imprisoned for their beliefs would be released.

***

The women set about gathering the few belongings they had been able to keep in prison.

"Come along, Peter," said one, her face alight with relief and happiness, "Pick up thy coat and bundle. The gaoler will be here soon to let us out. Thee must be ready to go home."

But her words were spoken too soon.

The Chief Gaoler regarded the order to release Quaker prisoners as one not to be carried out for another couple of days.

Friday, March 22nd 1672

By the day of their release the Friends' initial elation when they heard of the Declaration of Indulgence was quenched. The small shafts of pale late winter sunshine seeping through the high windows, lit a cluster of men and women standing, silent, subdued and dismayed, waiting for the door to be opened. On a grey early morning, a grey people. Grey clothes and grey faces. Many of the women were weeping as they tried to hold their torn clothes together. The gradually increasing light revealed the bloody scratches and grazes and the livid bruises.

***

Up until the previous day, non-Quaker prisoners, gaoled mostly for crimes involving stealing or prostitution, had shown a grudging respect for Friends' strict views, even to the point of curbing their filthy language and crude behaviour. But after the announcement that all Quaker prisoners were to be released, the other captives' pent-up feelings of hatred and resentment couldn't be contained any longer.

Throughout their imprisonment Quaker men had

successfully managed to shield their women against the possibility of sexual assault, but yesterday protection for the women disappeared, as Peter and the other Friends were set upon and beaten with fists and feet, by enraged prisoners. Imprisoned vagrants, thieves, highwaymen, beggars, pickpockets, all joined in the attack. Aggrieved non-Quaker women prisoners fought alongside their men, adding refinements like hair pulling and face-scratching, as, through it all, the gaolers turned a blind eye.

At the same time, frenzied criminals who'd privately found the modesty of Quaker women provocative, lost control, took their chances and threw women onto the floor, raping them brutally, while their anguished men being outnumbered, were overcome by the gaolers and other prisoners.

The walls of the stone cell filled with the sound of the women's screaming and begging for mercy. Some relief came when the men and women were locked in their separate night-cells and the cries changed to desperate sobbing before a sort of silence fell. In the men's cells there were more attempts at violence, but in the darkness it soon stopped, to be replaced by curses and insults. Some Friends slept, while other lay awake, listening to the night sounds of snores, whimpers, occasional cries from dreamers and the night-watchman's call of "All's well".

ഇർ

CHAPTER TWENTY-NINE

Wednesday, October 21st 1674

At first Elizabeth Littleton hadn't known whether to laugh or cry. Peter released a few weeks ago, from prison under the terms of the King's Declaration of Indulgence Act, had been re-arrested.

The Rector, Thomas Fletcher and two agents, Will Ridgely and Sampson Birch, helping him in his obsessive pursuit of Peter. In addition there were other influential supporters in the three persons of Joseph Martin, the Mayor of Stafford, Francis Moss, a Justice of the Peace and Henry Archbold, Chancellor of Lichfield Consistory Court. With the assistance of these influential men, a successful appeal was made to the Courts that Peter's release from prison under the King's Act of Indulgence was unlawful.

Peter, in his usual placid way, had submitted to being re-arrested, offering no defence in court. As before, having refused to swear the Oath of Allegiance, he was condemned to forty days in prison. At the end of that time, once again, with his repeated refusal to swear, he was sentenced to a further forty-day incarceration. He knew that this would be repeated until he 'repented', but was determined that he would not. He would die first, as Friends had done before.

Responding to the promptings of his conscience, he resigned himself to whatever would happen in the future, regarding his present situation as a necessary part of his personal testimony for Truth.

Monday, December 14th 1674

About eight weeks after being gaoled, while Elizabeth was visiting him, Peter felt the first symptoms of the fever. The last time she had been to see him he had asked her not to come any more, but she'd ignored his instructions and now she was here again. Today he was warning her for a second time, as they sat together on the floor of the cold and crowded cell.

"There is so much illness here," he said. "Thou art in danger of falling sick thyself. Stay at home, Eliza. Attend to thy duties there. I am well able to take care of my self."

Elizabeth was dismissive. "There always is sickness here," she said. "Every time thee has been in here there has been sickness. It is to be expected, with so much vermin and filth around."

She handed him the warm woollen overshirt she had laundered and dried by the fire for him. While he changed his soiled shirt for the clean one, she discreetly put a small amount of money in the bundle he always had by him. Slipping the shirt over his head Peter smiled as he recognised the smoky scent of the fire at home.

They ignored the noise and commotion around them and talked quietly for a while. They even kept the Silence for a few minutes; sitting on the damp stone floor, holding hands and waiting for God's word to be revealed to them, then Peter, anxious for his wife's health, insisted that she went home.

"Stay away from this hideous place." He cautioned her firmly. "Thee mustn't become ill. Thy responsibilities at home must be thy first thought. Thee doesn't need to come again until this fever has passed."

As she began to protest he stopped her.

"I shall be busy here, but shall send a message when all is well."

He spoke in a voice that would not be denied and then called through the grating for the door to be opened. They kissed and she walked away and out of his sight.

For fear of alarming her he'd not told her that he was beginning to feel feverish. He felt warm, too warm for the coldness of the cell; he felt cold, too cold to be running with sweat and he ached in every part of his body. The five people who'd died of the fever over the previous week had been covered in rose-coloured spots at the start of their illness and died after a period of semiconscious delirium. After Elizabeth left, Peter examined his body and limbs for spots but found none. It was not too late to take medicine to allay the gaol fever, if that was what he'd caught, but what he really felt he needed was fresh air.

He called out through the grating in the cell door. It was unusual for Peter to create any sort of disturbance and the gaoler, when he came, expected to be told of another death among the prisoners. Reluctant to make any close contact with the virulent infection, his only emotion was relief on finding that there was not another body waiting to be removed from the building. He listened while Peter made his request.

"Will thee allow me to walk out into the town for a while in order to buy medicines?"

It was quite usual for trusted prisoners to be temporarily released from prison to go out to buy food or even to visit their families if they lived close enough. There were ways of facilitating the privilege and procedures that had to be gone through. In Peter's case Thomas Fletcher, the priest who had brought him to court, would have to be applied to for permission. The gaoler explained this and Peter's heart sank. He was only too aware of Fletcher's hostility towards him and knew that he had been a thorn in the priest's flesh. There was, he thought, little chance of permission being given for him to leave the premises.

Thursday December 17th 1674

By the time the Reverend Fletcher's reply was received Peter knew that he was extremely ill. When the gaoler called him to the grill to give him the news, which wasn't good, he could see the poor state of the man. Peter, though still able to walk to the door, was burning with fever, the spots had begun to show and it was obvious that he needed medicine.

The gaoler told him that his request had been refused and Peter stood for a moment, silently staring at him through the grating, then he turned round to go back to his place on the floor of the cell.

Watching and pitying the dejected figure stumbling back

into the crush of dirty ragged prisoners, the gaoler felt an unexpected surge of pity for Peter. The man was a lunatic, he knew, but he caused very little trouble; in fact he'd helped many other prisoners to survive their ordeal. His wife was as mad as her husband, but of a tender nature. A woman with no airs or graces, gentle and kind.

The gaoler, a compassionate man among uncaring colleagues, shouted after the retreating Peter. "Come back 'ere!" and as Peter stumbled painfully back up to the grill, he whispered, "Look, I'll let you out, but yer on yer honour to be back before the church clock strikes eleven."

Peter fumbled in his breeches pocket and the gaoler heard the chink of coins. "Don't bother about that," he said, as he opened the door. "Keep it to buy yer medicines,"

"I thank thee," said Peter, "What is thy name?"

The gaoler hesitated. It was not a good idea to strike up friendship with some prisoners, and this man was one of those to be avoided.

"Hugh," he said

Sunday, December 20th 1674

Peter was back in the crowded cell. He'd managed to buy a few simples in the town.

For the looseness of the bowels which was a symptom of the disease, he'd got a remedy of isinglass boiled in milk with a handful of Archangel flowers. He'd also bought powdered lily root to be taken in cherry water. Where he was to obtain cherry water he didn't know, but he'd seen other prisoners suffer terrible convulsions and knew that the lily root would help to ease them. The apothecary had mentioned that it was useful to carry the powder, mixed with sugar, in his pocket and take a little often during the day. Before he secreted the medicines in his bundle he tasted it. Without sugar it tasted nasty, but it was the best he could do.

He settled himself to pray before sleep. The words "Thy Will be done," kept repeating themselves in his brain, over and over again. He tried to bring himself back into reality but the words would not leave him.

The following morning he woke and attempted to rise from the floor but his legs buckled beneath him and he fell down onto the foetid straw. In his sleep he had fouled himself. He wept, for the shame of it, then sleep overcame him.

As the day went on his sleep became more profound. He roused once or twice and once more attempted to rise from the floor, but there was no strength in his limbs, which felt heavy, paralysed. He tried to speak, but even that was impossible. He fell into a state of half-sleep, during which someone, Henry Bowman's wife, he thought it was, gave him a drink of water. The last thing he thought before the water dribbled down his chin and he drifted into semi-unconsciousness, was 'What was Henry Bowman's wife's name? What was it?'

***

"Thy Will be done. Thy Will be done." The words wriggled through his brain. Peter, silent and weak, was being shaken from his half-trance, half-sleep, by rough hands grasping his arms and legs. He heard shouts and the rattling sounds of metal, which were transformed by his imagination into the voices of devils, feeding the fires of hell.

***

At this time of year and in this weather, only essential work was undertaken around the yard and fields. Robert Davis, the young man taken on as a farmhand during Peter's imprisonment twelve years ago, was now experienced enough to deal with any of the routine work outdoors and so Elizabeth left him to it. She carried on with the organisation of the household duties, including caring for the old and infirm, Quakers and non-Quakers, who had taken up the Littletons' offers of help and lodging for as long as they needed it.

She still gave help with reading and writing to the few men and women living locally who wished to learn. Although her moral strength and resolution helped her through Peter's many terms of imprisonment, it was inevitable that at some time her physical health would falter. It was with Peter's most recent re-arrest, appearance at Court and gaol sentence, that the strain began to show.

***

Today, after leaving corn to be ground at the watermill in Ridge Lane, she was walking home pushing the empty handcart along the snowy path which ran alongside the riverbank. Her thoughts were on the things she had to attend to at home when she experienced the slight disturbance in her vision. She'd had it before; it often went away as quickly as it arrived, but sometimes, like today, it developed into dizziness and nausea. The glare from the snow didn't help.

When she got to the small stone bridge over the river, where the path and the green lane crossed, she stopped pushing and, resting the handles on the ground, moved round and sat down on the cart. Her body felt chilled the moment she stopped walking, so she wrapped her hooded woollen cloak more closely around herself and blew warm breath into the blue-tinged hands curved over her nose and mouth.

Although she was wearing high-soled pattens and had hitched her skirt above her ankles before she set out that morning, the hems of her skirt and underskirt were wet with melted snow. They would take hours, days even, to dry. She hoped that Robert was making sure that the fire didn't go out. At any time a cold hearth was an inconvenience. In weather like this today it was a calamity. She put her gloves back on and sitting hunched up, tucked her hands into her armpits. Closing her eyes, she tried to breathe regularly and steadily, to still the busy thoughts whirring about her brain. She attempted to relax her tired body, if only for a few moments, before she needed to start walking again. She would regain warmth lost, by the effort of once more pushing the cart across the fields.

"Are thee not well, Elizabeth?" A woman's voice sounded above her head. Elizabeth looked up into the anxious face of Alice Bowman, whose intense brown eyes were accentuated by the man's woollen hat pulled down over her head and down to her eyebrows.

"I'm just a mite tired," Elizabeth replied, "Thank thee for thy concern."

Alice nodded and taking Elizabeth's answer at face value, assumed that 'well' indeed meant 'well'. It brought to an end her interest in the matter of Elizabeth's well-being and she carried on with the matter in hand. "I was just coming to thy house," she said. "I have news for thee, of thy husband."

Elizabeth grasped Alice's hand, panic-stricken, "He's not well?" The question was both enquiry and reply.

"I went with Grace Wells to visit Tom yesterday and saw Peter," Alice answered, feeling Elizabeth's hand tightened on hers as she continued.

"No, Eliza, he isn't well. When I spoke to him he didn't know me. I fear he has the fever."

Elizabeth started to rise to her feet, saying, "I must go to him," but the dizziness came on again and she slipped, falling back onto the snow with a little cry of surprise.

"Thou'rt not well either," Alice said sharply. "Go to see him and thee put thyself in danger. Thee has responsibilities at home. He needs thee to be well." She thought quickly. "If thee is agreeable, I will go to see him from time to time and make sure that all that can be done for him is done."

Elizabeth, still shaken, still dizzy, could only find the strength to nod. She trusted Alice as she could trust no one else. She remembered that Peter had been very firm when he told her not to visit him and the thought eased her conscience. Alice's voice, quiet and steady, broke into her thoughts.

"Elizabeth, I will always tell thee the truth, even if it should be a hard truth. If I think his end is near I shall make sure he does not die alone."

For a shocked moment Elizabeth could only stare at Alice, her face blank, then she drew as deeply as she could on her inner store of emotional strength, saying, "I must get home."

Alice nodded, but seeing Elizabeth's unsteadiness, she knew that her friend was in no state to be left alone and so her voice was gentler when she said, "Come, I'll take thee home."

She started to help Elizabeth to her feet but it was clear that she was in no state to walk across the fields to the Littletons' house. "I'll take thee to my house, it's closer." Alice said firmly, but Elizabeth protested.

"Thank thee, no, Alice." Elizabeth tried to match Alice's firmness. "I can't impose on you. There is so much that I have to do at home."

Alice didn't seem to be listening.

Elizabeth, not so sure of herself now, continued, "The old people need me, Alice. There is nobody but me to make their dinner."

She fumbled with her shawl, and began to pick up the handles of the cart. "Robert is good around the farm but some of the lodgers are ill, and he doesn't know who has which medicine."

She made one last effort. "I must go home, Alice".

Alice had only half-listened, trying to think of a solution to the problem. Elizabeth wasn't well, it was obvious, but she wouldn't settle until she was in her own place. It was probably just the usual women's troubles and if so, she would eventually be able to finish the work which seemed to be so important to her. There was only one thing to do.

"Get in the cart," ordered Alice. Elizabeth opened her mouth to protest, but Alice pointed to the cart. There could be no argument.

***

And so it was that Elizabeth, despite her protests, arrived home in a handcart. She was greeted with relief by anxious lodgers who had expected their nurse, cook, teacher and friend to arrive home earlier. In fact Elizabeth had started to feel better shortly after she and Alice had set out, but she'd been too apprehensive of her benefactor's reaction to tell her. She'd been pushed across the snowy fields by a resolute Alice who, in spite of the difficulty she had with pushing, or alternatively pulling, the cart across frozen, uneven ground, regarded the journey as a challenge.

Stopping at the Littleton house only for a drink of weak beer and a piece of bread and cheese, Alice replaced her cloak and extra wrap, her hat and gloves. Putting back on the man's boots that she'd removed before coming into the house, she bade the occupants 'Good day' and left, to walk the four miles home across the moor to the steading.

CHAPTER THIRTY

Monday, January 4th 1674/5

Peter was in chains, held to a wall by his ankles. For ten or eleven days he'd been unaware of his surroundings, his companions, or any of his body's needs. Even if he'd have been well enough to, the irons on his wrists would not have allowed him sufficient movement to feed himself, neither would he have been able to remove his clothes or attend to his bodily functions. In the event, compassionate fellow-prisoners attempted to feed him and give him water to drink between his convulsions, with varying degrees of success. Two or three of the braver women prisoners took turns to try to administer medicines.

Then one day the woman whom he vaguely recognised, wiped as much as she could of his burning skin with cool liquid, speaking soothingly to him all the time, as if he was a tired child.

"There, there, Peter. Drink this. Thee'll feel better soon, please God"

And he did. After the cooling sponge he did feel cleaner and better, even if only for a short time. She came another day, or later the same day, he didn't know which. She left him feeling cooler, cleaner and better. It lasted a little longer this time.

Friday, January 15th 1674/75

The chained prisoners could not be moved into the night cells and the high day cell was quiet, or as quiet as it could ever be. Some sleepers were snoring, some of those sick of the fever whimpered a little. One or two of the recumbent figures twitched and grunted in their sleep.

The gaoler peered through the grating. Faint moonlight

reflecting on the snow outside, lightened the gloom through the high windows. He could just about recognise the outline of Peter's broad-shouldered shape as he lay on his side.

Quietly, very quietly, the heavy door was unlocked and opened, as quietly closed and locked again. Hugh trod silently between sleeping bodies, stopping frequently when one of them stirred or made a noise. After what seemed hours, he reached his target and softly tapped Peter's shoulder.

"I 'ad to do it, Master Littleton," he whispered. "I 'ad to. That bloody priest found out that I'd let you go out for medicine and 'e was going to report me to the Chief Gaoler." He waited for some response from Peter, but there was none. Hugh decided to carry on with his confession anyway. It had taken him many days to gather the courage to speak. Just because the prisoner hadn't answered didn't mean he hadn't heard.

"The priest said I 'ad to chain you up," The gaoler was sweating now, despite the chill of the cell. "If the Chief Gaoler'd found out about me letting you out, I'd've lost me job." He tapped Peter's shoulder again hopefully. "I've got a wife and four little uns. I can't afford to lose me job."

Peter stirred and the shock of the movement silenced Hugh. Suddenly he realised the danger of his situation and crept, as quickly and quietly as he could, to the door, let himself out and locked it.

Peter, free of the fever but in the deep sleep of the very weak, had heard nothing.

***

"There, there, Peter. Take a drink of water. That's it. That's better. Thanks be to God."

He recognised the voice this time, but it wasn't Elizabeth's. He remembered now. He had told her not to come. He wished he hadn't. 'Poor Elizabeth,' he thought before returning to oblivion

Another day he was aware of the same woman's voice asking, no, ordering, the gaoler to remove Peter's chains.

"How can thee let the poor wretch suffer like this?" she

210

said sharply. "What harm could it do to unshackle him? The poor man cannot stand, let alone run away. Let him free, in the name of God!"

Once again Peter thought, 'I know that voice,' soon, worn out by the noise of it, he lapsed back into semi-consciousness.

***

Then he awoke one morning aware of who he was, where he was. He was in the familiar cell, with light shining through the windows, high up in the wall. He tried to sit up but was hampered not by chains now, but by weakness.

"Welcome back, Peter!" a voice rang out across the cell. John Oreton, imprisoned at the same time as Peter, for not paying tithes or Easter Offerings, got up from his space by the opposite wall and came over to Peter, where he lay on the straw-covered floor.

"We thought thee would die, Friend," John said cheerfully, as he helped Peter to sit up. "And thee would have done but for the intervention of the good Lord in spirit and in the persons of Alice Bowman and other Friends who have looked after thee and many others sick of the fever."

"Elizabeth?"

The first conscious word that Peter had spoken for weeks sounded anxious, cracked and feeble, like that of an old man. John calmed him with a gesture. "She is well, but misses you most sorely, having stayed away as you said she must."

Peter slowly shook his head from side to side.

"Elizabeth," he said, and wept a little, before falling into an easy natural sleep in the arms of a Friend.

Friday, February 19th 1674/75

19. 11th. m. 1675.

Quarterly Meeting

Accounts of collections made from Knutton, Leek, Lyn, Uttoxeter, Morridge and Stafford, totalling £3.14.6.

8 disbursements were given, totalling £3.1.4.

The Quarterly Meeting called in order to discuss the business of the Friends was drawing to a close. The time had been taken up mostly with matters regarding the distribution of charitable donations to sixteen Friends who, for various reasons, were suffering financial hardship.

A recent appeal, which had gone out all over the county for Quakers to report their experiences of persecution, had brought in few reports. Many Quakers were reluctant to make a fuss or draw attention to themselves, for fear of reprisals. The few reports of persecution that had been offered were being written down in the back of the Quarterly Meeting Minute Book, as and when they were received.

Before the Meeting closed today a new entry was written, under the special heading 'Friends Suffering for the Truth in Staffordshire'. The entry was brief but telling:

'Peter Littleton committed to prison the 21 of the eight month ... there being at that time a mortal distemper in the Gaole whereof there died 5 persons in a few days space. The said Peter having the distemper, the Gaoler let him goe forth a little into the town to take something for the distemper. There came 2 agents of the priest, Ridgley & Birch, 2 furious persecutors, & threatened the Gaoler & caused him send for him to come in again, in great haste, in the Coldest time in winter. By which means his sickness increased for a time, yet through God's mercies, who is good to all that depend upon him, his life was preserved.'

There was silence in the room except for the scratching of the Clerk's quill and the regular tapping of the replenished point of it against the neck of the inkwell. When the entry was finished the Clerk laid down his pen and sat back on the bench, hands folded in his lap and joined the rest of the Friends present in a silent Meeting for Worship. All thoughts were of Friends who had suffered, and the absent Peter in particular. He was usually Clerk.

80 03

CHAPTER THIRTY-ONE

Saturday, July 17th 1675

Rosabella Chinnock opened her eyes and immediately closed them. The sun, shining directly on her face through a chink in the bed curtains, was dazzling. Cautiously she opened one eye a little then she tried both. She knew that after a while her eyes would become used to the light. This was something she had discovered all by herself.

There was a little fluttery feeling in her stomach this morning as well as the usual rumblings due to being hungry. Still half asleep, she knew that there was something special about today, but was too interested in observing her eyes' reaction to light to remember what it was.

Suddenly it came to her. It was her and Joe's birthday. She pushed off the bedclothes and sat up. Simultaneously Ruth came bustling into the room and drawing back the bed curtains, threw her arms exultantly around her daughter.

"Happy birthday, my darling," she said already close to tears. "What a lovely day it is, too. There are lots of surprises for you, and presents."

Ruth went to the door and called for Lucy, the young waiting woman who'd replace the nursemaid when Rosa was eight years old. Together they dressed the little girl while Rosa and her mother chattered excitedly.

***

Abel had told Ruth that, although it was the twins' birthday, he would be occupied with other matters outside the house that would keep him occupied for most of the day. At the moment he was in his office, discussing the day's work on the hone farm.

As Ruth, Rosa and Lucy sat around the table finishing their breakfast of bread and butter and weak beer, Rosa asked where her father was. Even on very busy days he usually at least put his head around the door to wish her 'Good morning', but today there had been no sign of him.

"Your father is very busy today, my dear," Ruth comforted her. "He has business to attend to in town, but he will surely see you before bedtime."

'Bedtime!' thought Rosa. 'I want him here, now!' And she pouted a little as she considered how long the time would be before she saw her adored father. But today was her birthday. She hadn't forgotten that it was Joe's too, but he was away at the same school as Abel's other sons had attended and she guessed that it would be Christmas before he came home. The twins saw one another very rarely now and though Rosa had been very distressed when her brother first went away, she was now accustomed to his absence. Occasionally, in the middle of the night, if she had a bad dream or it was a stormy night with thunder and lightening, she missed being able to creep into his bed and hold his comforting hand in hers.

After breakfast, even today, the morning was occupied with lessons. Any birthday gifts for Rosa wouldn't be given until later. Sometimes they were even left until the evening, when Abel was at home to watch 'My little Rose', as he called her, receive them. So today was likely to be a very long day if he was away all the time.

Rosa had sensed the atmosphere of secrecy in the house for some days. Her father appeared to be keeping something to himself. Sometimes, when she caught his eye, he had a little smile on his face and once he actually winked. She guessed that it was something to do with her birthday but had no idea what it could be. Any question to her mother only brought forth the reply, "I'm sure I don't know, my dear. Now run along, do."

Lucy's response was no more useful, "I don't know what you mean, Miss Rosa, but whatever it is, your father will always do his best by you."

Of the two replies, both expressing ignorance on the matter, Rosa only believed Lucy's, as her mother always blushed when she wasn't telling the truth.

***

Lucy's duties included teaching Rosa her letters and lessons would be attended to this morning, as on any other day. For her age, Rosa was progressing as well as any girl-child of her class could be expected to. She knew the names of most of the letters and the sounds of some. She had difficulty with the sounds made by combinations of letters and got angry and unhappy when attempting to learn the vagaries of the illogical pronunciations of, for example the 'bow' which meant a pretty knot of ribbon, and the 'bow' which meant bending forward like father did when greeting his business friends. She had yet had to meet the word 'bough'.

Rosa was learning her sums as well. This was where she excelled, but from Lucy she would never learn much more than she would require in order to manage her household when she married.

The standard of her needlework filled Ruth with despair. Lucy, a well-brought-up young woman from a respectable, though poor home, had been engaged on the strength of her proficiency with the needle and Ruth expected her daughter to have inherited her skill, but it simply didn't seem to be there. Rosa tried hard, but always seemed to spend more time unpicking her untidy embroidery than adding to it and sometimes she cried with frustration at her own lack of expertise.

Eventually the two hours of lessons were over and Rosa was free for a while at last. After dinner there would be a walk in the countryside with Lucy who was very knowledgeable about flowers, birds and the like. Rosa was usually quite interested to hear the waiting-woman's descriptions of the life-histories of small creatures such as butterflies, or the reason leaves fell from the trees in autumn, but what she really enjoyed was Rosa's stories of her own country childhood.

Today Lucy, though happy for Rosa on her birthday, was feeling a little sad. Today had been her father's birthday too, but he'd died the previous year. This was the reason that Lucy had needed to find work to support herself. Her mother, at home in a neighbouring village, had been left a little money on the death of her husband, but it was only enough to keep one daughter at home. Consequently Mistress Henderson had let it be known that her elder daughter, Lucy, then aged twenty years, would be available to help with the bringing up of a girl-child in a respectable household for a small wage and her keep.

The Chinnocks were always kind to Lucy, but they weren't her own family and there were times when, alone at night in the room next to Rosa's, she'd allowed herself to weep a little for the loss of her father and her home. She knew that today would be one of those days when she would be in great danger of being overcome by these sad thoughts, but she was a resourceful young woman and had learnt a way of dealing with what she inwardly called her 'downward-looking' days. The secret was busyness. This day, Lucy thought, was Rosa's day and she was determined that it should be a happy one.

***

During the afternoon walk, Rosa had become too excited to be receptive to Lucy's instruction. The sky was blue, the sun was shining, the little birds were singing. The world was a beautiful place, anyone could see that. Rosa didn't need to be told about it. Lucy, recognising her pupil's lack of interest, struggled to find something that, if only for a short time, would engage Rosa for more than the blink of an eye. Then Rosa, on her own account found the very thing.

They were walking along the edge of Croke's field, through which a branch of the stream flowed. "Let's look for fish," she shouted, and headed off, lifting her skirts and running through the parsnip crop, towards the water. Lucy followed her more slowly, picking her way across the uneven ground.

By the time she got to the bank, Rosa was already lying face down over the stream. Her sleeves were rolled up and she held onto a tuft of grass with one hand while the other was submerged to the elbow in the brownish water. Without looking at Lucy she breathed, half to herself, "It's lovely." Then, whispered, "Look!" Quietly, Lucy leaned forward before kneeling down to see what Rosa saw.

The trout hung there, motionless, hovering in the curve of the small, caressing, fingers. "I could pick it up if I wanted to," Rosa whispered, turning her head towards Lucy. And in that second the moment was gone, as the fish, disturbed by the movement, woke from it's trance and darted away.

Disappointed and annoyed with herself, Rosa stood up and began to look around for some other diversion. Lucy, getting to her feet, brushed her skirts down with her hands. There were a few dirty marks on her apron which would easily be removed. Then she caught sight of her charge. "Miss Rosa," she said, sharply, "Look at the state of your clothes."

Rosa looked down, surprised, at the mud and grass stains on her dress. She'd been quite comfortable, lying there on the bank, not felt the damp at all, unaware of the grubby state she would be in when she stood up. Ineffectually, she tried to rub the stains out with her hands, one of which was wet, while the other was dirty and in doing so she only managed to make matters worse. Lucy decided that the afternoon's lessons were over and the two made their sober way back to The Grange.

Ruth was unable to control a little scream at the sight of her daughter, who appeared to have been rolling in mud. Regaining a little composure she then fluttered around trying to think of how to deal with what had happened.

In the event it was Lucy who took matters in hand. She sat Ruth down, patted her hands and reassured the distraught mother that all would be attended to. Then she sent the now crying Rosa to the little cubby-hole off her parents' room where she slept, with instructions to take her shoes off and stand still until someone came to help her undress and wash. That done, she arranged for warm water to be taken to Rosa before going to her own space under the eaves, where she changed her apron before returning to care for the contrite little girl, still standing in her stockinged feet by her bed.

Rosa, serene, stood with her back to the looking glass hanging on the wall as Lucy dressed her in her new suit: petticoat, skirt and bodice. Made up by the best dressmaker in the district, the imported cloth for the two outer garments was cotton lawn, coloured rose pink and bought for his little Rose by Abel while on a visit to London. At the same time he also bought an imported filmy cambric wrap to cover Rosa's shoulders if the evening should be chilly. His daughter was to be dressed in cloth from France for her tenth birthday.

A pane of the new cotton petticoat was displayed in the front opening of the skirt. It had been embroidered by Ruth, with intertwined flowers, leaves and small birds in colours to complement the skirt and bodice. A birthday surprise for her daughter, it had to be stitched at night, after Rosa had gone to bed.

"There you are, Miss Rosa." Lucy ran her hands swiftly down the folds of the skirt and gave one more tweak to the shoulders of the bodice. "Do you want to look at yourself now?"

Rosa spun round to view her image, which she could only see from the waist up, behind the imperfections in the surface of the glass, to the glowing girl reflected there. Dragging a chair into position, she stood on it to admire the skirt and embroidered panel.

"Oh Lucy," she exclaimed, as she got down and put the chair back, "I'm pretty aren't I?"

Lucy smiled, excusing the child's vanity. It was her birthday. She could do no wrong. And indeed she was pretty.

***

Now all was sweetness and calm again. Rosa, walking sedately at Lucy's side, was being taken to show her parents how well she looked in her new clothes. Tonight she was to be allowed to eat with them. A proper grown-up meal with guests who were not all family and there would probably be a gift to be presented after it was over.

The first sight she saw when the door was opened was the table, laid with the best the Chinnocks had acquired in the last few years: pewter, silver cutlery of elegant design, and glassware. There were three or four kinds of fowl, beef, ham and pork, steaming dishes of vegetables and gleaming bowls of fruit. The second thing she saw as she turned to speak to Lucy was her brother, Joe, flanked by Ruth and Abel. Rosa's excitement subsided a little.

"Say good evening to your brother," Abel said, while Joe, freeing himself from his parents' embrace, smiled a little awkwardly and came forward to kiss her.

Rosa manage to say "Good evening, Joe." Her smile felt uncomfortable on her lips.

***

Later, as she helped Rosa out of her new clothes, Lucy said, "Have you enjoyed your birthday, Miss Rosa?"

The answer came after a deal of thought. The presence of her brother had not been her only gift. Her grandmother, a very old lady whom she only knew slightly and was a little frightened of, had given her a pretty necklace and one of her aunts-by-marriage had embroidered a purse for her. "Yes," said Rosa, "I have, thank you, Lucy."

Later, before she slept, she puzzled over her strange feelings about her brother. They had been such good friends once but now he was like a stranger. She even felt rather shy with him and she guessed he felt the same way. Then she thought about the beautiful clothes, the purse, the necklace, before turning over onto her side, and settling for sleep. She smiled as she remembered.

'The best thing about today was the trout.' she said to herself.

ഇ ൠ

CHAPTER THIRTY-TWO

Easter-Day 1677

"But Mam, it makes my arms ache!"

Over the still fields, brushed with a pale green wash of early growing shoots now that the sun had dispersed the frost, the wailing cry floated out from the barn.

"Stop grumbling, child. It makes my arms ache too, but it has to be done!"

Alice's answer was short and final, as they struggled with the annual task of filling the family's mattresses with fresh straw. Flock would have been softer and kinder to young skin, but although Alice knew they could probably afford it now, she would have no such extravagance in her house. Straw was available just for the effort of gathering it and, as she reminded Hester, "When it's done, the house will smell sweeter!"

Hester viewed the scratches on her arms, rubbed them briefly then returned to her work. Every spring the routine cleaning of the stone house took on a more intense nature than at any other time of the year. Once the weather began to become even a little warmer and dryer, some sort of frenzy would come over her mother, making her wash, scrub, polish and scour every part of the house which she could reach. Those areas that she couldn't get at she set one of her older, taller sons to clean, while she watched them, barking instructions.

Every person living on the farm, family, employees, young and old, found themselves caught up in her domestic rampage, even if the only thing the smallest ones could do to help was to absent themselves from the house.

At these times Hester suspected that her mother's vision, hearing and sense of smell, always good, became unnaturally acute. It seemed that Alice could see dust and grime, hear mice and rats and smell the tiniest traces of offensive odour, where up until now, there had been no sign of any of these things.

Another thing that was making Hester discontented was the thought that last year Ellen would have been helped her, but she'd left home. In November of the previous year the Bowman's eldest daughter, to her family's horror, had announced that she wished to 'marry out'.

***

Alice, outraged, had tried every strategy that she could think of to discourage Hester from taking this step. Not even the threat of being cast out of her family as well as the Meeting had any effect. Ellen was unyielding, thereby, Alice realised, truly demonstrating that she was her mother's daughter. At home two irresistible forces, Alice and Ellen, met. There was sadness, but no surrender on either side.

There had been interminable interviews with the Meeting's equally unbending Elders. The anger evident at home as well as at Meeting left all parties unhappy and unsettled. Inevitably, neither would give way and one day Ellen, determined to marry the handsome young non-Quaker man she'd fallen in love with, left home to stay until she was married, with a non-Quaker friend who lived in another part of Branslow.

***

Hester, feeling more disgruntled every minute, continued to fill the mattresses with straw, which for her, after prolonged contact, had lost its sweet smell. She also missed Ellen for the way she had sometimes acted as a buffer between Hester and her mother. The way that, talking to her older sister at night as they lay in bed together, Ellen could make her feel better about things that had been worrying her during the day. Ellen showed her different ways of looking at things. She was strong, like their mother, but, like Alice, could be gentle when gentleness and sympathy was needed. On the other hand Hester resented the way she'd been left to take on the older sister's domestic tasks, not to mention having to deal with her mother on her own.

Alice's voice roused her from her discontented twelve-year-old's thoughts. "Come on Hester. Thee can help me beat this one into shape!" The mattress that her mother had been working on was filled and sewn up. Shaking the straw into an even layer and thumping it hard with clenched fists would disperse and soften the straw a bit, and release some of the dust before it was taken inside. Hester left her own work to join her mother in beating the lumpy mattress to comfortable evenness. They worked together, chatting a little but mostly in silence broken only by occasional sneezes and the following laughter. The energy expended in beating the mattress released much of Hester's frustrated unhappiness.

Alice had guessed it would.

***

In the yard a few hens scratched hopefully about in the small wisps of straw left by the mattress filling as a white duck with a twisted leg made its slow, painful progress across the stones to the small pond by the gate.

Elsewhere, the youngest Bowman boy was leaning on a wall talking quietly.

"I think I should like to go to Americky, Samuel," said Richard to his very best friend. "The sun is always shining there, and there are strange trees with 'lishuss fruits on them."

He made himself more comfortable as he leaned with folded arms on top of the wall. "I'd like to sail on the sea in a great ship and see all the different lands."

Samuel grunted, but didn't reply. Richard was used to one-sided conversations with Samuel; they didn't daunt him one bit.

"I'd like to see all the strange people in those lands over the sea."

Samuel looked at him, smiling a little, but still didn't speak.

"I could do it, you know," Richard continued. "I could go when I'm grown up. When I'm fourteen - no thirteen." He did the sum in his head. "In five years I could get on a ship and go."

There was silence between them for a while, then Richard said, "Most of all, I'd like to go to - " he thought very hard.

What was the most exotic place that he knew of besides America? It came to him.

"I'd like to go to Scotland!" Another thought came to him. "'Ow old are thee Samuel?"

Samuel shook his head.

***

Above Alice and Hester's heads the two youngest Bowman daughters were living in the perfect dream which only little girls can experience. A few weeks earlier a stray cat had made the loft her home. She was welcome around the farm where her services as mouser would be appreciated.

There was already a feline tribe inhabiting any nook and cranny available to them. Mostly tortoiseshell or black-and-white cats, they lived by their wits, feeding on whatever prey they could find. The Bowmans would never have fed a farm cat any more than they would have fed a mouse or a rat. These feral cats bred every year and every year the weaker kittens died of starvation and cold. Thus the balance of nature between cat, mouse and rat was maintained as the surviving cats rarely amounted to more than four or five and they were sufficient to keep the mice and rats down to reasonable levels.

The visiting cat was a beauty and a treasure. Black cats were regarded with superstitious fear as witches and were often tortured before being hanged or drowned, but a black cat could be reprieved if it had even the smallest trace of white on it.

This cat was purest white, except for a round black spot on the back of the lower part of its left leg. It was also pregnant when it arrived, although nobody noticed at the time. The five kittens had been born about two weeks after their mother's arrival and Henry had been steeling himself to drown them in the duck-pond. Elizabeth, aged seven and four-year-old Little Alice had pleaded with their father to spare them and now spent all the time they could with Elspeth, as they called the cat, and her kittens.

The little girls had been ordered not to feed Elspeth or her kittens, "Thee must leave them to find their own food, daughters." Henry had said, quite sternly. "The mother will feed them, and will go out to hunt for 'er own food when she needs to. When they are grown, the kittens will learn from 'er how to 'unt for themselves."

At six weeks old, the kittens were already reduced to three. One had died when only a few days old and the other two days later. Both had been buried, with separate silent, tearful ceremonies, in the garden. The remaining three were bright and playful. They were called Tom, Sue and Joe, although the girls had no idea what sex the kittens were.

Today Elizabeth, Little Alice, Elspeth, Tom, Sue and Joe would spend most of the day together in the happy, peaceful world.

Their idyll was interrupted when Alice's head rose above the loft floor as she climbed the ladder. She gave little indication of any interest in the cat and her kittens as she called the girls down for their evening meal. Five of the eight mattresses required for the family were filled; the others could wait until tomorrow.

Alice watched them from the loft as her younger daughters climbed down the ladder. She stroked Elspeth and the kittens softly as they lay curled up in their nest and took a small piece of meat out of her pocket and gave it to Elspeth, before she descended the ladder herself.

As she followed her daughters across the yard to the house they were joined by Richard, who'd dragged himself away from his one-sided conversation with Samuel. His mother laid an arm across his shoulders. He was growing so tall, now, her youngest boy, dreamy and with poor eyesight. Alice sometimes worried about his future. But for now she knew that he was happy enough in his own quiet way.

"And what have thee been doing this morning, Richard?" she asked. "While Hester and I have been making comfortable new beds for thee and thy father and brothers."

Richard, walking with his hands held behind his back, kicked a stone before answering, "Oh, nothing, Mother." He took a deep breath and decided to broach the subject with his mother, before tackling it with his father.

"Mother, can I be a seaman when I grow up. Go on a ship to other lands?"

Alice was startled by the request but gave one of her stock answers, "We will think about it again when thou'rt older." And with that Richard knew from past experience that, for the moment, it was useless pursuing the matter.

As they reached the house door Henry and Cornelius caught up with them. "What now, brother Richard!" said Cornelius cheerfully, "Hast thee spent the morning talking to that pig again?"

***

Lucy Henderson sat with her charge, Rosa, Rosa's twin brother Joe and their parents in their privileged front row pew at Saint James' Church. The rest of the Grange employees and those who worked for other families, stood at the back of the church.

Lucy Henderson had proved to be of great value to Abel and Ruth Chinnock. Over the two and a half years of her employment by them she had proved herself to be the perfect teacher for Rosabella and a loyal servant to the household.

Rosa, now in her thirteenth year, would never be as accomplished at needlework as her mother, but did have other qualities. Although she was more interested in how the instrument worked than the sound it made, she played competently upon the virginals, as Abel had hoped she would. Also she could read and write better than either of her parents and possibly better than her brother. These accomplishments were the result of Lucy's instruction and encouragement.

Abel regarded his daughter benevolently. If she had a fault it was possibly in the matter of her appearance. For very important occasions, such as her Confirmation last year, she could be persuaded to take care not to spoil a pretty skirt or bodice, but for less special times she had to be reminded constantly. Left to herself she would run wild in the gardens so recently set out around the house, chasing butterflies, or she would be found sprawled on her belly, watching the progress of a beetle through the grass stems. Today she was presentable, clean and tidy; her hands demurely folded in her lap while Thomas Fletcher read the Old Testament First Lesson for the day.

Lucy sat looking equally demure. Her eyes downcast as she looked at her hands, also folded in her lap. Her quiet appearance hid thoughts which disturbed her

'Why?' she was thinking. 'Why do we do this? Twice, sometimes three times, every Sunday.' It had become almost mechanical. The same things said or read out at every service. Every movement predictable. 'Why is it always the same?' she thought. 'Why do I have to remain silent if the Reverend Master Fletcher says something that I disagree with? Surely I cannot be the only one who disagrees!'

She pulled herself together with an effort, despising and silently reprimanding herself for such wicked thoughts. The First Lesson finished, the congregation rose to its feet for the Second Lesson, the New Testament. Today the story of Christ's Resurrection.

Later, kneeling for prayers, hands together, Lucy watched through her fingers as the priest approach the altar. To her horror another wicked question entered her mind. 'Why does the priest wear those robes? Why doesn't he wear the same clothes as every other man in the church?'

She pulled herself together once again and tried to concentrate on her devotions. Nothing in her demeanour had betrayed her thoughts.

***

226

The Bowman family were as usual joined at their evening meal by the workers who lived at the farm, Daniel Brass, once the yard-boy, but now a valued stockman and Kate Watson, the house servant. Before eating, as usual, Henry gave thanks to the Lord.

"We thank thee Lord, for all thy gifts to us, but especially for our food tonight eaten in peace and quiet. We thank you also for the kindness of our friend, Daniel, who, although not in The Light, has worked with us for many years, without complaint. He is a link between us and those who would persecute us, which allows us that peace and quiet." In the few minutes' silence that followed, Daniel blushed slightly as he sat with bowed head.

***

He had come to the Bowmans as an orphan thirteen years earlier. For most of that time he had been treated in the same way as their own sons, so that he now regarded them as the nearest he would ever get to his own parents. He had never ever considered that he might join the religion of his employers, thinking them very strange indeed in the way they worshipped, but he recognised that he could not work for more considerate or fair dealing people.

The Bowmans had made a request to him shortly after that beautiful May afternoon when Henry had spoken to Alice about how they would continue in their faith more discreetly. Since then Daniel had willingly carried out a further duty in addition to his work with the farm animals. As a resident member of the household, aged over sixteen years of age, he had represented the family once a month at the parish church. Lip service, but it was enough to protect the family from further persecution for non-attendance and evidence that the law in regard to church attendance was gradually being relaxed in small ways.

In many parishes a lot depended upon the good will of the priest. Henry and Alice's decision to be more restrained and discreet in their resistance to the established church had also resulted in their no longer being seen as threatening. It was a ploy practised by many religious non-conformists, especially as they grew older.

***

Much to the disgust of Elizabeth, whose bed she shared, Little Alice was sick in the night. More frightened than anything else, Little Alice burst into noisy tears, calling for her father. It was Alice who went to see to her youngest, but she could not soothe the child, who still insisted that she wanted Dad. Henry, reluctantly, got out of bed and went to the now almost hysterical child. She immediately quietened when she saw him and he held her in his arms while Alice changed the bedclothes and pacified Elizabeth, who had started to cry in unison with her sister. By the time the bed was clean again, Little Alice was asleep.

Now all was quiet once more save for the night sounds of owls in the nearby barns, the occasional eerie cry of a vixen and the familiar sound of the house cooling and settling down for the night. Elizabeth and Little Alice slept, back-to-back, the older with her open hand between pillow and right cheek, the younger with a well-sucked right thumb half an inch from her slightly open mouth.

Henry and Alice lay on their right sides, he behind her, his left arm around her waist, fitting together like two matching spoons, listening to the well-known sound of the house and the land outside. Alice was just in the time between sleeping and waking, but Henry was wide-awake after having been disturbed. He tried to settle himself by centring down, as he did in Meeting for Worship, but then it would have been in waiting for the promptings of the Lord, now it was simply a way to steady and soothe his mind.

Suddenly he thought, 'Today was the day they call Easter-Day,' He thought about a previous Easter-Day when Alice had harangued the priest in the steeple-house just at the moment most holy to him and his congregation. Henry, in gaol himself at the time, had been proud of her when he heard about her

228

protestation but feared for her too. She'd been pregnant with Susan. Susan born to be too small, too frail, too ill and so soon to die. What a time that had been. But his Alice had survived, even though she had been sick in body, mind and spirit, she'd survived. His Alice. His jewel. His pearl without price. He drew her closer to him and held her as she slept. She stirred slightly and made a small noise then was quiet again.

***

In her room at the Grange, Lucy Henderson was also lying in bed. At home she'd shared her bed with two younger sisters. She'd often wished that she could have a bed and a room to herself, now she missed her widowed mother and her sisters more than she could say.

She wondered what their reaction would have been if they had known of the wicked thoughts she'd allowed into her mind this morning in church. Her mother would have been bitterly disappointed in her oldest daughter who'd been brought up in a household where church attendance, although not slavishly practised, was regular. Lucy resolved never to tell her mother about her doubts. She also resolved never to entertain them again, but had misgivings as to whether she'd be able to.

Lucy's late father had been a moderately successful tailor. It was a customer of his who, hearing that his friend Abel Chinnock was looking for a respectable young woman to govern the education of his daughter and knowing of Mrs. Henderson's reduced circumstances, immediately recommended Lucy. Mrs. Henderson and her daughters had been delighted and it had proved to be a successful appointment. Lucy knew how lucky she was to have been accepted by such respectable and respected people who were always kind to her. She was aware of the contrast between her life and the unhappy existences of many young women from fatherless families who left home rather than be a financial burden on them.

It had taken a little while for Rosa to recover from the loss of the nurse-maid who had cared for her for so many years, but with patience, Lucy was able to capture her charge's imagination and interest, and in time a friendship developed which, although neither of them knew it, would last until old age.

Even so, there were times when dear Rosa could be very difficult. She had such strange ideas, being more interested in small creatures such as beetles and ants, even smaller creatures. She had asked for a 'glass' for Christmas, and her father had bought her an expensive looking-glass for the wall, but to his surprise, his little Rose had seemed disappointed with the gift. Her lack of appreciation hurt him but he laughed loud and long, when, after a little persuasion, she confessed that she had wanted a glass that made things look bigger. From his next visit to London he returned with a magnifying lens.

Lucy smiled, remembering. Rosa had pestered everyone she knew to observe things through her glass and taken huge delight in the reactions of some of them to the sight of enormous wasps, flies and beetles which she had found in the gardens around The Grange. And not unexpectedly, it mattered not where she was or what she was doing, the child always seemed to have dirty hands and face, or a smudge or stain on her clothes.

Lucy sighed.

And yet, and yet. Rosa could be so warm-hearted and delightful when the mood was upon her. There'd been that initial stiffness between the twins when Joe, with special permission, came home from school for their birthday, two years earlier. Within a day or two they'd settled back into their former happy friendship, but it was not to last. Less than a week later Joe had to return to the school that he hated. He came home for a week at Christmas the same year and things were easier, with the twins spending much of their time together.

When Joe had returned to school after Christmas, Rosa had been very subdued and sometimes inclined to weepiness, apparently for no reason. Eventually Lucy managed to pierce the wall of silent sadness between them and Rosa, in a burst of tears, expressed the wish that she could go away to school too. Joe hated his lessons, but she yearned to learn "about everything" as she put it.

Lucy hadn't wished to lose her own position, but knowing how Rosa felt, she'd thought it was only fair that she should take Rosa with her and tell her employer about his daughter's aspirations. As she'd expected his answer had been a firm "No!"

Later, as tenderly as he knew how Abel explained to Rosa that Lucy's instruction in all matters was perfectly adequate. Indeed it was more than adequate; it was excellent. Rosabella, dear little rose that she was, must understand how lucky she was to have such a teacher and friend. She should also know that for a girl from such a family as theirs, to go away to school was out of the question. If there had been one, she could have attended a local Dame School, but none was available and that must be the end of the matter. With that Rosa, suppressing her tears, curtsied to her father and her mother, who had been hovering anxiously in the background, and ran out of the room followed by Lucy.

This Easter time, the Chinnock family were looking forward to later in the year, to the autumn, when Joe would be coming home, this time never to return to the hated school. From Michaelmas, by which time he and his sister would be thirteen years old, he would begin to work for Abel who hoped that the time his son had spent being educated would at least mean that he could help his father with the farm accounts.

***

Ridge Farm slept under a clear starry night presided over by the waning Easter moon, where Alice lay safe in the bend of Henry's arm. She had not been unaware of the significance of the day. With the strange telepathy of those who know well the working of a dear one's mind, be it parent, wife, husband, friend, brother or sister, at the same time as Henry, she, too had been thinking of that morning when, disregarding her pregnancy, she had raced down the aisle of the church full of furious fervour.

She rarely thought about that time, or the times which

followed. It was dangerous. The fear and confusion, sadness and despair, had turned her mind in the weeks and months following her arrest and it could turn again. She was thinking now of the poor, weak, demented creature she had been when Henry and Harry came to bring her home to her family.

She felt shame, now, that she could have distressed them all so much. Then Henry's arm slid between her left arm and her waist before curving, comfortably firm, around her. 'Safe,' she thought, 'Safe and sound.'

She slept.

* * *

She was standing on the ridge, looking down at the farm, watching Henry and the boys working. They were haymaking. For a moment she thought, 'It's the wrong time of the year,'

Then she saw that her husband and family were not working alone. Other people were there, not Daniel and the other farm hands.

Then the strangers turned and saw her, and she wasn't standing on the ridge anymore, she was nearer, and they were nearer; the Justice, smiling cruelly, and Goody Barton, with her hand out, asking for food.

Nearer still they came. The Constable, from the Meeting at the Buxton's, the soldiers, the stamping horses.

And she was at the relentlessly spinning wheel, with every tensed muscle in her body on fire.

And Susan, little dead Susan, was crying.

She tried to run to Henry, as he lifted and turned the hay, with a steady and easy rhythm, but her legs were leaden.

She tried to call him, but had no strength to her voice.

* * *

"Henry!"

Alice's waking scream for help tore through the house, waking everybody.

Harry racing down from the loft, thrust aside the curtain which separated his parent's sleeping place from the house-room and saw them, sitting up in bed, Henry with his arms tight around a weeping, shaking Alice, rocking her gently. He lifted his head from where his cheek had been resting on the top of her head and said to Harry, "Settle everyone down again, and go back to bed, son. Thy mother had a bad dream. There is nothing to concern thee here."

And he went back to comforting his wife.

CHAPTER THIRTY-THREE

Tuesday, January 20th 1680

Joseph Chinnock was enduring work in the farm office and Rosa, in the parlour with Ruth and Lucy, was, with equal fortitude struggling with the sampler she had started three years ago when she was twelve. Mrs. Denny was organising the household staff who now numbered five.

Ruth, with time on her hands, looked around herself for something to do. She'd tried to take up her own embroidery but cast it aside after about three minutes. She felt unsettled and unhappy. She rebuked herself mentally for her discontent, telling herself she had much to be grateful for. Staring out of the window, she felt somewhat ashamed of herself for her inability to cope with the problem that underlined all her agitation.

Abel, not knowing what was wrong, had suggested to her that she was tired but she knew that wasn't so. The fact was that Lucy, dear Lucy, was the root of Ruth's troubles at the moment. Always a quiet girl and now grown into a quiet woman, Lucy was the epitome of loyalty and conscientiousness, but a slow though definite change was taking place in her character. It was nothing that Ruth could pinpoint other than that there was a frustrating submissiveness about Lucy which had not been evident before.

A turning point had been reached on the morning of the Christmas just past. Lucy had refused to go to Church. On one of the two most holy days of the year, Easter and Christmas, when everyone must receive the Sacrament, Lucy had refused even to attend church, let alone take Communion.

Ruth was at first scandalised then she wept at Lucy's fall from grace. Abel had spluttered somewhat before retiring to his office until time to go to church. Rosa and Joe had stared at one another, astonished. Mistress Denny had been horror-stricken, and stated that the girl should be dismissed without a character.

The rest of the day had passed without Lucy's presence. She shut herself in her room and did not emerge until the following day, when she took up her duties with Rosa. This she did as if nothing had happened. She was quietly cheerful, as had become her habit.

Lucy was not domestic staff and so was not Mrs. Denny's responsibility. Ruth hated conflict of any kind and rarely rebuked any of the servants, but she knew that action of some kind ought to be taken and she herself must take it. She only knew one family, even if it was only slightly, who did not go to church. There was only one woman to whom she could confide her feelings without risk of incriminating herself.

She would visit her. This very day. Now.

***

Ten-year-old Elizabeth Bowman and sister Little Alice, aged seven, were sitting on the floor playing with a toy wooden dog which John Taylor had carved for their brother Richard about two years earlier, when there were the sounds of horses' hooves on the yard. Alice looked up from the dough she was kneading. She wasn't expecting anyone and the clatter of hooves always provoked remembrances of previous fears.

With a finger to her lip, she cautioned the girls to silence and moved over to the window, concealing herself as much as possible. Looking out to see who the visitor was, it was with mixed feelings of relief and irritation that she recognised Ruth Chinnock. She had never been to the house before. "What does she want?" she muttered to herself as she went over to open the door.

Ruth had ridden pillion behind John Denny, the stable hand, who was assisting her to dismount. She stood in the yard, uncertain of what her reception would be. Alice's expression was not welcoming and she didn't speak to her visitor, only moved to one side to allow her visitor into the house.

The two women stood looking at one another for a few seconds until Ruth, embarrassed by the silence, decided to open the conversation. Blushing deeply, she said. "Good morning, Mistress - " and before she could continue Alice reminded her, tersely, "My name is Alice." Ruth, a little upset by the interruption, which she thought ill mannered, was surprised into saying her own name, "Ruth." in a perfect imitation of the Quaker woman's tone.

Alice held out her hand for Ruth to shake then led her over to the table motioning to her to sit down, while she continued to knead the dough.

Ruth cleared her throat. "I hope you and your family are well?" She glanced towards the little girls playing by the fire, "What beautiful children," she said.

Alice allowed herself a small smile. In her innermost heart she knew she had beautiful children but always reminded herself that such credit was due to the Lord's will, not to herself or Henry

Ruth was waiting for a reply. Alice, awkwardly, said, "My husband is well, thanks be to God, although he sometimes suffers with the cough. My children, too, are all well, thank the Lord."

There followed a short silence during which the fire crackled, Elizabeth and Little Alice talked and laughed quietly between themselves as they played cat's cradle and the toy dog lay forgotten on the floor.

Ruth turned her attention from the bright flames of the fire and turned to look at Alice and once again timid blue eyes met unwavering brown.

"I think Lucy is becoming a Quaker!"

The words burst from her. She felt immediately that she'd not approached the matter properly. She'd said it wrongly. She'd made it sound as if Lucy had some dreadful disease - which, in some way, she had. At least the effects could be almost as bad. Could kill her, in fact.

Alice's response was unexpected. "I know," she said calmly. "She's been visiting us on occasion and asking us questions. She's been welcome at the Meetings for Worship which are held in this house."

Ruth gasped. Such meetings were illegal. Lucy, with everyone else attending, was taking a great risk. She thought it was possible that even she herself may be in danger simply by being in the house. She was so shocked that Alice noticed the sudden pallor of her usually pink cheeks and quickly she found a chair for Ruth to sit on, while she recovered.

Ruth eventually found words to express her concern and dismay. "Lucy was brought up in the Church. She was confirmed by the Bishop and took Communion at least once a month." She paused. "Until recently." Then she continued. "She always seemed so devout, a true member of the Church." Ruth shook her head. "I didn't know that she was having doubts. I thought she believed what we believed."

Alice divided the dough into six equal loaves and set them by the fire to rise. She was unsure as to how to deal with Ruth's distress and tried to console her, while not, at the same time, betraying her own beliefs.

"We believe in the Truth of God's presence in every man," she said, simply, when she returned to the table. "We believe that the Church is too concerned with ritual, the cup and the bread, the vestments, all the worldly richness that's in there. We believe God speaks to us directly and we to Him, in the spirit - "

Ruth flinched, ready to get up from the chair and leave this house of blasphemy but couldn't, for the power of Alice's certainty. This was a Truth that she was unwilling to hear. It wasn't the Truth as she knew it. Alice sat down again and there was silence for a few moments. Even the little girls were quiet now, listening interestedly to the grown-up's conversation, though understanding little of it.

Then Ruth regained her confidence, small though she knew it to be. She felt that she must retaliate for the sake of her own beliefs. "But we believe that we are the true religion," she said. "The Rector is the one who prays to God for us. We're not worthy enough to speak to Him ourselves. We can only approach him through the Rector. The beautiful things in the church are there in praise of God."

There was silence for a while, then Alice looked at Ruth almost shyly and said, hesitatingly, "I can understand that we both strongly believe that what we think is right. We both pray to the same God but you require a priest's intercession. We need no intercession. We are friends who cannot agree on this one thing. But we can still be friends who must each follow what we think is right. We believe in different Truths and will come to the same end."

***

Later that day Ruth told Lucy about her visit to Alice at Ridge Farms and spoke gently to her about her attendance at Quaker Meetings, saying only that she must take care.

ഇ ന്ദ

CHAPTER THIRTY-FOUR

Thursday, January 26th 1682

Quakers refused to bury their dead in Churchyards. A few Friends had bequeathed ground to use for funerals, but if no Quaker burial ground was available, Friends used their own land. The nearest burial ground was about 10 miles away from Branslow and Joan Webb's husband, William, was unwilling for Friends to have to travel so far in inclement weather.

He prepared to bury his dead wife in the garden she had tended for many years.

Luke Carter, one of Branslow's two Constables, had been told about the proposed burial by an informer, so he took advantage of the opportunity to harass and cause trouble for Quakers by relaying the information to the Rector, Thomas Fletcher.

William was being comforted by Friends, including John Taylor and Henry and Alice Bowman, when the Reverend Fletcher banged on the door, and demanded entrance. For the next hour the Rector attempted to persuade the grieving widower to bury his wife in the churchyard. When his bullying proved to be unsuccessful, he retaliated by telling William that he would still have to pay the church's usual burial fee, just that same as if he had used the churchyard. His last words before he left the house, had been to tell William that if he didn't use the churchyard, his wife's body would be seized by the Constables and buried somewhere in a ditch.

When John Taylor went to Peter to report it, about it a week or two after the funeral, he'd said, "I'd gone to see Will to console him on 'is wife's death and 'eard the priest saying these cruel things to 'im. I also 'eard the priest say, 'I would rather see all you heretics hanged, than lose one sixpence of my fee because of you.'"

Peter and John had exchanged resigned looks across the table.

"Even in death, we are not free of the church's torment," Peter said.

"But that's not the end of it, Peter," John continued. "The priest and 'is wardens got to know about the night funeral was to 'appen and on that night they sat in the house opposite, watching for most of the night. They'd wanted to catch us as we took the poor woman to 'er grave which we'd dug at the side of the 'ouse. But somebody 'ad told Will that we was being informed on, so the day was changed and after a quiet Meeting in the 'ouse, to keep 'er out of the 'ands of the church we buried 'er in a grave we dug 'astily in the back garden, without them knowing."

Peter, who hadn't been able to attend the funeral, nodded his head, " And now, six days later, poor Will is dead, and buried next to his dear wife." he said.

John was close to tears now and Elizabeth, who had been sitting spinning and talking to Mary, John's wife, saw his distress. She came over to him and laid her hand on his shoulder. "Dear Friend," she said, "Try not to trouble thyself too much, both are at rest now."

"I know that's true," said John, his eyes full of tears, "And I'm glad for their sakes. But so much trouble and disturbance over two of our peaceable people -."

Elizabeth went into the kitchen and returned with two cups of small ale which she placed on the table before the men, before returning to her spinning and Mary. John drank thirstily, then went on, "'Umphrey Woolrich was there and after the burial 'e prayed and preached about death and the uncertainty of life, but it was so fine and good, that we were uplifted, even though it was such a sad occasion."

He took another mouthful of beer, wiped his mouth and carried on. "But what we didn't know was that those cursed Church Wardens - "

Peter stiffened; John should not have used such strong

words about men made in God's image. Understanding Peter's reaction, John shook his head.

"I'm sorry for speaking so strong, Peter," he continued, "But they'd bin 'iding behind the 'edge again, watching. They went and reported to Justice Sneyd that there'd been an Unlawful Conventicle, as they call it, because 'Umphrey had prayed and preached."

***

There had been no doubt that Humphrey and anyone else present at the funeral would be fined, but Justice William Sneyd was known as a lenient man of moderate disposition, not unsympathetic to Quakers. The general feeling of Friends was that he had been unwillingly forced to prosecute by the priest. In due course the Justice dealt out fines ranging from as low as five shillings to some Friends, although Humphrey Woolrich's fine was twenty pounds for unlicensed preaching.

After the Court hearing Justice Sneyd's amiability was proved when he advised those who objected to the fines to appeal at the next Sessions, when he would see that they had their fines refunded.

One Friend, William Morgan, took him at his word, appealed and his fine of forty shillings was duly returned. This irritated the prosecuting priest so much, that he decided to take his revenge upon Humphrey Woolrich. The path he chose was the well-trodden one of ordering Humphrey to swear the Oath of Allegiance. Humphrey refused and was, inevitably, imprisoned.

John thought ruefully, 'Perhaps those who didn't claim their money back had the right idea.'

***

Like every other member of the Quaker community, the Bowman family were appalled by the incidents during the funerals of Joan and William Webb and the aftermath, even though disruption of funerals was not uncommon. The horror of it all had affected Alice profoundly and for a few weeks she was troubled by dark dreams from which she awoke with her heart pounding in her chest, unable to remember what demons had invaded her sleep.

Eventually she was able to overcome her fears, but she determined that such troubles would not attend her family's burials.

෨෬

CHAPTER THIRTY-FIVE

Tuesday, July 8th 1684

Two years later, recalling the incident and John's distress, Peter sighed. He was sitting on a stool at the small cluttered table by the window in the house room. As an Elder and Clerk to the Meeting it had been necessary, from time to time, for this precious space in the crowded house to be used for Society of Friends' matters. Minutes were usually written down as the Quarterly Meetings for business progressed, with Peter, as Clerk, occasionally asking for Friends to pause in their speaking to give him time to catch up with them.

Since 1677 he had become even more familiar with procedure at the County and Magistrates Courts, and with other Elders of the Meeting he now visited them on a regular basis as an observer and recorder of proceedings.

Today he was copying Friends' reports of their persecution and sufferings into a new book recently bought for the purpose. Giving himself a break from this necessary but depressing work, he leaned forward on his elbows and looked out of the window across the yard. A few fowl were scratching about and beyond them, in the field the last remaining hay stooks were drying before being taken to store in the barn. It was a glorious day, warm and sunny, the sight of it was in contrast to what he was writing about the cruel treatment of Friends.

With another sigh, before he returned to his work he glanced through the previous year's reports.

Hugh Ford, for non-attendance at church, had had a heifer taken, valued at one pound six shillings and eightpence in lieu of fines.

William Haywood and his wife for two instances of the same offence had lost two loads each of wheat and rye, valued at twentyfour shillings. In the same year, for non-payment of tithes, they'd had four pewter dishes taken, worth six shillings. Later still, for three further offences of not attending church, the bailiffs had taken away three loads of barley, worth eight shillings and sixpence, cheeses worth five shillings and one pound twelve shillings worth of barley and oats.

Samuel Sneyd, Richard Simpson and his wife and John Hall, all suffered loss of household goods and crops for refusing to pay the fines demanded for not attending the hated Steeple-house.

Peter had also recorded that he and his wife had been fined ten shillings for attending an illegal Meeting for the second time. They had refused to pay, so goods were taken from each of them to the value of one pound, twice the value of the fine.

Peter felt disappointed that an appeal for reports of persecution had only produced these few examples. It was only a few of the many who had suffered because they chose to worship God in a different way to the majority of people. It was unfortunate, but understandable, that they had chosen not to make public what had happened to them. It was quite natural, Peter supposed; they probably were reluctant to make any fuss or draw attention to themselves or their Meeting.

***

Because of the 1670 Conventicles Act forbidding religious Meeting Houses, many Quakers, like the Bowmans, while still practising the principles of Quakerism at home and in their working life, chose to observe silent Meetings for Worship at home with their families and Friends.

Others continued to risk using buildings used exclusively for Meetings, because even the small degree of secrecy implied by Meetings in private houses, was against their Quaker principles. These Meeting Houses were often occupied by Friends acting as wardens, but despite their presence, and various Acts of Indulgence or Tolerance declared by the King, Meetings were still in danger of being disturbed.

Two days ago Peter had been present at the incident in Stafford, which he was now about to record. He took up his quill and began to write in his large, well-formed, though untidy, hand.

6 5th.m. 1684

'We being Mett in the street peaceable before our Meeting House door, which by order of the Mayor was Locked up (to prevent our Assembling there) and as we were standing quietly together came with constables sergeants and wardens, Leese, the Mace Barer, who, to manifest his continued Envy, took away Peter Littleton afore the Mayor and pulled the stools from under some ancient women who, for their support and ease had got a few to sitt upon, and cast them about the street, and then returning to the Mayor with many invections in his mouth against us, told him he would turn informer and command the Justice of Peace upon the penalty of an 100 shillings, and offered to sware the peace against Peter Littleton if the Mayor would but tender it to him: With many more scurrilous expressions too many here to recognise, it is likewise to be noted that Leese did sware the peace Maliciously against some of our Friends...'

Once more an informer had been at work, in this case one had actually attended the Meeting in the guise of spectator. When asked to by Leese, unaccountably he had refused to swear that there had been any unlicensed preaching. Leese became angry and declared that if nobody else would, he himself would swear that there had been.

Those present viewed his threat to commit the sin of perjury in order to bring a case against Quakers as a sure sign that he preferred damaging them to the safety of a good

245

conscience. Some Friends had attempted to persuade Leese against his action and he'd fallen into a rage, calling Friends dogs and rogues.

During the disturbance, the stable door was broken down and one Friend's mare was taken, but returned before the thief could be prosecuted.

The next day warrants were issued to break into the Littleton's house and barn. Household goods including bedding were taken away and the next day the same officers removed all the remaining property, including fire-irons and cooking utensils, work tools and a parcel of chaff from the barn. The value of these goods was ten pounds, to cover six convictions of Peter and Elizabeth.

Peter turned from his writing to look across the room to where Elizabeth tended two of the elderly woman who'd been treated so badly. One of them had fallen to the ground when the stool had been pulled from under her, landing heavily on her right wrist and breaking her collarbone. The other had large bruises on her left shoulder and hip. Both of them had been severely shocked, firstly by the disturbance and then by the rough handling they'd received. As he watched his wife Peter thought, 'How does she stay so calm?' He was remembering the younger Elizabeth who worried so much. 'She has grown stronger with years and adversity.' For a moment she looked up at him, they exchanged smiles before each returned to their tasks.

໐໐

CHAPTER THIRTY-SIX

Friday, December 10th 1686

Alice Bowman often thought about the funerals of Joan and William Webb, but in common with busy women the world over, other things had got in the way during the intervening two years. Now the subject was becoming more important.

Henry, who had remained strong in mind and faith, had never properly regained his bodily strength since his repeated terms of imprisonment and his recovery from gaol fever. He'd suffered from recurrent winter chest infections before and invariably recovered, even though each time he was a little weaker. But this year, since the middle of November he'd been unable to 'get the better of it', as he said.

It was nearly midnight. Richard, the only Bowman son not yet to have married and set up his own home, was asleep in his bed under the eaves. His two younger sisters, Elizabeth, sixteen, and Little Alice, thirteen, slept in their curtained off part of the house room, unaware that Hester, the oldest sister remaining at home, was still awake.

Henry Bowman, sitting up in bed with pillows behind his back, slept, but lightly. Alice sat at his side. At this time of the day she would usually have been occupying herself with mending torn clothes, knitting stockings or spinning, but tonight all she wanted to do was look at her husband as he lay. He was thin and every breath was hard come by, his mouth open as even in sleep, he gasped for air.

She'd given him a posset of figs, liquorice and aniseed for his cough and a small amount of poppy to help him sleep.

Holding his nearest hand in hers, she thought, 'Thee will not be buried where any priest can have dominion over thee. I'll see to that, my love'. At that moment he opened his eyes, smiled at her and said, "I think I feel a little better, now, Alice. I think I'd like a drink and something to eat."

***

A few days later Henry showed more signs of improvement, but Alice hadn't forgotten her unspoken promise to him and a few days later, when she felt that she could safely leave him for an hour or two in care of nineteen-year-old Hester, she began to put her plan into action. It started with a walk across the fields.

ഇൽ ൽ

CHAPTER THIRTY-SEVEN

Monday, December 27th 1686

Harry had finished feeding the inside animals and was preparing to take advantage of the quieter time of year and sit for a while by the warm fire in the kitchen, before going home to his own wife and family. He was intercepted by his mother before he could enter the house.

"Don't take thy boots off yet, Harry. Come with me," she called across the yard, "I've got something to show thee." And, not waiting for his reply, she set off at a smart pace through the gate and along the track. Henry, frustrated, changed course and ran to catch up with her.

"Where are we going, Mam?" he panted when he reached her side.

Alice didn't answer. This was not a matter to be discussed. Her decision was made and Harry was only being involved because when the time came his presence would be necessary.

Harry knew better than to press the point. As they walked away from the house, he was curious to know what his mother had in mind, but Alice was clearly not about to tell him. She strode on, not speaking, intent on putting her plan into action.

A couple of fields from the house was a row of elm trees, empty now of leaves, their branches reaching high and wide into the winter sky. They grew on the eastern side of a piece of land, about 16 yards square, enclosed in a stone wall. It was full of rough grass and thistles, having not been cultivated for a number of years. It was part of a purchase Henry had made some years before, but had proved unsuitable for crops or grazing. There had been attempts to improve the quality of the soil when he had first acquired it, but he'd given up after a while. Sometimes they put the donkeys on it and it was kept as a spare temporary holding area for the sheep before bringing them under cover or sorting them for the market.

When they reached it Alice leaned on the wall and looked out over the field. "It's a sorrowful piece of land," she said, "But it's quiet, the trees shelter it and it's of little use for anything, but it'll be fine for my purpose." Without turning round she said to Harry, "What dost thee think?"

Harry was puzzled. He leaned on the wall beside her, "What have I to think about, Mam?" he said.

"A burial ground for Friends," was the reply. The tone of her voice didn't invite argument, but she had asked Harry for his opinion. She hadn't mentioned her plan to any member of her family, so the suggestion took Harry by surprise. He thought for a moment, then, "It's a long way from the lane, Mam," he said. "That narrow stone stile will have to go. Friends can't carry coffins over it -"

"We'll widen it and put a gate in," Alice interrupted. There was a determined expression on her face and her movements were impatient as she straightened up. "That's decided then," she said. "We'll see an attorney tomorrow and make it legal." She was making her way back towards the house, "Come on, Harry," she said as, once more, her son hurried to catch up with her.

When they parted at the yard gate Alice turned to Harry and said in a low, shaking voice, "I'll not have what happened to Joan and Bill Webb happen to my Henry." As mother and son stood in the yard there was the sudden rush of wings above them and they looked up to see the ghostly white mask and wings of a barn own setting out on it's night-hunt, lit by a bright moon in a dark sky.

Harry, in a rare show of affection, embraced his mother and kissed her, before saying goodnight and preparing to walk home.

***

Early the next day Harry and Cornelius set about taking out the half-buried and heavy stones of the stile and enlarging the entrance to the field. In the barn at Ridge Farm, Richard started to make the wooden gate to replace the stile. It was hard work for all of them and the weather was bitter but by sunset most of the initial outside work on making the entrance to the plot was done.

The work continued for the next week or so, with Alice dividing her time between the two sites when her household duties allowed, offering advice which was accepted gracefully and ignored, or bread, cheese and beer which they accepted gratefully and devoured.

Henry was mildly curious about their activities but asked no questions. He was too tired. Alice had that determined look about her which could presage anything from a special baked goose for dinner on a family member's birthday, to the annual, dreaded, thorough cleaning of the house. Any way, Christmas was coming and although the family did not celebrate Christ's birth, they took advantage of the opportunity to show their affection for each other with small gifts. Henry smiled to himself at the thought

ॐ

CHAPTER THIRTY-EIGHT

Monday, January 4th 1686/7

Alice and Harry drove home from the town, where they'd conveyed a deed of gift of a parcel of land for a burial ground 'for the use of the people called Quakers', to Friends and Trustees, John Hall and John Mellor.

Henry knew nothing about it until three weeks later, dying, he whispered to Alice as she lay by his side on the bed cradling him in her arms, "Don't let the priests know, Alice." She stroked his face, "Oh no, my love," she said. "Thee will rest in a place made specially for thee." As he looked up at her waiting for the explanation, she smiled at him and told him of the place, not far away, quiet, guarded by the elm trees, under the sun in summer, and the snow in winter.

"The skylarks will sing to thee," she said, "And the leaves on the trees will whisper in thine ears."

Henry closed his eyes for a while. When he opened them he asked, "Where are the children?"

"They're here," Alice replied and beckoned them to the bedside, then she rose from her place at his side and went to compose herself by busy-ness at the fire. Harry, Ellen, Cornelius, Hester, Richard, Elizabeth and Little Alice came to the bedside one by one, bade their father goodbye and kissed him before returning to their seats.

Henry died, quietly and gently, about half an hour later with his wife at his side. He was buried in the quiet field guarded by the elm trees during a Meeting for Burial attended by his wife, their many children and Quaker Friends.

80 03

CHAPTER THIRTY-NINE

Saturday, March 9th 1690

Abel and Ruth Chinnock sat in their customary chairs on each side of the hearth, where the fire was burning low. Ruth dozed as she leaned back in the chair, with her arms elbows resting on the arms of her chair and her hands drooping towards her lap, where her embroidery lay.

Abel raised his eyes from the almanac and regarded her affectionately. 'Why,' he thought, ' She must be fifty-something now.' He smiled to himself. He hadn't noticed the passage of time. Another thought occurred to him, as he did a rapid mental calculation. The result shocked him.

"I'm seventy-four!" he said out loud. Ruth stirred and opened her eyes, "What did you say my dear?" she asked. "I'm seventy-four!" Abel repeated. "I know, my dear," she said drowsily. She closed her eyes, settling back into her nap, saying, "Seventy-four. Well I never."

Her lack of concern didn't hurt his feelings, or intrude any further upon his thoughts. He realised that he'd now been married longer to Ruth than he'd been to his first wife. He was a grandfather to eleven children whose names he could only with difficulty remember, but knew it was five boys and six girls.

Earlier this year his little Rose, though still retaining her unladylike interest in creeping things, or grains of sand, or snowflakes, anything in fact which she could marvel over through her magnifying glass, had actually got married to the son of one of Abel's friends. As it happened, James Cosgill had the same strange interests as Rosa and sometimes Abel and Ruth found it difficult to understand anything either of the young couple talked about, but James was a good man and would be kind to Abel's little Rose, who had, of course, been the most beautiful bride ever. He chuckled. Whenever he thought of her, seeing in his mind's eye the little Rose whose two cupped hands would open to show her shocked mother a caterpillar or a ladybird crawling over her skin.

He looked again at Ruth. She'd been to see that Bowman woman again today. He'd also met her once or twice, but had always felt slightly uneasy in Alice's company. He felt that at any moment she would become the madwoman of that long ago Easter Day. Ruth, who at the time had been greatly upset by the incident, now counted Alice not an acquaintance, but a friend, although they still met only occasionally.

ଚ୍ଚ ଓଷ

CHAPTER FORTY

Saturday, August 30th 1690

Alice's health had been deteriorating for the last three or four months and Ruth had been visiting her more often. The visits had been short, with Alice not always seeming to appreciate them, but Ruth had become used to her strange friend's abrupt manner, knowing that it concealed a more sensitive nature than Alice would usually admit to. Both knew the value of their understanding of each other.

When Ruth visited her on this sultry summer afternoon, Alice was ill, so ill, in fact, that she had not risen from her bed for some time. This was unheard of in the Bowman family; Alice was always the strong one, the one who looked after everyone else in the family. Now it was she who was causing some concern.

She'd lost some of her enthusiasm for life for a while after Henry had died, but eventually had seemed to recover. It was only since the beginning of November last year that she'd been forced to take to her bed more often. Her joints were painful due to a lifetime of excessively hard and heavy work, often in cold and damp conditions. In addition, with the onset of winter she'd developed a cough and chest pains. With the beginning of the warmer weather, she'd seemed to recover as much of her health as could be expected of a woman of her age, but it was a short respite before all her symptoms returned at the end of July after helping with the hay harvest.

Ruth was worried when she saw how her friend's health had deteriorated but heartened when she realised that though her body was visibly weakened, Alice's spirit was still strong. As she sat on the chair by the side of Alice's bed in the house room they spoke together of general things, each other's families mostly, then Alice, sitting supported by pillows, beckoned Ruth nearer to her.

"I've made my Will. Last November, when I could tell how things were going with me. It's best to prepare," she said, her voice dropping to a hoarse whisper. "All my children are to benefit. They've all worked hard to make the farm thrive and they shall share what there is."

Alice paused, thinking about past family conflict and a trace of her former severity was in her voice when she said. "Even Ellen."

Ruth was surprised at this, knowing that this daughter had caused the family much heartache when she'd 'married out'. Alice continued, her voice strained through the wheezing in her chest.

"She shall have her share but I've made sure that her husband shan't get hold of it." She shifted position on the straw-filled mattress in an attempt to relieve the pain in her knees and hips before she spoke again.

"I expect that Ellen will be allowed back to the Meeting in time. It nearly always happens to those who have been cast out, after a while." She smiled up at Ruth, 'To forgive is divine,'" she quoted. "My sons shall be well provided for and all my daughters shall have marriage portions."

She closed her eyes, obviously tired and Ruth was rising from the chair, preparing to leave, when Alice called her back. She caught hold of Ruth's hand and said, simply, "Thee has been a good friend to me, Ruth."

Ruth replied, "And you to me, Alice."

Then, with quiet and affectionate words of farewell to Harry, Ellen, Cornelius, Hester, Richard and Elizabeth, Ruth left the house, never to see Alice again before she died the following month.

She was always to think of her sometimes-unpredictable friend as one of the most precious memories in her life.

Monday, December 29th 1692
And now she was witness to the passing of another great

heart. Alice Bowman's other friend was Elizabeth Littleton. Ruth had met her occasionally over the years and Lucy had told her of Peter Littleton's death. It was by chance that his funeral procession was making its way through Branslow, when Ruth and Abel were returning from an evening visit to Rosa and James.

On horseback or on foot, the solemn line of expressionless, black-clad Quakers followed the coffin as it made its way through the town watched by curious onlookers. Abel and Ruth, Tom and Grace Wells, and non-Quaker Robert Davis, who worked as odd job man and labourer for the Littletons, stood respectfully quiet as the mourners passed.

Dai Davis, Robert's father, was there with his friends Eddie Morris and George Palmer. George still held bitter memories of the way Quakers had disrupted his life and he, with many other people watching, had cause to hate the Quakers. The three friends stood silent, each with their own thoughts. Others in the street were openly derisive. Catcalls and missiles, thrown from the small crowd, were ignored and in the face of such passive reaction, the crowd's interest fell away and most people left, to go about their business.

Elizabeth walked behind her husband's coffin thinking of their life together. She was finding it difficult to believe that her tall, strong, robust man could be lying in the box being carried before her. It didn't look big enough. But it was true. She was on her own. They'd no children living. She'd no relatives nearby to help her, although Peter's cousins had been very kind to her. She'd no idea of what she should do after the funeral; no idea of her duties and responsibilities as executrix of his will. She felt truly bereft.

Looking up for a moment, she found herself staring into the face of Ruth Chinnock. They smiled, briefly and shakily at each other.

Ruth thought, 'I'll visit her in a few days. When she's settled a little'.

Quietly, sternly, stoically, the procession moved through Branslow and out past the Ockenden's cottage, and the

Johnson's, towards the place near the Bowman's steading, where Peter Littleton was to be laid to rest.

ଛୋ ଓଞ

CHAPTER FORTY-ONE

Thursday, January 5th 1693

The Advent wreath had been removed from the sanctuary of St. James' church, to be replaced by holly boughs tied with red ribbons for Christmas. They, in turn, had now been removed. The church, dark and quiet, settled itself down to wait until the preparation for the next festival, Easter. The evening was cold, crisp with frost, weaving a wreath of mist, around the square tower. The churchyard surrounding the church lay peacefully in the light of the frost-bright moonlight.

During the day the Wassailers had toured Branslow and the neighbouring villages, performing their unchanging ritual, being greeted by most people as a familiar ending to the Christmas season. Their reception at The Grange had been warm and hospitable, as usual, although Joe Chinnock took the place of his father, as Abel was feeling a little unwell. He admitted that it was partly due to age and partly due to a surfeit of enjoyment. Joe performed his duties well and seemed to relish his role as deputy head of the household.

The procession through Branslow had passed without incident, although there had been one or two sour looks for some individuals. The general opinion of the team was that they must be some of those Quaker people, but they'd caused no trouble.

In their stone cottage near the mill, John and Mary Taylor, born Johnson, heard the music and laughter, passing no comment. Their three children were woken from their sleep as they lay under the roof.

"What's that?" the youngest, four-year old Charles, whispered.

"It's those 'eathen Wassailers, Charlie," the eldest, John Junior, thirteen, told him.

"What's Wassailers?"

"You remember them from last year. They're 'eathens. Bad people. They play fiddles and drums and dance about like savages."

Joanna, nine years old, irritated by her brothers' chatter in the middle of the night, turned over with as much fuss and noise as she could manage, before saying, "I like it. It's - It's cheerful."

"It's wicked," said John Junior, dourly. He was disappointed in his sister. All three children were normally of rather solemn and dignified behaviour, but here Joanna was disagreeing with him.

Joanna sat up. "They said Dad was wicked when they sent him to prison for not going to church," she countered. "And we know he isn't. So p'raps the Wassailers aren't either."

"Shut up." said John Junior. "Thee wasn't even born then and I was only three, so what dost thee know?"

"How old was I?" asked Charlie.

"Go to sleep," said John Junior.

***

Their children's conversation was overheard by their parents, who smiled at each other. Neither spoke for a few seconds, then John said,

"Dost thee miss it, Mary?"

"What?" came the reply, although Mary knew what was in John's mind.

"The music. When thee joined the Meeting, thee wasn't free to enjoy it any more." He paused, then continued. "And thee liked to dance." Mary looked into John's eyes.

"I married thee because I love thee, John. It was no 'ardship to join the Meeting. I 'ave no regrets. We 'ave three children, after waiting a long time for them. All of 'em seem to be growing up with minds of their own, but loving the Lord. My 'usband is a man well-like and respected for the quality of 'is work, 'is honesty and uprightness and who loves me in return."

Mary stood up and walked over to John. Taking his hands, she raised him from his seat and said again, smiling. "I 'ave no regret, John."

***

The day finished at the Green Man. George Palmer had returned to the Wassailers a couple of years after the trouble with Frances had settled down. He, Eddie Morris, Dai Davis and his son Robert were still in their greenery, except for the black face paint, which they'd washed off. Now they removed their headdresses.

For George it was a double celebration.

Frances still lived in Dorset, but was now married to a modestly successful farmer's son. She'd recently given birth to a fourth child, their first boy. All the Wassailers, probably all the village, knew of George's daughter; he told anybody who would listen about her personable husband and their children. Many of George's acquaintances, although perhaps not going so far as to cross the road to avoid him, certainly tried to avoid accidentally giving him the chance to sing, yet again, the praises of his daughter and her family. Tonight, like all the Wassailers, George glowed with goodwill and a good supply of ale drunk on their procession around Branslow.

Brothers Humphrey and Billy Yates, who'd each beaten the drum as Pippit when they were small boys, now joined the rest after taking Humphrey's small son, Young 'Umphrey, back home to his mother, Joan Mason 'as was'. Six years old, with curly red hair and large brown eyes, Young 'Umphrey had become over-excited and exhausted after his first appearance as the new Pippit.

As Humphrey and Billy sat down the older men nodded affably in their direction.

"All right, is 'e?" asked Eddie Morris, who'd been secretly worried by Young 'Umphrey's tears. After taking a draught from his leather blackjack, Humphrey nodded and Eddie carried on.

"'E enjoyed 'imself, did 'e? Humphrey put down the half-empty blackjack and wiped his mouth with the back of his hand.

"Ah," he said. "'E'll never be as good as our Billy was, though."

"Oh no, our 'Umphrey," Billy protested. "There'll never be another one as good as you!" The two brothers grinned at one another and let the matter rest.

Jack the fiddler, grey-haired and a bit grumpy sometimes now, had finished tuning up. He nodded to the other fiddler, the tenor cornet player, the flute-player and the hurdy-gurdy man and they struck up with the old favourite, 'Drive the Cold Winter Away'. They'd play the new tune later, when Jack felt it would get the best reception. In the absence of the Pippit on the drum anyone whose hands were not occupied in grasping a blackjack, beat out the rhythm on the table.

**

The old tune seeped through the door and windows of the ale-house, floating over the frosty fields guarded by barn owls and foxes. Leafless trees, their up-stretched branches in dark silhouette against the chilly night sky, waited, ready for the fall of snow which would come before morning.

**

And so things go on.

Village celebrations continue, although their forms may change. Seasons follow seasons and nature, too, may change. Disagreements arise, fall and may, or may not, be resolved.

Great matters of politics, religion or morality will fill the minds of some, while the more immediate concerns of others may centre around how many lambs survive, what sex the new calf will be, or how long the harvest-time dry spell will last. Fond parents may agonise over whether so-and-so's son is a suitable husband for their daughter; a hard-bitten woman may save a tit-bit for a stray cat, or a growing boy may be envious of the small boy who now carries the drum.

And, somewhere above the moors, clouds sail across an boundless, everlasting sky filled with lark-song. Every heart-lifting note spills over rocky ridges, stone walls, grass, trees and shy flowers in gritty crevices, filling the ear and eye with delight and hope, while stone walls and tall elm trees protect an unmarked sixteen-foot-square field, in which brave hearts sleep in peace.

ℰᘉ ᑕℛ